ROSS O'CARROLL-KELLY

'Has delusions of adequacy'
Mr Crabtree, History

'Sets low personal standards and consistently fails to meet them'
Mr Clark, English

'He is depriving a village somewhere of an idiot'
Mr Lambkin, Biology

'I've never set eyes on the boy'
Mr Allen, Maths

'Reached rock bottom in fifth year and has continued to dig'
Miss Cully, Irish

'The next Ollie Campbell'
Fr Fehily, Principal

PAUL HOWARD hasn't done anything remotely athletic since running for and missing the 8.08am Dart from Greystones to Pearse Street on 12 February 2001. The last time he went to a rugby match he broke out in hives. The points he earned in the Leaving Cert barely reached double figures, but his record score on Larry Gogan's Sixty Second Quiz is 10. He's not much to look at and yet he does alright, thank you very much.

The Mis-Educa-tion years

Ross O'Carroll-Kelly

[As told to Paul Howard]

Illustrations by Alan Clarke

THE O'BRIEN PRESS
DUBLIN

This edition first published 2004 by The O'Brien Press Ltd,
20 Victoria Road, Dublin 6, Ireland.
Tel: +353 1 4923333; Fax: +353 1 4922777
E-mail: books@obrien.ie
Website: www.obrien.ie
Reprinted 2004, 2005 (twice).

Originally published in 2000 (without new material and revisions) as
The Miseducation of Ross O'Carroll-Kelly by the *Sunday Tribune*.

ISBN: 0-86278-852-8

British Library Cataloguing-in-Publication Data
Howard, Paul, 1971-
Ross O'Carroll-Kelly, the miseducation years
1.O'Carroll-Kelly, Ross (Fictitious character) - Fiction
2.Students - Ireland - Dublin - Fiction
3.Dublin (Ireland) - Social life and customs - Fiction
I.Title
823.9'14

4 5 6 7 8
05 06 07 08 09

Typesetting, editing, layout and design: The O'Brien Press Ltd
Illustrations: Alan Clarke
Author photograph, p.2: Emma Byrne
Printing: Cox & Wyman Ltd

Other books by Paul Howard

Ross O'Carroll-Kelly, The Teenage Dirtbag Years

Ross O'Carroll-Kelly, The Orange Mocha-Chip Frappuccino Years

Ross O'Carroll-Kelly, PS, I Scored the Bridesmaids

Hostage, Notorious Irish Kidnappings

The Joy - the shocking true story of life inside

The Gaffers, Roy Keane, Mick McCarthy and the team they built

Celtic Warrior

Dedication

To Laura and David Howard, for a life filled with love and laughter.
You made everything worthwhile. There aren't enough words.
Mum, we miss you every day x

Acknowledgements

Thanks to my mother and father for it all. Thanks to Mark, Vin and Rich for the interest you've taken in your adopted brother. Thanks to Matt Cooper, Paddy Murray and Jim Farrelly for taking a chance on an obnoxious little south Dublin shit, and thanks especially to Ger Siggins, who was there for the conception, the difficult birth and did most of the initial breast-feeding. For a whole myriad of other reasons too numerous to mention, thanks to Lady Dowager Genevieve; Wally; Ro and Johnny; Mick and Lorna who saved me from leeches; Mousey; Walshy; Paddy; Róisín; Dave; both Barrys; Fi and John and the lad Liam; Neil with the second name that goes on till Christmas and Liz; Karen with an e; Jenny Lowe and Claire Even Lower; Enda Mac; Lise with a totally unnecessary e; Fleur (!); Jimmy who's real name isn't Jimmy at all; Malachy; One F; at least two Michelles; Maureen, Deirdre and her south Dublin princess daughter Anne; Lisa and the Nordie Bogball Down Under Tour Party; and Dion and John from the cabal. Thanks to Ryle and Gerry for your restraint in never sending me a solicitor's letter. Thanks to Michael, Íde, Mary, Ivan, Lynn and everyone at OBP for accepting Ross into the OBP family. Caitríona, I miss you. And lastly – stay awake, these are the biggies – thanks to Emma for making these books look edible, to Alan for capturing our hero with the genius of your pen, and most of all to Rachel (Dublin 24), a brilliant editor who knows Ross better than I do. The funny bits are hers.

Contents

What's my name? I don't even bother answering him, just reef open the glove compartment and hand him my licence through the window, roysh, and he gives it the once-over and he goes, 'This is a provisional licence,' making no effort at all to hide the fact that he's a bogger. It's like he's actually proud of it. I go, 'Your point is?' and the way he looks at me, roysh, I can tell he just wants to snap those bracelets on me and haul my orse off to Donnybrook. He's like, 'Provisional licences are issued subject to certain restrictions. One is that you have a fully qualified driver accompanying you at all times.'

I turn around to the bird beside me and I go, 'Have you passed your test?' and she's like, 'Oh my God, ages ago,' and she storts rooting through her Louis V for her licence, which she eventually finds and I hand it to focking Blackie Connors through the window. He throws the eyes over it, roysh, then he hands it back to me and I'm thinking of taking a sneaky look at it myself, maybe find out this bird's name, because she's a total randomer and at some point between her telling me her name in Annabel's and us doing the bould thing out in her gaff in Clonskeagh, I've managed to forget what she calls herself. In the end I don't. The goy goes, 'Where are your L-plates?' and I have to admit, roysh, that he has me there, although he knows he can't lift me for it, which is what he'd really like to do. I go, 'Don't own a set. Never did. To me they're a total passion-killer,' and I smile at the bird beside me. Martinique rings a bell. The goy goes, 'Did you know that it's an offence for a driver operating a vehicle on a provisional licence not to display Learner plates?' but I don't answer because it's not, like, a real question, and he looks at my licence again – like it's a forgery or something – and he tells me to, like, stay where I am and then he walks back to his cor, roysh, and in the rear-view I can see him getting on the radio. The bird's there giving it, 'OH! MY! GOD! Why are you giving him such attitude? I am SO not being arrested, Ross. HELLO? I've got cello in, like, half an hour,' and I tell her to drink the Kool-Aid, the goy's only trying to put the shits up us.

I'm always getting pulled over by the Feds, especially here, just after you go under the bridge at, like, UCD. I'm too smart to get caught doing more than forty, but what happens is they see the baseball cap, they see the Barbie doll next to me and they hear 'Smells Like Teen Spirit' blasting out through the windows at, like, a million decibels. Boggers or not, they're not thick, these goys, and because it's a focking Micra, they know straight away that it's a young dude driving his old dear's cor and – probably out of total jealousy – they end up pulling me over. I'm still looking at the goy in the mirror. He's finished talking on the radio and now he's just trying to make me sweat, which I'm SO not.

People always ask me, roysh, how did I get this cool? Not being big-headed or anything, but they genuinely want to know how it is that I pretty much have it all – Dead Eye Dick with a rugby ball and the stor of the school team, good-looking, amazing body, big-time chormer, great with the ladies and absolutely loaded.

But to be honest with you, roysh, I wasn't always shit-hot. Between me and you, when I was in, like, transition year I was actually as big a loser as Fionn. I used to basically get bullied. I remember the day I found out that we didn't always live in Foxrock. Two or three fifth years were in the process of, like, stuffing my head down the toilet one lunchtime when one of them happened to go, 'Go back to the focking Noggin.' So that night, roysh, I went to the old man, who's a complete and utter dickhead by the way, and I go, 'Did we live in Sallynoggin?' – straight out with it, just like that – and he looks at me, roysh, and he knows there's no point in lying, so he goes, 'It was more Glenageary than Sallynoggin, Ross,' and he tells me it was a long time ago, before the business took off.

But that whole Noggin thing followed me around for years. If they weren't stuffing my head down the pan and flushing it, they were giving me wedgies, or setting fire to my schoolbag, ha focking ha. Then one day, roysh, I'm walking down the corridor, minding my own business and these two fifth years grab me in a headlock and drag me into, like, one of the locker rooms. They stort giving me the usual crack, roysh – 'Are you getting a spice burger from the Noggin Grill later?' and 'Are you going up to the Noggin Inn for a few jors?' – when all of a sudden, roysh, I hear a voice behind them go, 'To get at him, goys, you're going to have to come through me first,' and I look up and it's, like, Christian. So all hell breaks loose and the two of us end up decking the two fifth years and afterwards he tells me that Obi Wan has taught me well and I tell him he's the best friend I've ever had, which he is, roysh, even if it sounds a bit gay.

Of course the word went around, roysh, that we'd basically decked two goys who, it turned out, were on the S, and nobody laid a finger on me after that. Then the next year there was, shall we say, an incident that helped me complete the change from geek to chic – basically I got my Nat King Cole before anyone else in our whole year. AND it was with an older woman.

To cut a long story short, roysh, our school arranged this thing called The Urban Plunge, which was basically an exchange programme between us and a school from, like, Pram Springs. It was typical of the Brothers in our place. They knew we were loaded, roysh, and most of us would never have to work for a thing in our lives, but it was their 'Christian responsibility' to show us how people less fortunate than ourselves – meaning skobies – lived, as if we wanted to know.

The way it worked, roysh, was that you got paired off with some Anto or other – in fact, I think my one was actually called Anto. Anyway, he ended up half-inching everything in our gaff that wasn't nailed down. I remember the old man and the old dear, the silly wagon, walking around the house making a list of all the stuff that had disappeared, the old dear going, 'Your Callaway driver, darling,' and the old man shaking his head and writing it down. Of course Castlerock agreed to pay for everything on condition that they didn't involve the Feds.

But while this was all going on, roysh, I was getting my own back by scoring his older sister, we're talking Wham, Bam, that's for the old dear's Waterford Crystal limited edition votive, Ma'am. Tina was her name, roysh, a total howiya, but she was, like, twenty and I was, like, sixteen and by the time I got back from my two-week tour of duty in Beirut – every meal came with curry sauce, roysh, and they never answered the door in case it was the rent man or a loan shork – I was a legend in the school. The head-lice were gone after a couple of weeks and I settled well into my new existence as a complete focking stud.

'What speed were you doing?'

Glenroe's finest is back at the window. I was miles away there. I'm like, 'I think you'll find I was just under forty,' which he knows well from his speed camera. He's just trying to put the shits up me. He hands me back my licence and he goes, 'I'll let you go ... this time,' and I have to stop myself from going, 'Oh, I'm SO grateful, orsehole,' and he goes, 'Get a set of Learner plates when you're in town, Rod.'

I'm there, 'Rod? *Rod?* It's Ross! Ross O'Carroll-Kelly! You might not know the name now, but by the seventeenth of March you will.' He goes, 'Why? What's happening on that day?' The smell of turnip and spuds off him. I go, 'What's happening on that day? That's the day I become

Ross O'Carroll-Kelly, living focking legend.'

CHAPTER ONE
'Comes to class unprepared'

'**Mister O'Carroll-Kelly,** will you pay attention please.' That's what Lambkin says. He goes, 'Entertaining the troops as usual,' but I'm not, roysh, I'm actually about to spew my ring all over the desk, and we're talking totally here. If I'd known we were going to be looking at an actual focking cow's eye this morning, roysh, I think it's pretty safe to say I wouldn't have been out on the batter last night. And Oisinn's not helping. He was more hammered than I was, but he's got a stomach like a focking goat. He's got it in his hand, roysh, and he's, like, squelching it and you can hear all the, I don't know, guts inside. The goy actually wants to see me spitting chunks.

The teacher's going, 'How do we see? Well, the eye processes the light through photoreceptors located in the eye, which send signals to the brain and tell us what we are seeing. There are two types of photoreceptor and these are called rods and cones,' and then he walks around handing us each a scalpel, and I'm thinking he couldn't seriously be suggesting we ... He goes, 'These photoreceptors are sensitive to light. Rods are the most sensitive to light and therefore provide grey vision at night. Now there are a number of differences between the human eye and the cow's eye, which I will discuss as we proceed with the dissection.'

I'm just, like, staring straight ahead, trying not to think about what we're about to do, when all of a sudden Oisinn taps me on the shoulder and – HOLY FOCK! – he's somehow managed to stick the focking eyeball onto his forehead, roysh, and he goes, 'Look at me, Ross, I'm from Newtownmountkennedy,' and I laugh and heave at the same time and old focking Lamb Chop throws me a filthy, basically telling me that I'm pushing my luck here.

He's going, 'Cones are, in the main, active in bright light and enable you to see colour. There are one hundred million rods located in your retina compared to just three million cones.'

I just need to get through this class, then I'll hit the canteen and get a Yop or something to settle my stomach. But Oisinn knows how close I am to hurling here and it's become, like, a challenge now. He turns around to Fionn and goes, 'Gimme your glasses,' and Fionn's like, 'Why?' and Oisinn just grabs them off him. Then – this is focking horrific – he puts the eye basically onto his own eye and then he puts on Fionn's glasses, which sort of, like, hold it in place. Then he turns around to the rest of the class and goes, 'ESMERELDA!' and the whole class cracks up, roysh, and Lamb Chop, who's been writing some shite or other on the blackboard, turns around and goes, 'O'CARROLL-KELLY!' and he looks at me in a way that basically says Last Chance Saloon, and of course I can't tell him that I'm doing fockall, roysh, because I can taste the vom at the top of my throat and if I open my mouth it's coming out. Oisinn throws Fionn back his goggles and Fionn's, like, majorly pissed off, trying to clean them on his shirt, but of course they're covered in, like, blood and shite and all sorts, but I'm trying not to, like, think about it.

'If you walk inside from the sun,' – this is Lambkin again – 'you can't initially see anything. This is due to the activity of the cones and the lack of activity of the rods. Similarly, when you leave a cinema during the day, it's the rods that are mainly activated and the cones have to adjust to the sunlight.'

I'm thinking, I better actually listen to some of this shit because it might, like, come up in the Leaving. Then I hear Oisinn going, 'Ross! Ross! I know you can hear me!' and I'm trying my best to, like, ignore him. Rods and cones, I get it now. He just, like, grabs me by the back of the neck, roysh, and spins me around so that I'm, like, facing him and then – Oh! My! FOCKING! God! – he pops the eyeball into his mouth like it's a focking Bon Bon and then – get this – he actually bites into the focking thing and all this, like, blood and yellow goo and everything just, like, squirts out of the side of his mouth and, like, dribbles down his face and I just go, *Weeeuuuggghhh!* and basically explode.

There's vom everywhere, all over my Dubes, the desk, my biology book, the floor. I'm like a focking volcano. It just keeps coming and coming. Goes on for about ten minutes and everyone's just, like, staring at me, and when I've finished I've got, like, my face on the desk and the table feels nice and cold against my cheek, and I'm slowly getting my breath back and Lamb Chop's basically speechless and I'm thinking, I don't even remember having a kebab.

XXX

Castlerock boarders are Total Knackers it says in, like, black morker on the bus shelter opposite Stillorgan Shopping Centre, roysh, put there by some tool who doesn't realise that (a) writing graffiti actually makes *him* a knacker and (b) so does getting the focking bus. Nothing against public transport myself, but the old pair are basically rolling in it enough for me and the old 46A to lead parallel lives. The old dear, who's a total focking weapon, pulls up in her Micra – total shamer – and I hop in, and she's all smug and delighted with herself because she's just been to the printers to collect the posters for this anti-halting site group she's involved in, Foxrock Against Total Skangers or whatever the fock they're called, and she says that Lucy and Angela are going to be SO pleased with how they turned out, basically not giving a fock how long she left me sitting around waiting.

I go, 'I am SO late,' but she makes a big deal of ignoring me, roysh, humming some stupid Celine Dion song to herself, and I pretty much know what this is all about. Last week, roysh, the old man found out I've been, like, skipping my grinds. It's already January, roysh, and I basically haven't gone to one. The old Crimbo report comes and I ended up failing, like, six of my seven exams, and of course the old man's going, 'Don't be too down in the mouth, Kicker. I'll phone that Institute tomorrow and see if I can't get to the bottom of it.' I'm like, 'What are you banging on about, you dickhead?' and he goes, 'Well, you're not stupid, we know that. My brains and your mother's, that's a formidable combination, with a capital F. No, they're obviously not teaching you the right things. No, wait a second, maybe it is the school after all. Yes. Clearly they've either miscalculated your marks, given you the wrong report, or simply didn't understand what it was you were trying to say.' The tosser actually thinks I'm the next Stephen what's-his-face with the focking voicebox. *My eyesight is very important to me.*

So thinking of the old man, roysh, trying to help him not make a *complete* tit of himself, I end up telling him that I haven't been doing the grinds. He has an eppo, of course, reminding me how much they cost him – we're talking two thousand bills, the scabby focker – and then he asks me, roysh, what I've been doing every Friday night and Saturday morning, and I tell him I've been, like, hanging around town and shit, not mentioning, of course, the fact that I've been going on the batter with the goys. So the old pair have a major freak out, and we're talking major here – they basically don't understand the pressure of being on the S. All this results in the Mister Freeze treatment, which suits me because I hate having to talk to them. Anyway, the schools cup storts in two weeks and they'll be all focking over me then, you mork my words. Still can't believe I failed six of my seven exams. Actually, it was news to me that I even took English.

The goys are already sitting in Eddie Rockets when I arrive. Oisinn's wearing the old beige Dockers chinos, brown dubes, light blue Ralph and a red, white and blue sailing jacket by Henri Lloyd. He high-fives me, then he hugs me – nearly breaks my back, the fat bastard – and he goes, 'YOU THE MAN, ROSS,' seven or eight times in my ear. JP high-fives me and tells me he's glad I took the idea of having a nosebag offline. JP's also wearing beige Dockers chinos, brown dubes, light blue Ralph and a red, white and blue sailing jacket by Henri Lloyd. Aoife leans across the table and, like, air-kisses me on both cheeks, totally flirting her orse off with me, while Sorcha gives me daggers and goes, 'We've already ordered,' and I look her in the eye and I know she basically still wants me.

Oisinn goes, 'Question for you, Ross. If anyone can answer this, you can,' and I'm there, 'Shoot, my man.' He goes, 'Is it proper to wear Dubes with, like, formalwear?' and of course I'm there, 'How formal is formal?' and he goes, 'We're talking black trousers, we're talking white shirt, we're talking black blazer.' I rub my chin and think about it. The food arrives. JP is having the Classic without dill pickle, bacon and cheese fries and a large Coke. Oisinn is having the Moby Dick,

southern chicken tenders, chilli fries, a side order of nachos with guaca-
mole, cheese sauce, salsa and hot jalapenos and a chocolate malt, the
focking Michelin man that he is. Sorcha is having a Caesar salad with
extra croutons and Romanie lettuce. Aoife is having a bag of popcorn
which she has hidden inside her baby-blue sleeveless bubble jacket.
She's looking over her shoulder every few seconds, roysh, going, 'I
have to be careful. Me, Sophie, Amy and clarinet Deirdre got focked
out of the one in Donnybrook last week for ordering, like, a Diet Coke
between us.' and Sorcha says that is, like, SO *Duhhh!* And Aoife's there,
'Totally. It's like, OH my God! HELLO?' and Sorcha goes, 'No, it's more
like, OH MY GOD!' and Aoife's there, 'Oh my God! *Totally.*'

The waitress, roysh, is a total babe, we're talking Kelly out of 90210's
identical twin here, and when she drops the last of the food over she
turns around to me and she goes, 'Do you want to order something?'
and I go, 'Well, what I want and what I get are probably two different
things,' and I'm hoping it didn't sound too sleazy, roysh, but she just
goes red and out of the corner of my eye I can see Sorcha giving me
filthies, and we're talking *total* filthies. I go – cue sexy voice, roysh – I'm
like, 'Could I get a, em, dolphin-friendly tuna melt, maybe a chilli
cheese dog and a portion of, like, buffalo wings,' and she writes it down
and then, like, smiles at me and when she focks off Sorcha goes, 'That
girl is SUCH a knob.' I'm there, 'You don't even know her,' and she
goes, 'HELLO? Her name HAPPENS to be Sian Kennedy and she's doing, like, morkeshing in ATIM.' Aoife goes, 'She is like, *Aaaggghhh!*' and
Sorcha goes, 'Totally.'

Oisinn's there, 'Ross, you never answered my question, dude,' and
I'm there, 'I don't know why you have to rely on me for this stuff,' secretly delighted of course, and then I'm like, 'Dubes are traditionally a

casual shoe.' I look at Sorcha, who stirs Oisinn's chocolate malt and then takes a sip from it. I go, 'But to be passed off along with formalwear, the Dubes must – and I repeat *must* – be black.' Oisinn whistles. JP goes, 'They can't be brown?' in a real, like, suspicious voice. I go, 'Too casual for black trousers. Beige definitely. Black's a complete no-no.'

Sorcha's mobile rings, roysh, and it's, like, Jayne with a y, who used to be her best friend until she caught me wearing the face off her in Fionn's kitchen on New Year's Eve, which was basically one of the reasons Sorcha, like, finished with me. Anyway, roysh, they're obviously back talking again and they're blabbing on about some, like, dinner porty they're organising, but then all of a sudden Sorcha turns around to her and goes, 'Is Fionn there with you?' and of course immediately the old antennae pop up, and I'm wondering what that four-eyed focker's doing sniffing around – looks like Anna Friel this bird, I'm telling you – and JP must cop the look on my face because he goes, 'Message to the stockmorket – friendly merger going down between Fionn and Jayne with a y.' I'm there, 'And for those of us who don't speak morkeshing?' and he goes, 'They're going out together, Ross,' which is news to me, roysh, because I've been seeing her on the old QT for the past three or four weeks and she asked me to, like, keep it quiet, the complete bitch.

Sorcha must cop my reaction, roysh, because she's suddenly going, 'Ross, I'm talking to Jayne with a y. Fionn's sitting beside her. Do you want a word with him?' and I go, 'Tell him I'll pick him up for rugby training in the morning,' playing it Kool Plus Support Band. I run my hand through my hair, which needs a serious cut. Might get a blade one all over this time instead of, like, just the sides, seeing as the Cup's about

to stort and everything.

Sorcha hangs up and of course she can't let it go. She goes, 'Oh my God, they make SUCH a cute couple, don't they?' and Aoife's there, 'Yeah, it's like, Rachel and Ross cute,' and Sorcha goes, 'No, it's more like, Joey and Dawson cute,' then she turns to me and she's like, 'You've gone very quiet, Ross. Not jealous, are you?' Where's my focking food? I'm there, 'Not at all. Been there, done that ... worn the best friend,' and she's bulling, and we're talking bigtime.

The waitress comes over and I decide to up the old ante. She's putting my food on the table, roysh, and I'm giving it, 'You're Sian Kennedy, aren't you?' and she goes, 'Yeah,' and I'm there, 'First year morkeshing in ATIM?' and she goes, 'Yeah, I know your face. You go to Annabel's, don't you?' and I'm seriously giving it, 'Sure do. Maybe I'll see you there tomorrow night?' and she goes totally red, roysh, and she's there, 'Em ... yeah,' and I go, 'Cool,' and she's like, 'Bye,' and I'm giving it, 'Later.'

Oisinn and JP both high-five me and Aoife goes, 'Oh my *God*, you don't ACTUALLY fancy her, do you?' and I go, 'She looks like Kelly off 90210,' and Aoife goes, 'But she's a sap, Ross. A total sap,' and out of the corner of my eye I can see Sorcha's face is all red, the way it gets when she's pissed off. I'm on match-point now. She turns around to Aoife and she goes, 'So, do you think I should go?' and Aoife's there, 'What?' and Sorcha's like, 'Do you think I should go?' Aoife's there, 'Oh my God, you SO should. I'm telling you, you SO should go,' obviously wanting me to ask, roysh, but I'm in the game too long to fall for that one. But JP – the loser – he goes, 'Go where?' and Aoife's like, 'She's been invited to the Gonzaga pre-debs,' and JP's there, 'By who?' and Sorcha goes, 'Jamie O'Connell-Keavney,' all delighted with herself and she's looking at me for a reaction, roysh, because she knows damn well we have Gonzaga in the first round of the Cup.

The goys look at me for a reaction too, roysh, but there's no way I'm, like, taking the bait. JP goes, 'That is SO not cool, Sorcha. That is SUCH an uncool thing to do,' and Sorcha's like, 'Why?' and JP goes, 'Because Gonzaga are our TOTAL enemies,' and Oisinn nods and goes, 'Tossers.' Sorcha goes, 'Jamie's not like that. He's SUCH a cool goy,' and Aoife's there, 'What do *you* think she should do, Ross?' As subtle as a kick in the old town halls. I pop the last piece of tuna into my mouth and I go, 'If she wants to go, that's cool. I think she should do what makes her happy,' and JP's going, 'Yeah, but not with someone from Gonzaga ... Oh my God, we are SO going to kick their orses now,' and him and Oisinn high-five each other.

Aoife gets up to go to the toilet and Oisinn goes, 'That's three times she's been in there since we arrived. What kind of load could she possibly be dropping off? It's not as if she ever eats anything.' Then he says he can definitely taste dill pickle on his Classic and he takes the top off the bun to investigate. Sorcha takes off her scrunchy and slips it onto her wrist, shakes her head, smoothes her hair back into a low ponytail, puts it back in the scrunchy and then pulls five or six strands of hair loose. It looks exactly the same as it did before she did it.

Aoife comes back, wiping her mouth, calls one of the other waitresses over and asks can she have a glass of, like, water. The waitress asks us if we want dessert and Oisinn and JP both order the Kit Kat Dream and Sorcha orders the New York toffee cheesecake with ice cream and cream. Aoife goes, 'OH MY GOD! Do you KNOW how many points are in that? Have you, like, TOTALLY lost your mind?' and Sorcha goes, 'I'm not counting my points anymore,' but before it arrives the guilt gets to her, roysh, and she takes one mouthful, then pushes the rest across the table to me. I just pick at it, roysh, then I get up to go. JP goes, 'You heading home?' and I'm there, 'Yeah. Big training session tomorrow. Got to, like, keep my focus.'

I walk up to the counter, cool as a fish's fart, tell Sian what I had and she tots it up. I hand her twenty bills and tell her to, like, keep the change. Then I tell her I might see her tomorrow night, which is, like, Saturday, and she says that would be cool. Behind me I can hear Oisinn saying he's sure he can taste dill pickle on his burger and he is SO not paying for it. Aoife goes, 'See you tomorrow night, Ross. Annabel's,' but I totally blank her and go outside. I stand in the cor pork and try to ring the old dear, but the phone's engaged and so's her mobile. Her and that focking campaign of hers. I try Dick Features, but then I remember he's out at the K Club tonight with Hennessy, his orsehole solicitor.

I stand out on the road for ten minutes looking for a taxi, roysh, but there's fock-all about. I don't focking believe this, but there's nothing else for it, I'm going to have to get the focking bus. Mortification City, Wisconsin. I cross over to the bus stop. There's two birds there. Skobies. One is telling the other that Sharon — no, Shadden — is a dorty-lookin' dort-bord. The bus comes and I let them get on first. I hand the driver two pound coins, roysh, and he tells me to put the money in the slot, which I do. I pull the ticket and wait for my change but the tosspot storts driving off. I go, 'What do you think that is, a tip or something?' and he goes, 'Sorry, bud, we don't give out change. You have to take your receipt into O'Connell Street to get yisser change.' I go, 'Are you trying to be funny?' and he's there, 'Sorry, bud?' I'm like, 'O'Connell Street?' and he goes, 'Yeah, you know where Dublin Bus is?' and I'm there, 'No. I don't *do* the northside,' and I sit down. He probably had one of his mates lined up to focking mug me.

I sit downstairs. There's a funny smell off buses. Actually it's probably the people. I take out my mobile and, like, listen to my messages.
Some bird called Alison phoned and said OH MY GOD! she hoped I remembered her from last Saturday night and she couldn't remember
whether I was supposed to phone her or she was supposed to phone
me, but she decided to call me anyway and if it's after midnight when I
get this message I should phone her tomorrow, but not in the morning
because OH MY GOD! she's just remembered she's at the orthodontist
and she gives me the number again.

XXX

It's Saturday morning, roysh, and I'm hanging, but try telling that to the
old man. He comes into the sitting-room where I'm trying to watch
MTV, roysh, and of course straight away I grab the remote and higher
up the volume. The Prodigy SO rock. The dickhead doesn't even take
this as a hint, roysh, just marches straight in and storts giving it loads,
like we're long-lost friends or something. He's there, 'I expect you
heard me getting up in the middle of the night,' and I know he's
basically dying for me to ask why, but I'm not going to give him the
satisfaction. He goes, 'Difficulty sleeping, Kicker. Got up and had a
glass of milk, which can sometimes help. Hope I didn't wake you.' I just
look at him, roysh – give him this total filthy – and I go, 'Well, given that
I fell in that door at half-six this morning, I don't think so. I was
probably still in Reynords.'

He goes, 'The reason I couldn't sleep, in case you're wondering, is all
this halting site nonsense. It's not that we're anti these types of people.
That little one who sings off Grafton Street? Tremendous fun. Your
mother will tell you, I wouldn't pass him without putting a few pence in

his tin and whatnot. But a halting site in Foxrock? It's just not appropriate. I'm thinking about them as much as anyone else. They wouldn't be happy here. Good lord, Ross, who is that chap?' I don't answer him, roysh, and he goes, 'Who is he, Ross?' and I'm there, 'Are you focking deaf? I said his name's Keith Flint.' He's there, 'Very peculiar-looking individual, isn't he? I suppose they can do all sorts with make-up.'

I just, like, shake my head but he still doesn't take the hint. He goes, 'Travelling people. *Travelling*. It's like when that client of Hennessy's woke up one morning to find three caravans on that little patch of grass opposite his house. In *Dalkey* of all places. Year of our Lord nineteen hundred and ninety-seven. Six months they stayed. As he said – you'll have to get Hennessy to do the voice for you – he said, "I don't know why they call them travelling folk, hell, they never bloody move." Because he's a terrible snob, old Wilmot Ruddy. A great old character, even if he is a bit much at times.'

Shania Twain comes on. I would, before you ask. The old man's still blabbing away. 'You do understand, don't you, that I've nothing against these people? I'm all for them. I just happen to think they'd struggle to fit in, inverted commas. Can't say that to these councillors, of course. Racism, that silly woman accused me of. There were times, of course, when all you had to do was pop a few hundred pounds in an envelope and hey presto you had the council on your side. These are changed times, thank you very much indeed Mister G Kerrigan of Middle Abbey Street, Dublin 1.'

I look at him and I go, 'Are you still here?' He winks at me, roysh – actually focking winks – and he goes, 'I've got my Mont Blanc pen out, Ross. Which can mean only one thing. Yes, I'm going to write one of my world-famous letters to *The Irish Times*. Oh, I love the letters page of

The Irish Times. The cut and thrust of the debates on all the important issues of the day. The cheeky humour. Throw in a witticism or two at the
start and you've got a winner on your hands. Winner with a capital W.
Let me read you what I've put down thus far,' and he whips out this
sheet of paper, roysh. He's there, 'Have a listen to this: I need only say
the words 'Hiace van' and 'Family Allowance Day' to evoke the image
of–' and straight away, roysh, I'm there, 'If you're not out of this room
in five focking seconds, I'm leaving home.'

XXX

I place the ball on the ground, stand up and raise my head slowly.
Christian's behind me going, 'One of the great taboos of the twentieth
century and no one's prepared to talk about it.' I look down, take five
steps backwards and look up again, tracing the line of the posts
upwards. Christian's still in my ear, giving it, 'It's, what, twenty years on
and there's never been any discussion on the subject.' I take three steps
to the side, look down at the ball, lick my fingers, run my right hand
through my hair, do my usual dance on the spot, then I run at the ball.
Just as I'm about to kick it, roysh, Christian goes, 'I mean, far be it from
me to tell George Lucas his business ...' and of course I end up skying
the focking thing to the right of the posts and there's this, like, chorus
of OH MY GODs from the Mounties on the sideline.

I'm just there, 'Fock's sake, Christian, you're supposed to be helping
me practice,' basically ripping the dude out of it, and he looks at me,
roysh, like I've just dropped a load in one of his Dubes. Of course I
stort feeling bad then, roysh, basic softie that I am, and I go, 'Look, I'm
sorry. It's just this Gonzaga match. Storting to feel, like, the pressure,
you know. What were you saying?' He goes, 'I was talking about the in-
cestuous undertone running through the first half of the original

trilogy. Have you not been listening to me? I'm talking about the sexual frisson between Luke Skywalker and Princess Leia.' I just go, 'Oh, roysh,' and try to look interested, he *is* my best friend, the focking weirdo.

He goes, 'Okay, you might think it was a harmless, hand-holding, carry-your-books-home-from-high-school kind of attraction. When Leia kissed Luke in the central core shaft ...' I'm there, 'Kissed him *where*?' and he goes, 'The central core shaft? Of the Death Stor? Before they swung across the gorge? Okay it was just a peck on the cheek, like the one she gave him in the main hangar deck on Alderaan. But there's no doubt they were the main love interest in *A New Hope*. Then in *Return of the Jedi* we found out they were brother and sister all along. We're talking *twins* here!' I'm there, 'Your point is?' and he goes, 'My point is, if George Lucas knew that these were Anakin Skywalker's kids, why the fock were they playing tonsil hockey in the medical centre on Hoth at the stort of *Empire*?'

I'm just, like, staring at the dude. He's totally lost me. The goy's focking Baghdad. He walked up to two Virgins on the Rocks at the Trinity Open Day last week and he went, 'What planet is this? What year is this? Where is your water source?' But like I say, roysh, we've been best friends since we were, like, kids, so I just go, 'That's a good point,' and he tells me not to worry about Gonzaga, he heard they're running on empty this year, and he tells me to let go of my conscious self and trust my instinct.

XXX

'I'm thinking of sleeping with you.' That's what Erika says to me when I meet her for lunch. We're talking Erika as in Sorcha's friend Erika. We're talking Erika who's the image of Denise Richards Erika. We're talking Erika as in total bitch Erika who never sleeps with anyone who's never been on 'Lifestyles of the Rich and Famous'. And she doesn't even look up from the menu, roysh, she just goes, 'Don't have the split pea soup, the croutons are always stale. I'm thinking of sleeping with you,' and I sort of, like, resent the fact that she thinks she could basically have me any time she wants me, even though she could. She looks up and she cops the delighted look on my face, roysh, and she goes, 'Not for pleasure, Ross. It's just that I know you're on the rugby team this year. And you're the goy all the girls will want to be with.'

The waitress comes over, roysh – bit of a hound, truth be told – and I order a roast beef sandwich, a portion of fries and, like, a Coke. Erika asks for just a latte, roysh, and the waitress points to a sign on the wall, something about a five quid minimum charge between twelve and two o'clock. The waitress is like, 'Can you read?' which is a big mistake, roysh, because quick as a flash Erika goes, 'Yes I can. You're the one earning three pounds an hour for collecting dirty dishes, remember.'

The waitress – she's actually a bit of a howiya – she goes, 'Between twelve and two the tables are reserved for *lunch* customers,' and Erika just, like, looks her up and down, roysh, and she goes, 'Just bring me a latte and you can charge me five pounds for it,' and the bird doesn't know what to say, roysh, obviously no one's ever said that before. Erika goes, 'Five pounds is hordly expensive for a cup of coffee anyway. Have you ever been to Paris, dear?'

She's, like, fascinating to watch when she's in this kind of form. The waitress, roysh, she mutters something about having to ask the manager and as she's walking away, Erika goes, 'On second thoughts,' and the bird turns around and Erika's like, 'I will have something to eat. I'll have the spaghetti bolognaise,' and she closes the menu and hands it to her. She goes, 'And that latte. *Thank you,*' real, like, sarcastic. Then she turns to me and goes, 'Where was I?'

I'm there, 'The thing is, Erika, I'm very flattered to think that you'd want to be with me, even for the reason you said. But maybe *I* don't want to be with *you*.' She looks at me, roysh, through sort of, like, slanty eyes, and she goes, 'Listen to yourself, will you? Do you think I'm blind or something? Do you think I haven't seen you looking at me and practically salivating? You can't help yourself around me. You want me, Ross. You always have,' and like an idiot, I go, 'That's true. But what about Sorcha? She's your friend. And she still has, like, feelings for me? And I wouldn't do anything to—' Erika just goes, 'Don't give me that, Ross. More than any other goy I know, you think with that,' and she points at my ... well, let's just say she points down.

The food arrives. Erika gives the waitress a filthy, roysh, and the waitress puts the plates on the table and throws her eyes up to heaven. Erika pushes her spaghetti bolognaise away from her, like it's infected or something. She goes, 'Don't kid yourself, Ross. Two squirts of *Issey Miyake* and that black Karen Millen top I have that you're always trying to look down and you'd be mine.' I go, 'And you'd do that? Even if it hurt Sorcha?' and she's there, 'Ross, have I got the words 'social worker' tattooed on my forehead? Do you think you're talking to someone who actually *gives* a shit about other people? Do you think I actually *enjoy* listening to Sorcha going on about how she is SO over you, then telling me she's going to lose a stone before the summer and "OH! MY! GOD! Wait until Ross sees me then." She's a sad case.'

She still hasn't touched her food. She goes, 'Face it, Ross. I'm the object of your desire. I'm the object of many men's desires. Whether I sleep with you or not is entirely up to me.' The next thing, roysh, her phone rings and she answers it and goes, 'Well, talk of the devil,' and of course I'm on the other side of the table, doing the actions to tell her not to tell Sorcha I'm here. 'Where am I?' she goes. 'I'm in town, having lunch with the love of your life ... yes, Ross. He's just been admiring my black top, the Karen Millen one?' The next thing, roysh, she puts the phone down on the table and goes, 'She hung up, the silly girl.'

I cannot focking Adam and Eve this, roysh, but twenty minutes later or whatever, we're both getting up to go and Erika gets the plate of spaghetti, which she hasn't eaten a single mouthful of, and she just, like, tips the whole thing onto the floor. It's one of those, like, wooden floors and she's made a total mess of it, and she just goes, 'Oops,' as in I've just done that accidentally on purpose. Then she walks straight up to the waitress, roysh, and she goes, 'Oh dear, I am SUCH a klutz. I seem to have spilled that food you made me order all over your clean floor. I really don't envy you the job of cleaning it up,' and before the waitress has a chance to say anything back, she goes, 'You obviously think you're made for something better than taking orders in a restaurant. But until Aaron Spelling discovers you, this is it for you, dear.'

She's incredible. She's right. She could have me like *that*.

XXX

I'm in the kitchen, roysh, lorrying the chicken and pasta into me, loading up on the old, I don't know, carbohydrates I suppose, what with this match coming up, when all of a sudden Knobhead comes into the kitchen with the portable, like, clutched to his ear, roysh, and he's going, 'What do you mean you won't be publishing my letter?' and at a guess I'd say it's someone from *The Irish Times*. He's going, 'Elements of it could be construed as being racist? What a lot of nonsense, pardon the French ... Weddings? Yes, that was just a bit of good-natured fun, to stop it getting too heavy and political. In fact, I think I may have actually spelt the word machete with two Ts instead of one. But look, I'd be willing to take it out if it meant ... Well, many of them *don't* tax or insure their cars, that's a fact ... Carpets? How can a reference to them selling poor quality carpets be construed as ... Hello? Hello? I think she might have bloody hung up on me.'

Tosser.

XXX

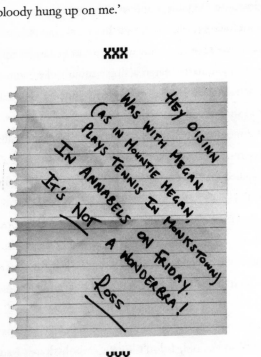

XXX

'Fucus is a multicellular alga consisting of an unbranched filament in which all of the cells are cylindrical and haploid and each has a cell wall surrounded by mucilage.' This is what passes for basically conversation among the birds. Sophie's going, 'Each has a chloroplast which is wound spirally inside the cell wall and the nucleus is suspended in the cell vacuole by threads of cytoplasm and–' Sorcha's, like, shaking her head. She goes, 'Sophie, HELLO? That's not fucus. That's, like, spirogyra,' and Sophie's giving it, 'Couldn't be,' and Sorcha's like, 'HELLO? I got an A in this at Christmas, remember?' Sophie sort of, like, squints her eyes, roysh, like she wants to rip Sorcha's face off and goes, 'They're practically the same focking thing anyway,' and Sorcha, being a total bitch, goes, 'No they're not. Spirogyra is a simple-structured, filamentous alga commonly found in ponds and ditches. Fucus is a multicellular marine-living brown alga commonly found on the seashore. They are SO different. We're talking habitat, structure, the way they reproduce. Ross, grab a seat. Is anyone else coming to the Ladies'?'

No one moves, roysh, so she focks off on her own. The second I sit down, Sophie goes, 'How the FOCK did you go out with that girl?' and I probably should defend her, roysh, but I just, like, shrug my shoulders instead and Sophie gives it, 'She is SUCH a bitch. Oh, and Ross, she still wants you.' Chloë goes, 'Sophie, oh my God, don't be a bitch yourself,' and Sophie's there, 'Fock HER. Ross, she talks about you all the time. I told her she's making a fool of herself. I was like, "Sorcha, you're one of my best friends, I don't want to see you get hurt," but she's like, "He's the love of my life." Oh and you know that song, 'I've Finally Found Someone'? It's, like, Bryan Adams and Barbra Streisand? Well, that's *your* song. She even bought the CD. She is SUCH a sap. *Ssshhh*, here she is back.'

I ask Sorcha if she wants a drink, roysh, and she asks me to get her a vodka and Diet 7-Up and as I'm getting up to go to the bor, roysh, I tell her in front of the rest of the birds that she looks really pretty tonight, and she looks at me sort of, like, suspiciously, then she asks me if I need money and I'm there, 'It's a compliment, Sorcha. I like your top. And your hair really suits you like that. You look really well,' and she looks like she's about to die of focking happiness and it really pisses off the others.

The goys arrive while I'm up at the bor, we're talking Oisinn, JP and Fionn. I come back with the drinks, roysh, and Oisinn tells me he wants a word, sort of, like, pulling me to one side kind of thing. I'm there, 'What's on your mind, dude?' He goes, 'Ross, you know Sooty's asked me to captain the S this year?' and I'm there, 'I know that,' and he's like, 'I just wanted to make sure there were no, I don't know, hord feelings, as *you* were the logical alternative.' I'm there, 'It's cool, Oisinn, you're an amazing rugby player and a natural leader. I'd bleed for you. You *know* that.' He's like, 'Hey, not on my Dockers,' and I just, like, laugh and admire his new chinos. He goes, 'Anyway, look, I've got something to ask you. Ross, I'd like you to be my vice-captain.'

I am, like, so, I don't know, filled with pride at that moment, roysh, that I nearly, like, burst into tears. I try to speak, roysh, but the words don't come out. He just goes, 'I know, buddy. I know,' and we just, like, hug each other – we're talking a goy's hug, though – and then, like, high-five each other, then go back over to the goys. Fionn's on the Cokes, roysh, because we've all got, like, grinds tonight, as in History, and the fact that Einstein there is getting History grinds himself proves that it's not me who's thick, it's that Crabtree's basically a crap teacher. JP's also supposed to be going, but he has a pint in front of him and he's drunk, like, half of it already and maybe I'm taking the whole vice-captaincy thing a bit too seriously, roysh, but I get this serious urge to tell him he's going to have to lay off the sauce when the serious stuff begins, though that would make me a bit of a hypocrite, roysh, given that I've got a pint of Ken in front of me myself. It's still a couple of weeks before we play Gonzaga, I suppose. There's probably going to be quite a few blow-outs between now and then.

Sorcha is telling Sophie that fucus vesiculosus is dioecious and you can see Sophie getting, like, frustrated, roysh. She shrugs her shoulders and asks what THAT means and Sorcha goes, 'HELLO? You don't have to KNOW what it means. You just have to remember it and write it down in the exam,' but when Fionn thinks no one is listening I hear him telling Sophie that dioecious means there are, like, separate male and female plants, the four-eyed basic knob-end.

My phone rings and it's, like, Dick Features, trying to get all *in* with me again, probably been telling all his dickhead mates that I'm playing outhalf on the S this year. He's like, 'Hey, Kicker,' and of course I don't say anything back to him. He goes, 'Hello? Hello, can you hear me?' and I'm there, 'Yes I can hear you. Unfortunately. What do you want?' He goes, 'Oh, just thought I'd, em, give you a call. See did you hear the team Warren Gatland's picked for the England match.' I just go, 'Pathetic,' and hang up. No one in the group seems to notice except, like, Sorcha, who gives me this smile, like she understands what I'm basically going through.

Chloë says that – OH! MY! GOD! – she has been eating SO many sweets since she storted work on her special study topic for honours History and Sophie says – OH! MY! GOD! – she's become addicted to Smorties and Skittles and is getting SUCH a study orse it's not funny. She goes, 'HELLO?' JP says he doesn't give two focks about the Leaving, roysh, because no matter how bad he does, he's going to end up working for his old man, who's, like, an estate agent, as in Hook, Lyon and Sinker?

I knock back the rest of my pint and get up to go. Oisinn goes, 'Shit the bed, Ross, you're John B,' and I'm there, 'I'm only going in because the old pair have guilted me into it.' And as me and the goys are leaving, roysh, Fionn sort of, like, sidles up to me and goes, 'Did you read that stuff he gave us last week about Sinn Féin and the 1918 election?' and I stop and look at him as if to say, you know, what the fock do you think? He just, like, nods, like he gets the message. Stupid focking question.

XXX

I'm already, like, half-awake when the old dear comes into my room. She goes, 'Ross, it's half-past eight,' and I totally blank her. She goes, 'Ross, it's half-eight,' and I'm like, 'I FOCKING SAID I ALREADY KNOW,' and of course she storts going, 'Don't use that kind of language to me. I'm just saying, you're going to be late for school.' I'm there, 'No shit, Sherlock,' and she takes the hint and focks off downstairs, the stupid cow.

Oh my God, I need a serious shower this morning, roysh. My hair and my face are all, like, sticky and they smell of orange. I reach down and feel around the floor, roysh, and find my dark blue 501s and my blue Chaps jumper with the stors and stripes on it and they're, like, sticky as well. Sorcha basically threw a Bacordi Breezer over me in Annabel's last night, roysh, had a total knicker fit when she saw me giving it loads in front of Sian, and we're talking total here. Wasn't even going to go out, roysh, but the goys talk me into going for a few scoops in Kiely's and – surprise, surprise – we ended up in Annabel's.

The second I walk in, roysh, I spot Sian up at the bor with a few of her mates, trying to play it Kool and the Gang but failing miserably by looking over every twenty seconds. I'm playing it cool like Fonzarella. Get the Britneys in – Ken for Christian and Oisinn, Probably for JP and, I don't know, a focking wine spritzer for Fionn. Half an hour later

Sian's so gagging for me that I'm storting to, like, feel sorry for her, so I mosey on over and I'm like, 'Hey,' and she goes, 'Hihoworya?' and I'm there, 'All the better for seeing you. You look so ... different. Without your Eddie Rockets uniform, I mean,' and she goes, 'OHMYGOD OHMYGOD OHMYGOD, SO embarrassing!'

Has to be said, she's looking pretty hot. Kelly from 90210, eat your focking heart out. She's wearing a black strapless mini dress which I, like, compliment her on and she mentions it's from, like, Morgan and also that her pony mules are Karen Millen, roysh, and apparently her leather jacket is a real Lawrence Streele, or that's what I overhear one of her friends saying to someone else. I introduce myself to her crew. Get in with the friends and it's green lights all the way. Melissa is a complete babe. Olwen is a total dog. In case you're interested – which I'm not – Melissa is wearing a white mini dress by Fenn Wright and Manson and sandles by Gucci. Olwen is wearing a black gypsy top by Prada, black trousers by Prada and black boots, also by Prada. I'm thinking, it's a pity Prada don't do paper bags. There's, like, ten or fifteen minutes of this crap, roysh, everyone dropping the names of labels, it's like sitting through an episode of 'Off the Rails' and I have to pretend I'm actually, like, interested and at one point, roysh, I just go, 'Clothes are SO impor-tant,' and I don't know what Melissa thinks I said, but I see her mouth something to Sian and I'm pretty sure it's, 'He is SO nice.'

I stort flirting my orse off with her then, we're talking Melissa. Does no harm to make a bird, like, jealous. I'm there, 'You used to go to school in Killiney, didn't you?' and she goes, 'Oh my God, how did you know that?' and I'm there, 'Because you did *West Side Story* with the sixth years in our school last year.' She's like, 'OH! MY! GOD! I am SO embarrassed. HELLO? Total shamer,' and I'm there giving it, 'No, it was cool,' and she's there, 'Oh my God, Oh my God.' Then she goes, 'You're in Castlerock, aren't you?' and I'm there, 'Sure am, baby,' playing like SO focking cool. She goes, 'Oh my God, do you know Jamie McIvor?' and I'm like, 'He's in my Art class, I think. I've only been once.' She goes, 'Oh my God! I'm taking him to my debs,' and I'm there, 'He's a good guy,' even though he's a focking asswipe, and she shakes her head and goes, 'I can't believe you know Jamie McIvor,' and when she thinks I'm not listening, roysh, she turns around to Sian and goes, 'OH my God! He is SO gorgeous.'

Olwen, roysh – not being a bastard or anything but the girl's a focking hound – she tries to get in on the act then, asking me who else I know in Killiney and I name a few birds I've been with, we're talking Elinor Snow, Amie Gough, Bryana Quigley. Their ears all suddenly prick up. Sian's there, 'How do you know Bryana Quigley?' really sort of, like, accusingly, if that's a word, and I go, 'I was with her twice during the summer. Met her in Irish college,' and Melissa and the focking moonpig just, like, turn their heads away and I ask Sian what the problem with Bryana Quigley is and she goes, 'Don't go there, Ross. Do NOT even go there.'

Melissa turns around to me and she goes, 'Hey, you're on the senior rugby team, aren't you?' and I'm there, 'Guilty as charged,' trying not to be too big-headed. She goes, 'We were thinking of going along one night to watch you practice your kicking, weren't we, Sian?' and I'm there, 'Hey, the more the merrier,' but Sian's not happy, roysh, she's giving Melissa a filthy, probably unhappy with the vibes going back and forth between me and her, and Melissa takes the hint and focks off to the jacks, bringing the Token Ugly Mate with her.

Sian goes, 'That girl is SUCH a sly bitch. Wouldn't trust her as far as I could throw her.' I'm like, 'How long have you been friends?' and she goes, 'Since we were three. She always does that, storts, like, flirting her orse off with goys I like.' There's my in. I go, 'So you like me, yeah?' and she goes red and sort of, like, looks away. I move in for the kill. I'm there, 'Don't be embarrassed. I've liked you for ages,' which is horse-shite, roysh, but birds love hearing that stuff. She goes, 'Oh my God!' and, well, to cut a long story short, roysh, I end up being with her.

The next thing, roysh, I open my eyes and who's standing over us only Sorcha. I think it's the smell that I get first – she's wearing the *Allure* by Chanel that I bought her for her birthday and a face like a well-slapped orse. She goes, 'Didn't take you long, did it, Ross?' Sian's still, like, wearing the neck off me at this stage. I'm there, 'Hey, Sorcha. How's things?' She doesn't say anything, just, like, stares at me. Sian's copped her now. They're both looking each other up and down. I go, 'Sorcha, you were the one who finished it,' and she looks at me and goes, 'HELLO? Because you were with one of my friends,' and I'm there, 'That wasn't my fault. I told you before, *she* came on to *me*.' 'Oh roysh, and now you've moved on to someone like *her*,' and she basically gives Sian daggers.

Of course Sian's not having that. She's there, 'OH my God, sorry, WHO the fock do you think you are?' It's actually a bit of an ego boost having two birds fighting over you like this. A lesser man than me would basically get a big head over it. 'I'm Sorcha Lalor,' Sorcha goes, 'and I know who you are and where you're from. Collars Up, Knickers Down.'

She can be very funny at times, Sorcha. I'd actually just taken a mouthful of Ken and nearly spat it all over the focking place. I go, 'Oh yeah, the Whores on the Shore!' sort of, like, laughing to myself, maybe try to defuse the situation. Sian looks at me like it's, I don't know, some sort of, like, betrayal. Then she looks at Sorcha and goes, 'It's better than Mount Anything,' then she turns around to me and gives me this, like, total filthy, pretty much to tell me to get rid of Sorcha. Now. And if I'm going to get beyond base camp tonight, I know I'll have to.

I go, 'Look, Sorcha, you ended it and as far as I'm concerned you basically did me a favour. We're both free agents. Just get over it,' and with that she ends up throwing pretty much a full Bacordi Breezer over me. Aoife and Sophie and all those arrive over and take her away, telling her that I'm SUCH an orsehole and that I'm, Oh my God! SO not worth it, roysh, and there's also that bird Nikki, who's, like, repeating in the Institute and as they're heading off I notice for the first time what a great orse she has.

Sian goes, 'I SO can't believe you went out with that knob,' and even though I probably should defend the girl, I end up going, 'I don't want to talk about the past. I only want to talk about the future. And that future is us,' and I throw the lips on her again, because if I'm honest I actually couldn't be orsed talking to her anymore. Didn't get any further than that. Turns out she's one of these birds who wants to go out on, like, dates before she'll let you pick her lock. End of the night she gave me her number, roysh, but I've no intention of ringing her.

Anyway, the upshot of all this is that I'm feeling pretty shabby this morning, roysh, and I'm not sure if I'm going to be able to get my head together for this, like, talk we're supposed to be getting from Sooty – Mr Sutton – who's, like, the coach of the S. He says the game against Gonzaga is, like, the toughest first-round draw Castlerock has ever got in the competition, although I heard he says that every year, just to make sure all the goys are, like, totally focused, put their heads down and work.

I finally get my act together and get out of the sack. Probably had three or four scoops too many actually. I have a shower and lash on my beige chinos, my All Blacks jersey and my brown Dubes, then head down to the kitchen. I grab a carton of, like, milk and stort, like, knocking it back. Didn't know the old dear was standing behind me. She goes, 'Ross, I've told you before to use a glass. Honestly, sometimes I wonder whether you were brought up in Foxrock or one of those frightful council estates.' I go, 'I'm eighteen. I'm not a focking kid,' and she goes, 'That's why I can't understand why you act like one,' playing the whole Responsible Parent act. I go, 'Shut the fock up and gimme your cor keys.' She goes, 'I need the car today, Ross. Friday is lunch with the girls in Avoca Handweavers. You know that,' and I just shake my head and go, 'What did I do to deserve someone like you for a mother? I need a focking lift.' So she drops me off at the school, the stupid wagon, and as I'm getting out of the cor she goes, 'What time will you be home?' and I just, like, totally blank her. We're talking totally as well.

Sooty – he's a good goy, roysh – he puts us all sitting in, like, a circle, roysh, and he goes, 'Heavy night on the sauce last night, lads?' and everyone's, like, breaking their shites laughing because, like, Sooty knows most of us usually head out for a few on a Thursday, but he basically doesn't give a fock. He's pacing back and forth, going, 'No, lads, in all seriousness. I want to say to you what I was saying to Father Fehily just this morning. We can't underestimate these fellas we're playing next Friday. They are serious players. Gone are the days when Gonzaga were considered the poor relation of the Leinster Schools Senior Cup. They have a great team this year. If you win this game, I guarantee you won't have a more difficult match until the final. So what I'm saying is that I want you to get your heads down for the next few days, lads. Lay off the sauce, lay off the late nights.'

He goes, 'I've spoken to your various teachers and they've agreed to excuse you all from homework for the weekend. It's like I said to you before, the Leaving Cert doesn't matter a damn. You can sit it again next year. I want to make sure you have time and space to concentrate on the job in hand. Do your gym work. Focus on your own game. Now, I want to do an exercise with you, if I may.'

He stops pacing backwards and forwards. He goes, 'It's an exercise aimed at building trust and morale. I want to go around you all individually and ask you what your goals are.' Which is what he does, roysh. JP goes, 'I guess to make everyone in the school proud of me.' Fionn's there, 'Well, Castlerock has a long and storied history and its victories in the Leinster Schools Cup are an integral part of that tradition. I guess I'd like to become part of it,' the steamer. Oisinn goes, 'I want to win the Cup because the old man said he'd buy me a Golf,' and we all totally crack up.

Sooty's like, 'No, lads, it doesn't matter what your own personal motivation is, as long as you are focused on the matter in hand, ie, winning the match. What about you, Ross?' I rub my face. I should have actually shaved. He goes, 'Well, Ross. What are your expectations?' I look up, roysh, we're talking really slowly here, shrug my shoulders and I just go, 'My expectations? Only one ... Kick ass!' And with that, roysh, the whole place goes totally ballistic, everyone's suddenly, like, standing up on the tables and screaming and cheering and giving it, 'YOU THE MAN, ROSS! YOU THE MAN!' And I look over at Sooty and he's, like, standing on the desk at the top of the room and he's, like, punching the air, going, 'KILL! KILL! KILL!'

xxx

JP grabs my orm, roysh, and shakes me and he's like, 'Ross, are with you us?' I snap out of it and I'm there, 'Sorry?' He goes, 'I asked you can you hear them?' and I'm like, 'Who?' and he's there, 'Our supporters.' I'm basically too focused to hear anything, but then I listen, roysh, and I can hear them, outside the dressing room, going, 'WE WILL, WE WILL ROCK YOU – FOCK YOU, ANY WAY YOU WANT TO,' which Sooty is supposed to have banned, though it won't even get mentioned at, like, assembly tomorrow if we kick orse today.

Yesterday, me and Oisinn were asked to give a speech at, like, choir practice, roysh, just to let the rest of the school know how much their support means to all the goys and, like, how we have to totally frighten the fock out of the Gonzaga crowd today. And they're doing us proud alroysh, judging by the noise they're making.

At this moment in time, I think it's pretty fair to say we're all, like, fairly tense and worked up. One of the goys, Simon – we're talking second row, he's, like, crying, roysh, and Oisinn's, like, hugging him and telling him to focus. Christian high-fives me, as does Fionn, while JP and one of the other goys, Eunan, are standing with their foreheads pressed together and giving it, 'GONZAGA, YOU ARE TOTALLED! YOU ARE TOTALLY FOCKING TOTALLED!' going completely apeshit basically. Even Oisinn storts losing it, punching one of the lockers, going, 'WE'RE CASTLEROCK. CASTLE-FOCKING-ROCK!'

Has to be said, roysh, the speech Father Fehily gave us this morning has, like, totally fired us up. He was like, 'I think I'm on the record as saying, quite a long time ago now, that I believe schools rugby is a gift from the Lord Himself. Yes, indeed. In fact, I like to believe that had

Our Lord had a little bit more time to compose His Sermon on the Mount, he would have given a little mention to the Leinster Senior Schools Cup, maybe leaving out the bit about the meek inheriting the Earth if he was under some class of time constraint. *For verily, I say unto thee that schools rugby is truly blesséd. Tend it, guard it and nourish it, for it is written.'*

It was pretty emotional stuff, I have to say. He was like, 'We here at Castlerock have decided to declare this year ... the Year of the Eagle. Yes. Yes, indeed. The eagle is the most magnificent of all of the manifold species of bird that God has given us. Strong and clever, the eagle rules the skies with a majesty that simply takes the breath away. And I draw an analogy between the eagle and the students here at Castlerock. Like the eagle, you are the very best of your species. The élite. You are better than everyone else in the whole world and the success of the school's rugby team – oh blesséd thing – is an expression of your superiority over people from other schools.'

I had, like, tears in my eyes at that stage. He was there, 'To add, if I might, a serious note – the perpetuation of the purity of our race depends on you. One day, difficult as it is to imagine, you will all leave this institution of education and social advancement. It is my earnest hope that you will take with you the moral principles and Christian lessons we have inculcated in you, when you go off to work for investment banks that destroy the Third World, or management consultancies that close down factories and throw poor people onto the dole. But ... oh but, oh but ... Verily, I say unto thee that what's more important than any of that is the good name of this school. And that is why it is *vital* that this Year of the Eagle proves he really is ... KING OF THE SKIES!'

The whole place went ballistic, roysh. I looked around and, like, everyone – we're talking me, Fionn, Simon, even Oisinn – was, like, bawling their eyes out. Then all of the goys on the S had to, like, stand up and walk up onto the stage and everyone in the whole crowd was, like, cheering and screaming, roysh, and then everyone sang the Castlerock anthem, 'Castlerock Above All Others', which has been the school song since, I don't know, the Thirties or something. It was actually Fehily's old man who wrote it. It's like:

> *Castlerock boys are we,*
> *There is nothing that we fear,*
> *Bold and courageous we morch,*
> *Danger will never faze us.*
> *We will sully the school's name never,*
> *You know we belong together,*
> *You and I forever and ever,*
> *Onwards and upwards we morch.*
> *We'll shy from battle never,*
> *We need our Lebensraum,*
> *We'll take the Rhineland,*
> *And the Sudetenland,*
> *Ein Volk, Ein Reich, Ein Rock.*
> *Castlerock above all others,*
> *Castlerock above all others.*

I'm telling you, roysh, if we'd played the game there and then, we'd have put, like, two hundred points past those tossers. Even, like, two hours later, every time I think about it the hairs on the back of my neck just, like, stand on end.

Oisinn stands up and tells us it's time to kick ass and a couple of the goys, obviously realising how much is riding on my kicking today, grab me by the shoulders and stort giving it, 'YOU THE MAN, ROSS! YOU THE MAN!'

We walk out of the dressing-room and the noise is, like, deafening. You'd basically swear there was only one team playing if you heard it. The Gonzaga crowd are being totally drowned out. It's all, like, 'WE ARE ROCK, WE ARE ROCK, WE ARE ROCK ...' The nerves just, like, disappear when I hear it. It's like Fehily said, it really does feel as though God wants us to win. I know I have to focus, though, so I kick a few balls from, like, different angles and I just know in my hort of horts that I'm not going to miss anything today. And the crowd are going, 'WE'VE GOT ROSS O'CARROLL-KELLY ON OUR TEAM, WE'VE GOT ROSS O'CARROLL-KELLY ON OUR TEAM ...'

I'm so focused on my own game during the warm-up, roysh, that I don't even look at the opposition. When I do, I have to say I'm not impressed. A few of them look like they should be on the old Slim Fast plan. Then I see that tosser who asked Sorcha to the pre-debs, we're talking Jamie O'Connell-Keavney, and I notice he's, like, captain, which shows you how hord up they must be. I just walk straight over to him and I go, 'You're history, dude.' He just, like, looks me up and down, roysh, and he goes, 'Yeah, Sorcha said you were a spa,' and I'm there, 'That is *it*. That is SO it. You are totalled. You are totally focking totalled,' and it takes the two biggest goys on our team – we're talking Oisinn and Simon – to drag me away. Oisinn's going, 'Save it for the game, Ross,' which I know is good advice.

And it's basically what I do. I settle whatever, like, butterflies are left by kicking a penalty after, like, two minutes. Christian – delighted for the goy – he scores an amazing try pretty much straight afterwards, which I convert, and Gonzaga are in total disarray. There's, like, twenty minutes gone and we're already 22-0 ahead and, not being, like, crude or anything, but we're pissing all over them. And I can't take all of the credit for it either. It's just one of those games when basically every cog in the machine works. Our pack destroyed them. Oisinn and Simon must have won nine or ten of their lineouts. Eunan, our scrumhalf, gave me so much good ball, JP didn't put a foot wrong at the back and even Fionn had a stormer outside me, though I'd never tell him that. The man of the match, for me and pretty much everyone, was Christian, who ended up scoring, like, three tries, and as we were walking off I was like, 'The Force was with you today,' and he goes, 'It was with all of us, young Skywalker,' which is fair enough. All the crowd are giving it, 'WE'RE RICH AND WE KNOW WE ARE, WE'RE RICH AND WE KNOW WE ARE ...' and the buzz is totally cool. Of course I ended up kicking five penalties and five conversions – we won, like, 60-6 – and you should have seen that tosser's face, Jamie whatever-the-fock-he's-called, about halfway through the second half when he kicked his first penalty and I went up to him and storted giving it, 'Happy birthday to you ...' He just, like, pushes me, roysh, and I push him back and I go, 'Do you want to finish this now?' and I swear to God I'm about to, like, deck the focker when Oisinn comes over and reminds me that I've already shown the retord who's boss.

And I SO did.

CHAPTER TWO
'Has minimal attention span'

I call out to Fionn's gaff and his old pair open the door. Not his old man, roysh, not his old dear, but the two of them. And they both hug me and tell me it's absolutely wonderful to see me, which is, like, slightly over the top given that I met them in the Frascati Centre on Thursday night, which they also thought was wonderful, and then they tell me to come into the kitchen because they're having quiche and it's got, like, artichokes and hickory bacon in it and it's wonderful. They walk me towards the kitchen, basically holding one orm each, and they sit me down at the table and they tell me it's wonderful that Fionn has made the school team, roysh, and they tell me that Fionn's grandfather also played centre on the great Castlerock team of the Thirties. Oh and that was also wonderful as well.

They completely freak me out, these two. My old dear's got these two sort of, like, porcelain apples with big smiley faces hanging up in the kitchen, roysh, and that's what Fionn's old pair remind me of, two focking apples with big mad shiny faces, red cheeks, the lot. They even colour-coordinate the way they dress, for fock's sake. She's got on a pair of beige slacks and a charcoal grey cardigan, roysh, and he's wearing beige cords. And they're all over each other, roysh, all this putting their orms around each other and giving each other, like, compliments.

I don't know how Fionn sticks it basically. If I go to watch telly and my old pair are even sitting next to each other, roysh, I go into the next room to borf.

Fionn's old man asks me how the studies are going and I tell him I haven't been to a single class since before Christmas, when you can basically get away with murder. He goes, 'Wonderful. Old Maximus Barry still doing the rounds, is he?' and I'm there, 'Yeah, I have him for French this year. Or is it Maths?' and he goes, 'He was there in my day, you know. Wonderful. And old Halitosis Henderson is still the first year dean, I believe. I shouldn't be unkind, of course.'

Fionn's sister Eleanor comes in. We're talking Carolyn Lilipaly here and I've been there twice and that wrecks Fionn's head. She goes, 'Hi, Ross,' and she air-kisses and hugs me, roysh, then says she heard we were doing *Wuthering Heights* as our novel – which is focking news to me, of course – and if I want any notes on it she can give them to me. I'm there, 'That'd be a huge help because I'm finding the book quite challenging. Hey, give me your mobile number and I'll ring you during the week,' and she gives it to me. Putty in the hand. She's got on the old boots and jodhpurs, roysh, and she announces that she's going riding, and I am SO tempted to comment it's not funny, but I manage to, like, bite my lip. It's hugs and air-kisses for everyone in the audience and then she focks off.

The old dear finishes setting the table, then she asks if Lorcan, Fionn's wanker of a little brother, is in and the old man says no, he's out with his pals on their skateboards, roysh, and suddenly she's like, 'Ewan, ask Ross now, before Fionn comes downstairs.' The old man goes, 'Rather delicate though, darling. Can't just blurt it out, can you?' and the old dear goes, 'But it's important that we know.' He's like,

'Ross, being young is a, what's the word, a wonderful time in anyone's life. But it's a difficult time, a time of confusion, of inner conflict, of bodily changes, of feelings we don't understand ...' The old dear goes, 'Oh for heaven's sake, Ewan. Ross, we think that Fionn might be gay.'

I go, *'Gay?'* There's, like, silence in the kitchen. They're looking for an answer. I look down at the table and I go, 'Oh, I get it now. The quiche.' The old dear goes, 'Well, we heard there's all sorts of things they eat, didn't we, Ewan?' He goes, 'I'll tell him about the sun-dried tomatoes. Ross, we bought a jar of sun-dried tomatoes, I suppose as a test more than anything. Popped them in the cupboard. Two days later the jar was empty. Now Eleanor didn't eat them. She has her allergies. And Lorcan wouldn't have touched them. It had to have been Fionn.' The old dear jumps up from her seat, yanks open the cupboard and goes, 'He's made a big hole in that crumbled feta cheese as well.' She closes the cupboard, sits down again and goes, 'These are just little bits of clues we've been putting together. But it's not just the food. I mean, I've suspected for years. Probably since that day I caught him cutting pictures out of that *Freemans* catalogue that came through the door. I think a mother knows, deep down. Ross, you need to tell us.'

I look away, roysh, doing my best not to crack my hole laughing. I go, 'He begged me not to say anything. I just feel I'm letting him down telling you this.' The old man goes, 'But he's our son, Ross. It's important that we know what he's going through.' I just, like, pause for about ten seconds, roysh, just for, like, dramatic effect, then I go, 'Okay. You're right. He's gay,' and the old dear jumps backwards, roysh, and claps her hands and sort of, like, squeals and goes, 'My son is gay! That's wonderful. I have to ring Alannah and Stephen. And Helen. Oh and the girls from golf.' The old man goes, 'Whoah, Andrea. Slow down there.

It would be unfair to let any of this out until Fionn tells us himself. And he'll tell us in his own time.' The old dear's, like, staring off into space and she's like, 'We could arrange a dinner party to announce it ... Oh, Ewan, we've been so fortunate. Three wonderful children. One of each.'

I'm seriously about to explode here, trying not to laugh. The old man goes, 'Wonderful. And Ross, bit delicate this as well, but you and Fionn aren't–' and I go, 'FOCK OFF! ... I mean, no. No, I'm, em, I'm actually normal.' He goes, 'Thought that, Andrea. Hasn't even looked at the quiche. Well, each to his own. And this young lady who's been coming to the house. This Jayne. Lovely girl. Her father's with Grabbit and Leggit Solicitors, and I go, 'She's actually mine. As in *my* girlfriend. Fionn is sort of, like, using her as a cover.' I'm actually shocked at how easily this stuff is coming to me. The old dear puts the quiche back in the fridge, roysh, and she goes, 'Because they spend hours up in that room and, without wishing to sound smutty, there's never a sound out of them.' Maybe he is a steamer. I'm like, 'I think they just talk about fashion and make-up and 'Ally McBeal'. They get on great as friends. It's often the way,' and the old man's there, 'We know. We got all the information off the Internet.' The old dear goes, 'We thought we should know everything. Autoerotic asphyxiation and what have you.'

Of course the next thing, roysh, Fionn walks into the kitchen with a book in his hand and I'm wondering has he heard any of what was said because he gives me this look, roysh, basically a filthy, but then he just goes, 'Hey, Ross. Sorry. Running a bit behind schedule. Bit wrecked actually. Was out with Jayne last night. You know Jayne with a y, don't you?' and I go, 'Yeah, the girl you're, em, going out with. What were you doing up so late? Looking at the new *Family Album* catalogue?' but he doesn't get it. I nod at the book and I go, 'What are you reading?' and he's like, 'It's a play,' and out of the corner of my eye I see his old man nodding his head at the old dear and she smiles back. Fionn goes, 'It's *Shadow of a Gunman*,' and I'm there, 'What? Hang on, how many books are on this course?' He's like, 'It's not *on* the course. *The Plough and the Stars* is. I'm actually reading *around* the course at the moment. I think they're going to hit us with a question about O'Casey's penchant for humanising political drama this year.' I go, 'Yeah, wake me when it's my stop. Come on, are we going?'

Fionn's old pair are looking at him, roysh, and they can't stop smiling, to the point where he actually has to ask them if everything's alroysh. They say that everything's wonderful and his old dear tells him she's so proud of him and I have to leave the room because I'm about to crack up in their faces.

XXX

The doorbell's been ringing for the last focking twenty minutes, roysh, and I've been screaming for someone to answer it, but it looks like I'm going to have to. The old pair must have gone into town. I look at my phone and it's, like, eleven o'clock and I'm wondering who in their right mind could be calling to the door at this time on a Saturday morning. I throw on my grey Russell Athletic T-shirt, roysh, and go down to answer the door, and who is it only Sorcha. She's obviously heard about the result of the Gonzaga match and is trying to, like, work her way back in. Before I get a chance to ask her what the fock she wants, roysh, she hands me a bottle of *cK One* and she goes, 'A peace offering.'

I'm freezing my towns off standing there in my boxer shorts, roysh, so I end up having to ask her in. I had it in my mind to be a total, like, dickhead to her, but it's only when we get into the kitchen, roysh, that I notice how well she looks, and we're talking totally here. She's obviously dressed for my benefit, roysh, because she's wearing that charcoal grey cashmere polo neck, the Calvin Klein one that I admired when I met her two weeks ago in The Bailey, and the Donna Karan boot-cut trousers she shelled out two hundred bills for and, unless I'm very much mistaken, the Dolce & Gabbana boots her old pair bought her for Christmas. She's basically dressed to kill and I actually want to be with her.

I give her a hug, roysh, and say she must be cold. She's not wearing a jacket, even though it's, like, freezing outside, but she is wearing a pink scorf and pink gloves and also her Chloe aviator sunglasses, though as a hair-band. She goes, 'Yeah. It's, like, SO cold out there.' I'm going, 'You're up early,' and she's like, 'I'm heading into town. The sale's storting in BT2 today. Dad gave me some money. Wondered did you fancy coming in with me?' I'm there, 'Don't know. I'm pretty sore after the game. Bumps and bruises,' and she goes, 'Please, Ross. You know what they say. It's just no fun, shopping for one.' I'm there, 'Yeah, fine. Want some coffee first?' and she goes, 'I'll make it while you get dressed.'

I open the cupboard to try to find where the old dear keeps the gourmet shit she buys. I'm, like, throwing boxes and jors and stuff around, roysh, trying to lay my hands on it and Sorcha comes over to help me and OH! MY! GOD! the smell of that *Issey Miyake*, roysh, I'm going to end up basically hopping the girl in a minute. She finds the coffee and she goes, 'I saw what Tony Ward wrote about you,' and I go, 'Haven't seen the paper yet.' She's like, 'He described your kicking as peerless,' and I'm there, 'Well, he's always had it in for me. Pure jealousy because he never achieved the heights in the game that I did.' She gives me a funny look and goes, 'No, Ross. It's actually good what he said. Peerless is good.' I whip out a packet of Jaffa Cakes and I'm there, 'Oh, roysh. That's cool, but we've still got a long way to go to the final.'

I tell her I'm going upstairs to get changed and she asks me, roysh, what I'm going to wear and before I get a chance to, like, answer she asks me to wear the French Connection shirt she bought me for our six-month anniversary, the light blue one, and my DKNY jeans and I don't know why, roysh, maybe it's just that, like, old habits die hord, but I end up doing what she says. As I'm walking out of the room, I grab my glacier blue lambswool V-neck, which I tie around my waist, to make it look like she hasn't totally dressed me, and also my Ralph Lauren baseball cap. A splash of *Carolina Herrera* and I'm ready.

'Is that *Carolina Herrera*?' she goes and I nod, and she's there, 'Ois-inn?' and I'm like, 'Yeah,' and she goes, 'So he's still working in the airport? In duty free?' and I'm there, 'Just on Saturdays. The amount of birds he ends up chatting up at that perfume counter ...' Sorcha's standing next to the sink. She still has her gloves on and she's, like, holding her mug with both hands. She blows into her coffee before she takes, like, a tiny sip. I'm there, 'So what did you say you're buying today?' and she doesn't answer, roysh, just keeps sort of, like, smiling at me, which freaks me out, and then eventually she goes, 'Who's Alyson?'

Fock.

I'm there, 'Who?' and she's like, 'Alyson? With a y?' So I'm there pretending to be wracking my brains, going, 'Alyson with a y ... doesn't ring any bells ...' and she's like, 'Your mum left you a note on the table, saying she phoned last night. Apparently you left one of your CDs in her car.' Snoop Dog, yeah. I'm there, 'Oh, that Alyson with a y. Look, Sorcha, she's only, like, a friend,' and she just, like, bursts out laughing and goes, 'I'm not jealous, Ross,' and I'm there, 'No skin off my nose if you are. We're both–' and she goes, 'Free agents, I know. Look, Ross. I came here today, well, portly to clear the air. I've been doing SUCH a lot of thinking and – OH! MY! GOD! – I was SO out of order that night in Annabel's, throwing drink over you. I guess when I saw you with that Sian what's-her-name I just totally flipped. I thought at first it was because she thinks she's all that on the hockey pitch when in fact she's a TOTAL knob. Then I realised it was because I still have strong feelings for you ...'

Fock the shopping. I put my orms around her, roysh, and get ready to throw the lips on her when all of a sudden she goes, 'Ross, what the hell do you think you're doing? I have feelings for you, but not in that way,' and I just, like, pull away. She goes, 'Like I said, I've been doing SUCH a lot of thinking and I won't deny there's still something there. But I accept that it's over between us. Me and you as, like, girl-friend-boyfriend, it's not healthy. But I still want us to do stuff together. I value your friendship too much to ever want to lose you.' I've made a total tit of myself here, which was her plan all along, and I end up going, 'That's what I want too. Come on, let's hit the shops.'

Sorcha's driving the RAV4 her old man bought her for her eighteenth. She's got the new Robbie Williams album on and she totally loses it when 'Angels' comes on, going, 'OHMYGOD OHMYGOD OHMYGOD, that is my favourite song of, like, ALL time,' and when it's over she asks me to, like, hit the button and play it again and we listen to it for the second time and then she turns around, roysh, and she tells me that it SO reminds her of Josh, and when I don't ask her who Josh is she tells me he's this amazing goy she met in Reynords a few weeks ago, he's in UCD, has an amazing body and plays Gaelic football. I go, 'Is he a bogger?' and she's like, 'He's *actually* from Dalkey,' and I say basically fock-all after that, which must make her day. I thought she'd be all over me like a rash after the Gonzaga result, not playing hord to get.

I spend the rest of the drive in, flipping through a magazine that was, like, on my seat when I got in and there's an article in it about shedding those unwanted pounds after Christmas and the headline is, like, WHAT YOU EAT TODAY, YOU WEAR TOMORROW.

We pork in the Stephen's Green Shopping Centre and Sorcha links my orm as we walk down Grafton Street and steers me into BT2. The place – I can't believe it, roysh – it's full of skobies. It's the sales that attract them, JP always says, like flies to a rotting dog. We're talking major skobefest here and these two birds – REAL howiyas – they stort giving Sorcha filthies. So I'm just there, 'Sorry, do you two have a problem, aport from the obvious?' and one of them gives it, 'Fookin poshie bastard,' and I go, 'Fock off back to your own side of the city,' and I turn around to Sorcha and I'm there, 'Pram Springs on tour.' She's like, 'What do you expect? They're offering, like, seventy percent off some of these clothes. It's bound to attract those sorts of people,' and I'm there, 'I know. It's like TK Maxx. Every focking skanger in Dublin is wearing Ralphs since they opened.'

Sorcha ends up buying a blue fitted jacket by Dolce & Gabbana, black knee-high boots by, as far as I remember, Alberta Ferretti, a black hooded evening dress by Elle Active and two white sleeveless T-shirts from, like, French Connection. Then we go and look at, like, the men's clothes. I notice that the black and white Ralph sweater I bought before Christmas is reduced from a hundred and ten bills to, like, fifty-five and the blue and white striped Polo Sport rugby shirt the old pair got me for Crimbo is reduced from, like, a hundred and fifteen bills to, like, eighty.

I turn to Sorcha and I'm there, 'This is totally unfair. I've a good mind to ask for the manager.' She goes, 'Cheer up, I bought you this,' and she hands me this bag, roysh, and she goes, 'Open it,' and I do and it's, like, a blue Armani Jeans baseball cap with a white AJ insignia on the front, and I take off the cap I already have on and put on the new one and Sorcha says it SO suits me. She's like, 'You don't already have it in blue, do you?' and I'm there, 'No,' and she's like, 'Thank God for that. Because I, like, bought it and then I got this, like, horrible feeling that I saw you wearing one in the Red Box a couple of weeks ago,' and quick as a flash, roysh, I'm there, 'Maybe you're thinking of Josh,' and the second I bring up his name, roysh, I regret it because I know I really shouldn't give her the pleasure. She just, like, smiles at that, roysh, and goes, 'I just bought you that to say thanks for coming into town with me,' and then she goes, 'Come on, I'll shout you a cappuccino.'

We're about to hit Café Java, roysh, when all of a sudden who do we bump into only Hennessy, the old man's penis of a solicitor. I crack on not to see him at first, roysh, trying to, like, distract Sorcha's attention into the window of some shop, which turns out to be the focking Scholl sandle shop, *duuuhhh!* But she cops him in the reflection of the window, roysh, and she goes, 'OH! MY! GOD! Ross, isn't that your dad's solicitor? Hennessy?' and she turns around – the dope – and she calls him and of course he's straight over.

He's like, 'Hello, Ross. Hello there, young Sorcha. Ross, I have to agree with every word Tony Ward said. Peerless is right. The trusty right foot. Gonzaga simply had no answer to it. It's like your father said, first round of the Leinster Schools Senior Cup or not, Warren Gatland will have taken note of that performance,' and he says all of this to me, roysh, without taking his eyes off Sorcha, and of course she hasn't copped him practically drooling over her. She goes, 'Are you doing some shopping?'

He goes, 'Getting a few last-minute things, darling. Flying out tonight,' and she's like, 'Oh my *God*, where?' and he's there, 'Bangkok. These tribunals are a licence to print money. I can't spend the bloody stuff fast enough. So it's Bangkok. You wouldn't believe the things that are still legal over there.' Of course this comment passes completely over Sorcha's head, as does the sly little look he has at her top tens.

She goes, 'Mrs Coghlan-O'Hara must be SO looking forward to it,' and he laughs and he goes, 'You don't bring coal to Newcastle, darling,' and he looks at me for the first time and winks. When he's focked off, roysh, Sorcha says that OH! MY! GOD! he is SUCH a nice man and it, like, frightens me how easily she's taken in by people.

We hit Café Java and end up getting a table near the window. She takes off her gloves and her scorf, roysh, and she, like, lays them down on the table and then storts looking through the menu. She orders a feta cheese salad, roysh, with tomato bread and no olives and a Diet Coke, and I order a club sandwich, which comes with, like, a side order of Pringles, and also a Coke, but I'm still Hank afterwards so I order, like, a ciabatta filler and then a Chocolate Concorde.

Sorcha says she's been eating SO much shit lately, trying to get her head around her special topic for history, which is the war poets, and she is SO not having dessert, although she ends up eating half of mine when it arrives. I order a coffee and she has, like, an espresso mallow-chino, which she plays with for, like, ten minutes with her spoon, making different shapes out of the marshmallow as it melts on the surface. I can tell there's something on her mind. Eventually, roysh, she puts down her spoon, takes off her scrunchy, slips it onto her wrist, shakes her hair loose, then pulls it back into a low ponytail again, puts the scrunchy back on and then pulls four or five or strands of hair loose. It looks exactly the same as it did before she did it. She goes, 'Ross, there's something I want to ask you,' and I'm there, 'Shoot,' and she goes, 'Okay, I'll come straight out with it. Will you come to the UCD Orts Ball with me? Just as, like, friends?' I'm there, 'But neither of us is in UCD.' She's like, 'Emma's got me two tickets. Please?' I go, 'Why don't you ask lover-boy? That Jamie O'Connell-Toss Features.' She's like, 'He's a loser, Ross.' I'm there, 'And what about this Josh tool?' She goes, 'Look, I'm asking *you*.' I let her sweat for a few seconds and then I go, 'Okay. But just as friends.' I'm dying to be with her, roysh, but I'm not getting into that whole going-together scene again.

She takes out a pack of Marlboro Lights and I go to squeeze the lizard. I wash my hands, splash some water on my face and then, like, take out my mobile. I have four new messages. Keeva phoned to say she is SO embarrassed and she's never done anything like this before, but she got my number from, like, Christian and she's probably making a TOTAL spa of herself but she really enjoyed that night, we're talking the night we were together, and she wondered whether I wanted to go out to her house in, like, Clonskeagh to maybe watch a DVD, or, like, go for a drink, or maybe something to eat, or the cinema and she leaves her number, roysh, and she tells me I can phone her back, but not on Saturday morning because she has, like, hockey. And I'm thinking, yeah she's right, she is making a total spa of herself. The next two messages are hang-ups, but I can see that they've both come from Sian's number, one at half-eleven last night and the other at, like, a quarter-to-nine this morning, which means she's probably been up all night brooding over the fact that I haven't rung her, the focking sap. The fourth call is from some bird called Claire who says she's, like, Sian's best friend and she tells me I'm a total orsehole for the way I treated her and she doesn't know why Sian is constantly falling for dickheads like me. Then she screams 'DICKHEAD' down the phone four times and tells me that any girl who has ever been with me says I have a small penis. I snap the phone shut and check myself out in the mirror again. I have to say, roysh, I'm looking pretty well. Then I go back to the table where Sorcha is handing the waitress her credit cord and asking her can she bring her a glass of Ballygowan. She goes, 'Still.'

XXX

Fionn goes, 'Ross, can I ask you something?' and I kind of know what's coming. I'm there, 'Shoot.' He goes, 'Did you say something to my old pair the other day?' Of course quick as a flash, roysh, I'm there, 'Like what?' and he goes, 'I don't know. They've just been acting really, I don't know, weird around me. They just keep smiling at me all the time. And the old dear keeps telling me that if I ever need someone to talk to ...' I go, 'She's probably just being, like, supportive. It's a difficult, confusing time for us all, Fionn.'

XXX

Erika always looks as though she's in a fouler, roysh, and I can actually picture her face when she answers her mobile. I'm there, 'Hey, it's Ross,' and I get nothing back. I'm there, 'Erika, it's Ross,' and she goes, 'So you know your own name, great. What do you want?' I'm like, 'Just, like, a chat,' and she's there, 'What kind of an idiot are you, calling me while I'm horse-riding? The ringing could have panicked Orchid,' and I'm there, 'Well if the phone scares the horse, why do you bring it with you when you're on him?' and it's probably in case Brad Pitt calls, or Matt Damon, or one of the other five men in the world she'd *actually* be prepared to sleep with. But she doesn't answer, roysh, she just goes, 'This conversation is boring me,' and she hangs up.

XXX

I need a sheet of paper, roysh, so I turn to the back of my copybook and rip out the last page, which of course means the first page comes out with it, though that doesn't matter a fock because I haven't written squat all year, even though it's, like, January. I write on it,

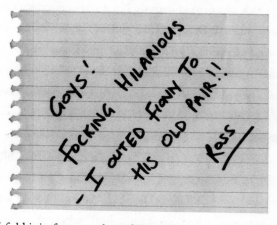

And I fold it in four, roysh, and I write like,

OISINN

on the outside and I hand it to Christian beside me and I tell him to, like, pass it down the line to Oisinn, totally forgetting that Fionn's sitting next to him and when he's handed the note to pass on, roysh, he's too engrossed in the lesson to look at the name that's on it, roysh, and he opens it while still looking at the blackboard and then he looks down and – FOCK IT! – he reads it. Then he turns it over, roysh, and he sees Oisinn's name on it and he looks back up the row and he knows it's from me. He just, like, gives me a filthy, then rips it up into, I don't know, fifty pieces.

The next thing I hear, roysh, is Ms Cully – we're talking Bet Down City, Idaho here – and she's going, *'Cad a bhí ar siúl nuair a fógraíodh na comhbhuaiteoirí don Duais Nobel in Oslo i 1998?'* and I'm just sitting there, roysh, staring at her, not having a focking bog whether this class is, like, French or Irish or what, but of course everyone's looking at me, roysh, waiting for my answer, so I take a gamble that it's Irish and I go, *'Tá me on the S,'* which I have to say, roysh, I'm pretty pleased with. Everyone cracks their holes laughing and she ends up asking some swot, Fionn actually, who's her focking pet. He's like, *'Bhí sé in mbun oibre i nDoire ag seoladh plean eacnamaíochta don chathair agus David Trimble ag filleadh abhaile ó thuras geilleagrach i Meiriceá nuair a fógraíodh in Oslo gurb iad a bhuaigh Duais Nobel na Síochána i 1998. Luach saothair a bhí ann do John Hume agaus dá bhean, Pat, as ucht na hoibre eachtach a rinne siad le triocha bliain anuas,'* and it's all *an bhfuil cead agam dul go dtí an focking leithreas* to me. Ms Cully's there, *'Ceart go leor,'* and Fionn's gone, *'Go raibh maith agat,'* and then she's like, *'An bhfuil tusa ar an S freisin?'* and he's like, *'Sea,'* and I don't know what the fock's going down here but she just, like, looks at me and shakes her head.

So after that, roysh – him basically making me look stupid – I decide there's no way I'm, like, apologising to him over the note, blah blah blah, so I decide to just, like, brazen it out, if that's the word, and after class I end up walking down the corridor behind him and I'm going, 'My name is Fionn. For Irish, press one. For French, press two. For Spanish, press three,' ripping the piss out of him basically, and of course he ends up flipping the lid, roysh, he spins around and he goes, 'What are you going to do when you finish school, Ross?' and the question catches me sort of, like, unawares, roysh, because I was expecting him to call me a tool or a knob or something like that. A spa or a wanker. Or a dickhead or a tosspot. Or a penis. I go, 'Em, nothing, I suppose,' and he nods his head and he's like, 'Just live off your old man's money? You don't aspire to anything better than that, Ross? You don't want something more for yourself?' I'm there, 'That's easy for you to say. You've got brains to burn,' and he goes, 'We've all got focking brains. It's how we use them that's different,' and I end up telling him that the only reason I give him such a hord time is because I always feel as thick as pigshit when I'm in his company and I'm probably jealous because he's amazing at rugby and at, like, learning.

I go, 'Look, I'm sorry about telling your old pair you were a steamer. There'll be no more of that shit, I promise. Are you coming down to the canteen? I'll shout you lunch, just to show there's, like, no hord feelings,' and he goes, 'I'm gonna skip lunch. I've got a meeting with the French Exchange Club,' and I have to bite my lip to stop myself calling him an Activities Nerd. He goes, 'Why don't you come along?' He senses my, like, reluctance, if that's the right word, and he goes, 'Come on. You never know what you'll get out of it.' So I end up tagging along, roysh, and on the way down to B6 I turn to him and I go, 'Fionn, can I just check with you – that wasn't French we were talking in that class back there, was it?' and he's there, 'No, that was Irish,' and I'm like, 'Thank fock for that. I thought I might have made a total tit of myself there for a second.'

So we head in, roysh, and it's like a focking Fionn lookalikes club in there, all glasses and anoraks and A4 pads on the table with blue and red biros and different coloured highlighter pens at the ready. It's the focking Valley of the Dweebs. This complete tool, roysh, I think I actually gave him a wedgy when we were in transition year, although he's obviously managed to blank out the experience because he turns around to me and he goes, '*Mon dieu*, a new member,' and straight away I go, 'Hey, don't get your hopes up. I'm just checking out the vibe.' He goes, '*Comment vous appellez vous?*' and I look at Fionn and he goes, 'He's asking you your name,' so obviously I'm like, 'Ross.'

Aidan's the tosser's name and I'm actually pretty insulted that he doesn't know who I am. He's obviously got no interest in rugby, the weirdo. He goes, '*Ah, Ross. Vous dites, "Mon nom est Ross", ou "Je m'appelle, Ross". Et je m'appelle Aidan. Bienvenu.*'

I'm just, like, staring the focker out of it. Everyone in the room's just, like, smiling at me and it's freaking the shit out of me. Fionn turns around to him and he goes, '*Il fait parti de l'équipe de rugby*,' and Aidan, who two years ago was down on his knees in the lobby, roysh, begging me not to hang his boxers off the Christmas tree in the library, suddenly thinks he's, like, shit-hot with his, '*Ooh la la! Nous devons parler plus lentement*,' and Fionn goes, '*Non, non. Il faut que nous parlions en Anglais.*'

Aidan goes, 'Ross, have you an interest in participating in the French Exchange Programme?' which I recognise as English, just about. He's even got me answering in this focking froggy accent. I'm there going, 'What *ees* involved?' like the tool that I am. He goes, 'Well, in collaboration with the languages laboratory, we've devised a ...' and I decide I've already heard enough of this shit and I go, 'Some frog comes to live in my house with me and then I go over there and live in his house with him?' He thinks for a few seconds and then he goes, 'Essentially, that's it,' and straight away I'm like, 'Not eenterested, *hombre*,' which is pretty good, I have to say, and I get up to go because my stomach's rumbling and I'd eat a scabby dog at this stage.

The next thing, roysh, Fionn slides this, like, file in front of me and goes, 'Aren't you going to at least look?' and I just throw my eyes up to heaven and I open it, anything for an easy life, and – HOLY! FOCK! – I cannot believe it. I go, 'You never said there'd be ... birds involved,' and Fionn goes, 'But of course if you're not interested,' and as he reaches over to take the file back, roysh, I grab it with both hands and I go, 'I never said that.' He smiles, roysh, and he's there, 'Beautiful, isn't she?' and I have to say she is, roysh, she's totally babealicious, a ringer for Natalie Imbruglia, and she's wearing this, like, swimsuit thing, huge top tens, and I've an old Woody Harrelson just looking at her. Fionn goes, 'Her name is Clementine,' and I go, 'I'll take her.'

Of course that's not good enough for this Aidan tool. He laughs, roysh – he's looking to get decked – and he goes, 'It's, er, not as simple as that, Ross,' obviously planning to bail in there himself. I'd love to see her face when she walks through the Arrivals gate and sees Bill focking Gates looking back at her. She'd be on the next plane back to, I don't know, Paris or wherever the airport in France is. It turns out, though, he knows he's out of his depth. He goes, 'First, you have to write a letter to her, to introduce yourself, let her know something about you. And she will write to you and you can decide whether you are suitable,' and I'm looking at the picture and I'm thinking, 'She's suitable alroysh.'

I stand up and pick up the file and I go, 'Fionn, you'll help me write the letter, will you?' and he goes, 'Absolutely,' and I'm there, 'Alroysh, I'm in. Now you're going to have to excuse me because I'm absolutely Hank at the moment. So I'll leave you to get on with whatever it is you do in here. *Asta la vista*,' and then I'm out the door.

✗✗✗

'*Tommy Girl* really is the any-time fragrance,' Oisinn is going. And there's, like, three or four birds around him – we're talking total stunners here – and they're hanging on his every word. He takes the tester down off the shelf, roysh, and he takes this bird's hand – you'd say it was Sharleen Spiteri if you didn't know better – and sprays a little bit on the inside of her wrist and he's going, 'It's a blend of Cherokee rose, camellia and blackcurrant flowers, cedar, sandalwood ...' I'm thinking the dude has GOT to be making this shit up. He's going, 'Wild heather, apple blossom, mandarin, tangerine, Dakota lily, jasmine and violet.'

Then suddenly this, like, announcement comes over the air, roysh, and it's like, 'Would all passengers on Aer Lingus flight EI102 to New York please proceed immediately to Gate 26, where your flight is now boarding and is about to close,' and one of the birds, roysh, she goes, 'We'd better be quick. Our plane is going to go without us,' and it's only then I realise they're Septics. I'm about to try and bail in, roysh – give it a bit of, 'New York, huh? The Windy City' – but I know they're, like, too engrossed in Oisinn's act to listen to any of my killer lines. Actually, I'm too engrossed myself to even use them.

He goes, 'Now *Sensi* is, in my humble opinion, the flagship of Giorgio's fleet, and I once told him as much. It's the fragrance that combines Oriental romance with Italian spirit, a rich blend of akazia, kaffir-limette, orgeat, jasmine, palisander and – who can forget? – benzoe.' *Who can forget? – benzoe?* I'd rip the piss out of him later in front of the goys if these birds didn't look like they're all about to jump his bones. He goes, '*Sensi* is a fragrance that's as warm as love itself.'

Fffzzz. He sprays a bit on one of the other bird's wrists – we're talking Nigella Lawson except sexier – and she smells it and she looks at Oisinn and I swear to God their eyes sort of, like, linger. This is *Oisinn* we're talking about. He's fat and ugly and I've just seen him send four total stunners weak at the knees. He ends up selling them a shitload of perfume, we're talking seven bottles between them, and off they go like they've just met focking Tom Cruise.

He doesn't seem to have been aware of me standing there. I go, 'Look at Tom Cruise there,' and he looks at me and goes, 'Ross, how the fock did you get through Departures without a boarding cord?' and I'm there, 'Remember that security pass that you thought you lost?' and he's like, 'Yeah,' and I go, 'Well, you didn't ... Have to say, Oisinn, when you told me you were going back working Saturdays, I couldn't focking understand why. To be honest, I always thought this job was a bit ... faggy. My eyes have been opened here this morning.'

He checks out these two air-hostesses who walk in – not Ryanair, decent-looking ones. He goes, 'There's no jobs going, Ross,' crapping it in case I try to muscle in on what he's got going here. I'm there, 'You know me, Oisinn. Not really interested in working. Although the hours you spent studying that shit are really paying off. Actually, seeing those Septics hanging out of you reminded me that we're both doing pretty well on the old foreign bird front at the mo.' He looks, like, intrigued, if that's the right word, and he goes, 'Do tell.' I'm there, 'Oh, it's nothing really, just that I'm going to be getting it together pretty soon with a French exchange student with the biggest airbags you've ever seen. Looks like that bird who used to be in 'Neighbours'. We're talking Natalie Imbruglia. Gonna be some hot lovin' going down.'

He goes, 'Yeah, I heard you were in with the Nerd Herd yesterday. Fionn set that up for you?' and I'm like, 'Fair focks to the goy, Oisinn. I mean, I know we've not always seen eye to eye – probably a bit of jealousy on his port because of my rugby skills, success with the fairer sex, etc, etc – but he's, like, sound. Looks after his mates.' Oisinn goes, 'Pity that,' and I'm like, 'What?' and he goes, 'Just saying it's a pity you two are all palsy-walsy again. I've a focking geansaí-load of women's cosmetics and fragrance catalogues that I've got to throw out. I was going to suggest that you maybe slip them under his bed next time you're in his gaff for his old dear to find,' and I go, 'He's doing me a serious turn here, Oisinn. Wouldn't be fair to do it to the goy,' and we both look at each other and break into a smile and I'm there, 'Go on, then. Give them to me.'

So he bends down under one of the checkouts, roysh, and he storts reefing all this stuff out – we're talking brochures and shit – when all of a sudden one of the Septics is back – it's the Nigella Lawson one – and her face is, like, really, really red, and at first, roysh, I'm wondering is it, like, an allergy to the perfume or something, but then I realise it's, like, embarrassment. She runs down, roysh, and she hands Oisinn this, like, piece of paper and she goes, 'I have never done anything like this in my life before. But that's, like, my phone number? And my cell's there too.'

Hand it to him. The goy's a ledge.

✗✗✗

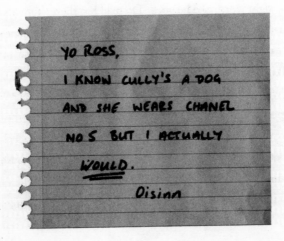

YO ROSS,

I KNOW CULLY'S A DOG

AND SHE WEARS CHANEL

NO 5 BUT I ACTUALLY

WOULD.

Oisinn

XXX

Okay. It's the third week in January. It's what, four-and-a-half to five months to the Leaving? I decide to knuckle down to a bit of study. There's no basic rule that says you can't play rugby *and* get a decent Leaving. Okay, Physics. No, fock that. History? Boring. Sorcha's doing it anyway. I'll get the notes off her the night before the exam. English. Yeah, not a bad idea. English is easy. It's just, like, reading, roysh? Where to stort is the problem. There's, like, a stack of books, we're talking poetry and plays and all sorts of bullshit. I pick up my book of past papers and just, like, open it at a random page.

'Kavanagh's poetry concerns itself with what it means to be a poet; a poet in a sometimes indifferent and ultimately beautiful world.' Consider his poetry on your course in the light of this statement. Your answer should be supported by relevant references or quotations.

Fock that.

XXX

In *Gay Times* this month the magazine's cinema critic asks why there aren't more romantic comedies with a gay theme. There's an article on gays in the Premiership and a feature on how the Internet has revolutionised the sex lives of hundreds of gay men. I wait until the shop has cleared out, then I go to pay for it, putting it face-down on the counter. The old goy in the shop goes, 'It's Ross, isn't it? You're Charles O'Carroll-Kelly's boy, aren't you?'

Fock!

I'm there, 'Can you just take for this?' and I slap ten bills on the counter and I'm like, 'Keep the change,' and I go to pick up the magazine but the focker's too quick for me. He's there, 'Let's see what it is first,' and he flips it over and he goes, 'Oh dear. What have you got yourself involved in?' I'm there, 'I haven't got myself involved in any-thing. It's not *for* me.'

'None of my business,' he goes, flicking through it. He storts reading out the focking headlines, roysh, at the top of his voice, going, 'THERE'S NOWT AS QUEER AS FOLK! SINGER-SONGWRITER TOM ROBINSON ON WHY HE'S RETURNING TO HIS TRADITIONAL ROOTS.' I'm there, 'HELLO? I said it's not *for* me.' He goes, 'FAIRY ACROSS THE MERSEY! AN EXCLUSIVE NO-HOLDS-BARRED REPORT ON THE GAY SCENE IN LIVERPOOL.' I go, 'Will you keep your focking voice down.' Two birds I know to see from Loreto Foxrock have just walked in. He goes, 'COTTAGE BY THE SEA! HOW LONELY MEN ARE FINDING LOVE IN THE PUBLIC TOILETS ... OF MORECAMBE.'

The two birds are over at the popcorn. The goy's like, 'Does Charles know you're out of the broom cupboard or what's this they call it?' I just, like, snatch the magazine off him. I go, 'It's not for me, you fock-ing brain-dead tool. It's for a friend of mine.' He just, like, taps the side of his nose and goes, 'Mum's the word.' I'm there, 'I want a large brown envelope as well.' He goes, 'Got them right here under the counter.' I stick the magazine into the envelope, roysh, then I borrow a pen off the goy and write Fionn's name and address on the outside. Then I rip the envelope a bit so the word GAY is showing. The goy goes, 'Whatever are you up to, Ross?' I'm there, 'HELLO? Will you focking butt out? Do you sell stamps?' He goes, 'I've a book of local ones, Ross. Letter rate. I've no scales, though, to weigh that. I wouldn't have a notion how much it'd cost to post something like that.' I'm there, 'Just gimme ten locals then.'

He gives me the stamps. The birds arrive down at the counter. One of them asks if he has any popcorn other than cheese popcorn. I think Oisinn was with one of them once. The goy says no, he just has what's there and the two birds throw their eyes up to heaven and go down the back of the shop to get a bottle of Volvic each. I stick the stamps on and turn around to the goy. I'm there, 'There's a postbox outside, isn't there?' He just, like, nods. I throw the tenner at him.

I'm on the way out the door and he goes – the birds *had* to have heard him – he goes, 'Being gay isn't the end of the world, Ross. I know they're old, but your parents can always try for another child. Or adopt.'

XXX

We're in Annabel's, roysh, and I've got these two Mounties eating out of my hand, we're talking Zara and Eloise, both absolute babes. Zara's a *little* bit like Angel from 'Home and Away' it has to be said, and Eloise is a total ringer for Julia Roberts and I've pretty much decided, roysh, that it's Eloise I'm going to be with. She's actually giving it loads, roysh, going, 'I saw you play against Gonzaga. I thought you had a great game,' and I'm going, 'You're not just saying that because you want to be with me, are you?' and she takes it the way I meant it, roysh, as a joke and she sort of, like, slaps the top of my orm and tells me I am SO big-headed it's unbelievable.

Zara decides to get in on the act then, roysh, and she asks me if I remember her and I ask her where from and she goes, 'HELLO? I'm on the Irish debating team. We had a debate against your school, like, two months ago?' and I'm there, 'Hey, yeah. Your speech was amazing,' even though I don't remember ever clapping eyes on her before in my life, roysh, and even though I haven't a focking breeze when it comes to Irish and the only words I know are, like, *tá* and *sea* and *agus* and it's pretty hord to make a sentence out of them.

Eloise tells Zara that she is SO going to have to stop reminding her about, like, school, because she basically hasn't done a tap all year and OH! MY! GOD! if she hears the words 'trigonometry' or 'vectors' again she is going to ohmygod scream and I'm standing there, roysh, trying to work out what subject she's actually talking about and whether I'm taking it as well. She says her parents are giving her SO much hassle over, like, studying and shit? And she's applied to do, like, International Commerce with French in UCD but it's, like, OH! MY! GOD! SO many points. On top of everything, she says, she's also deputy head girl this year and she's been asked to, like, arrange the music for the graduation, because she plays the piano, even though her playing has SO gone to seed since she got mono – 'we're talking, like, glandular fever?' – and she still doesn't know what song she's going to choose as their farewell song, roysh, or whether it's even up to her, but it's definitely going to be either 'Never Forget' by Take That, 'Hero' by Mariah Carey, or 'Wind Beneath My Wings' by that Bette Midler, which is OH! MY! GOD! her favourite song of, like, ALL time.

So she asks me which one I'd choose and like any great outhalf, roysh, I'm quick to see the opening. I go, 'Hero,' and she asks me why, roysh, and I tell her it's because I like love songs. She goes, Oh my God, I wouldn't have had you down as a romantic,' and I can see her, roysh, trying really hord to believe it. I get another pint in and ask her if she wants another vodka and Diet 7-Up and she's there, 'Cool.' Zara saw the odds were stacked against her and focked off somewhere. I go, 'You've probably heard a lot of bad stuff about me from other girls,' and she doesn't answer. I'm there, 'It's all bullshit, Eloise.' Fock, I nearly called her Zara. I'm giving it, 'They all want to get to know the real me, you see. And I'm not prepared to open up until I find the girl I truly love and want to spend the rest of my life with. Can I kiss you?' She looks like she's going to, like, die of focking happiness. Before she can answer, roysh, I move in and throw the lips on her and there we are basically wearing the face off each other for twenty minutes until I get bored and stort wondering what the goys are up to. I tell her I have to drain the snake, then I head off to look for Christian and Oisinn.

When I find them, roysh, they're having a toast to the greatest rugby team in the world – us, of course – and how we're going to total Sker-ries in the second round of the cup next week and when we say total we're talking totally total. Then Oisinn and JP, roysh, break into a cho-rus of, like, 'WE'VE GOT ROSS O'CARROLL-KELLY ON OUR TEAM, WE'VE GOT ROSS O'CARROLL-KELLY ON OUR TEAM ...' and everyone in the whole club is, like, looking over and we're just there, 'OH MY GOD! we SO rock.'

Christian tells me I'll have to leave my droids outside because they don't serve their kind in here and before I can ask him, roysh, what the fock he's bullshitting on about, Fionn – *oooh, my face is sponsored by Weatherglaze* – goes, 'Goys, do we know anyone called Julian?' and of course I have to turn away to stop myself cracking up in the dude's face. Fionn goes, 'Ross, I swear to God, if I find out you're ...' and I'm there, 'What?' playing the innocent. He goes, 'We had a truce, Ross. I'm sorting you out with a hot, seriously French Natalie Imbruglia lookalike and all you can do is ...' and I'm like, 'What the fock are you talking about?' and he goes, 'Some goy keeps ringing my house looking for me. Always when I'm out. Keeps leaving the name Julian,' and Oisinn goes, 'Well, he's got to be a bender with a name like that,' and I'm there, 'Don't look at me,' but Fionn just stares at me, like he's trying to make up his mind whether to believe me or not, and I have to get the fock away before I laugh, so I head off to the can. After six or seven Britneys, the old back teeth are floating.

So there I am at the trough, roysh, and the next thing Oisinn appears beside me, with this big focking grin on his face. He goes, 'I take it that was you,' and I'm there, 'You think I'd be capable of doing something like that?' and he's like, 'You're pure evil, Ross O'Carroll-Kelly,' and I'm there, 'Hey, careful with that thing, you're focking splashing my Dubes.' He goes, 'Sorry about that. Hey, gimme your mobile.' I'm there, 'Why, are you going to have a hit and miss on that as well?' He's like, 'Just give it to me.'

I hand it to him, roysh, and he flicks down through the old directory and presses Fionn's home number. His old man answers, roysh, focking Ned Flanders himself. He's like, 'Heeee-llo?' and Oisinn, roysh, he puts on this, like, faggy voice and he's like, 'Oooh what a lovely masculine voice – as the chorus girl said to the disgraced bishop of Galway. Is Fionn in residence?' I can hear Fionn's old man going, ''Fraid not at the minute. Expect he's out with his chums,' and Oisinn's there, 'I bet he is. I bet he *is*.' I'm up against the wall, roysh, holding my sides I'm laughing so much.

Oisinn goes, 'I'm ringing from Toni & Guy, the ladies' hairdressing people, just to let him know that we received his application for the trainee stylist's job. I've given it the once-over – as the chambermaid said to the elderly peer with the pronounced limp – and we'll be calling him for an interview next week,' and I can hear Fionn's old man going, 'That's wonderful! Andrea, come and share this wonderful news ...'

By the time he hangs up, roysh, I pretty much need oxygen I'm laughing so much and when we head back out to the goys, of course, neither of us can look at Fionn without cracking our holes and I'm pretty relieved, roysh, when someone suggests grabbing a load of cans, hopping into a Jo and heading out to Donnybrook to Simon's free gaff. His old pair are in New York for the week. His pad is amazing, roysh, a big fock-off one on Ailesbury Road. He actually looks quite shocked when he opens the door. He was probably upstairs having an Allied Irish, but when he sees the cans, roysh, he's going, 'Welcome to my humble abode,' then he goes, 'Anyone score tonight?' and I'm like, 'I nipped that Eloise one. She's wanted me for ages. I was always going to give in, in the end,' and he nods and goes, 'Darned Mounties. They always get their man.'

I high-five the dude, roysh, and then we hit the kitchen and get stuck into the cans and it turns out to be an amazing night. We're all sitting on the floor of his sitting-room, roysh, knocking back the Britneys, then we move onto the shorts, we're talking vodka and Red Bulls to stort with and then Simon produces a bottle of Sambucca that his old man brought back from, I don't know, Greece or somewhere.

Oisinn says he ended up with Ellie Whelan last week, roysh, and of course we're all going, 'As in first year Agriculture in UCD, used to be head girl in Loreto on the Green?' and he goes, 'Ugly *as* sin,' like it's a plus point, and we're all there, 'Yeah, it's the same Ellie Whelan alroysh.' Turns out, roysh, he nipped her in Annabel's last Friday night and he rings her up on Saturday and asks what she's doing that night and she's like, 'I don't have any plans,' which was pretty obvious, roysh, because with a face like that she'd hordly be expecting Brad Pitt to stop by. So Oisinn takes her into town, roysh, lashes the old wheels into the old man's porking spot just off Baggot Street and they hit Café en Seine and she's, like, knocking back the Bacordi Breezers and of course

Oisinn's drinking Coke because he's, like, driving? One o'clock in the morning, roysh, they head back to the jammer, Oisinn lashes on the Love Affair on Lite FM and they stort getting hot and bothered in the back. So anyway, roysh, Oisinn drops the hand and Ellie pushes him away and he asks what the Jackanory is, does she not, like, fancy going to heaven and back, and she says it's not that, roysh, it's just that, well, she's up on the blocks at the moment.

Oisinn goes, 'I flipped, of course. I said, 'You never told me that before I spent the best port of thirty sheets on drinks for you.' I'm there, 'So what did you do?' Actually, this Sambucca is going down a bit too well. Oisinn goes, 'What do you think? I threw her out of the cor. Wasn't moving, of course.' Fionn's like, 'Oisinn, that is the most callous thing I've ever heard. You left a girl in town on her own, late at night, just because she was menstruating?' and quick as a flash, roysh, Oisinn goes, 'What do you take me for, Fionn? I dropped her down for the Nightlink. I'm nothing if not a gentleman,' and I crack my shite laughing and I high-five the dude and Christian high-fives him and then I high-five JP and then he high-fives Christian and Christian high-fives me.

So we're all hammered off our tits, roysh, and of course the games stort then. First it's, like, Chariots of Fire, roysh, which – if you've never played it before – is where everyone gets a long strip of jacks roll, roysh, and you shove one end up your orse and then, like, light the other end, and the last one to pull theirs out is basically the winner. Then there's, like, Mince Pie, roysh, which is where everyone whips down their kacks, puts a mince pie between the cheeks of their orse and then there's, like, a race? Everyone had to peg it to the bottom of the gorden, roysh, touch the wall and get back to the house, without dropping the pie of course. Then you had to squat, roysh, over your pint and drop it in. The last one to do it has to drink the pint of the goy to his immediate roysh. I end up losing one game of that and three games of Soggy Biscuit, which is ... no, forget it.

I wake up the next morning, roysh, on the floor of, like, Simon's room, still wearing the clothes I went in last night, except there's vom all over them. I must have been borfing my ring up. I open my eyes a little bit, roysh, and I can see three figures standing over me. From their voices, roysh, I know it's Fionn, JP and Simon. JP's going, 'Is he still alive?' and Simon's like, 'Yeah. A miracle. I've never seen anyone eat so many soggy digestives.' Fionn's there, 'I suppose we'd better wake him up. Double biology in half an hour. It's that test today on the respiratory system,' and I'm listening to this, roysh, but I haven't even got the strength to go, 'Yeah, roysh!'

XXX

Eloise leaves a message, roysh, and says she knows it's, like, the second time she's phoned this week and – OH! MY! GOD! – she doesn't want me to think she's a stalker – she SO doesn't – but she forgot to say in her last message that she really enjoyed the night we were together and if I want to call her, here's her number.

I'm like, Take the hint, girl.

XXX

'Skerries,' Fehily goes. 'SKERRIES! The very name evokes a sense of misery ... and of dread. God created the Earth and he did it in seven days. But man ... MAN CREATED SKERRIES. Who else but iniquitous man could have conceived of a town where winds and rains not seen since the time of Noah bring misery to thousands of people huddled inside their holiday homes? Where fishermen return from another fruitless day on the over-fished Irish Sea to find solace in solvent abuse, where heroin is distributed free to children as young as two, and harlots – common whores, my children – walk the main street, offering their sorry wares as early as nine o'clock on weekday mornings and ten-thirty at weekends? Verily I tell thee that unto thee falls a great responsibility today.' Fehily's giving us his usual pre-match pep talk and I have to say, roysh, it's real lump-in-the-throat stuff.

He goes, 'Does not the Book of Revelation prophesy what will happen at Belfield this very afternoon? Does Revelation 17:1 not tell us: *And there came one of the seven angels which had the seven veils, and talked with me, saying unto me, Come hither; I will shew unto thee the judgement of the great whore that sitteth upon many waters.* Is the village of Skerries not that whore?

'Does Revelation 19 not relate to us the bloody crimes committed by the great whore? And when it speaks of the King of Kings, the Lord of Lords, is it not Castlerock College – this holy, sanctified institution – that is being referred to? I quote Revelation 19:11: *And I saw heaven opened, and beheld a white horse; and he that sat upon him was called Faithful and True, and in righteousness he doth judge and make war. His eyes were as a flame of fire, and on his head were many crowns; and he had a name written, that no man knew, but he himself. And he was clothed with a vesture dipped in blood: and his name is called The Word of God. And the armies which were in heaven followed him upon white horses, clothed in fine linen, white and clean. And out of his mouth goeth a sharp sword* – YOU, MY CHILDREN, TAKE THY MARK – *that with it he should smite the nations* – AS WELL AS MISERABLE FISHING TOWNS IN NORTH DUBLIN – *and he shall rule them with a rod of iron: and he treadeth the winepress of the fierceness and wrath of Almighty God. And he hath on his vesture and on his thigh a name written, KING OF KINGS, AND LORD OF LORDS. For true and righteous are his judgements: for he hath judged the great whore, which did corrupt the Earth with her fornication, and hath avenged the blood of his servants at her hand.'*

It's like, Whoah! Major round of applause. He just raises his hand, roysh, and with, like, a flick of his wrist, the room is silent again. He goes, 'Verily, I say unto thee that great will be the temptation to keep the score down to double figures today, as a mark of sympathy for a group of players who should in truth be playing more Earthly games, such as soccer. Don't give into temptation. Don't give the devil a foothold that he might gain a stronghold.'

Another round of applause. He goes, 'The army which we have formed grows from day to day; from hour to hour it grows more rapidly. Even now I have the proud hope that one day the hour is coming when these untrained bands will become battalions, when the battalions will become regiments and the regiments divisions, when the old cockade will be raised from the mire, when the old banners will once again wave before us: and then reconciliation will come in that eternal last Court of Judgement – the Court of God – before which we are ready to take our stand.

'Then from our bones, from our graves will sound the voice of that tribunal which alone has the right to sit in judgement upon us. For, gentlemen, it is not you who pronounce judgement upon us, it is the eternal Court of History which will make its pronouncement upon the charge which is brought against us. The judgement that you will pass – that, I know. But that Court will not ask of us: "Have you committed high treason or not?" That Court will judge us ... who, as Germans, have wished the best for their people and their Fatherland, who wished to fight and to die. You may declare us guilty a thousand times, but the Goddess who presides over the Eternal Court of History will, with a smile, tear in pieces the charge of the Public Prosecutor and the judgement of the Court: for she declares us guiltless.'

XXX

The Skerries match turned out to be a piece of piss. All through the game, roysh, their fans – so-called fans, there was only, like, ten of them there – they were giving it, 'DADDY'S GONNA BUY YOU A BRAND NEW MOTORCAR,' and of course quick as a flash, roysh, our goys were like, 'SKANG-ERS! SKANG-ERS! SKANG-ERS!' and if that doesn't fock their heads up enough, roysh, we ended up scoring ten tries – three from man-of-the-moment, me – and I also kick seven conversions and, like, six penalties and we win basically 82-6.

I have a shower, roysh, and throw on my threads for going out, we're talking my blue and white check Dockers shirt and my Armani jeans. Sooty tells us we were a credit to ourselves today and to our race and then he goes, 'But don't forget, goys, you're only in the quarter-finals. Don't go too mad on the beer tonight,' and of course we all, like, cheer, as if to say, Yeah, roysh!

Christian got, like, a box in the face off one of their goys – the focker never even got sin-binned – and he has, like, a huge shiner and he's looking pretty pleased with himself because it'll guarantee him the pick of the scenario when we hit Annabel's later. Some official dude comes in and he storts having, like, a chat with Sooty and then they go over to where Christian's sitting, roysh, and they ask him whether he wants to cite the skobie who pretty much decked him. He goes – and this is amazing, roysh – he goes, 'No. He comes from a disadvantaged background. Those people have enough problems putting food on the table while staying on the right side of the law. I don't want to add to that,' which I have to say, roysh, is a pretty amazing thing to say. I go, 'Not sure I'd be so forgiving. Fair focks to you,' and he's there, 'It's cool, young Skywalker.'

So we're heading out, roysh, and who's waiting outside the dressing-room – for FOCK'S sake – only Knob Brain with his orsehole solicitor. He's there, at the top of his voice, roysh, going, 'HERE HE COMES! HERO OF THE HOUR! ANOTHER MILESTONE IN THE HISTORY OF IRISH RUGBY. AND NO SIGN OF GERRY THORNLEY. THE PAPER OF RECORD HAVE SENT A *FREELANCE*!' I walk straight up to him and I go, 'Will you keep your big focking foghorn voice down? Now give me some sponds.' He goes, 'Off for a celebratory beer or two with the chaps, are we?' and I'm there, 'It's none of your focking business where I'm going. Two hundred sheets should cover it.' As he's fishing through his wallet, roysh, Hennessy, the big focking oily sleazebucket, goes, 'A fine game, Ross,' and I just shrug my shoulders and go, 'Cool,' because it costs nothing to be nice. As he's peeling off the wedge the old man's giving it, 'I shall be placing a phone call to a certain Mister Malachy Logan Esquire in the morning; find out why it's wall-to-wall coverage of Ireland versus France and there'll be barely a word in tomorrow's sports pages about the Leinster Senior Cup second-round match at Belfield and the birth of a new star.' I trouser the sponds, roysh, and I turn around to him, in front of Oisinn, JP and a couple of the other goys, and I go, 'You are the biggest focking tool on the planet,' and then we hit Kiely's.

I see Fionn's already there talking to Sorcha's friend, Aoife, who he's been seeing since he broke up with Jayne with a y and Aoife broke up with Cian, our tighthead prop. She actually looks amazing – not a pick on her, I don't know what she's doing with him – and I make, like, a resolution to try to be with her in the not-too-distant future, if only just to fock his head up. I walk over and I go, 'Now that's what I call style.' She has, like, a Castlerock jersey tied around her waist. I'm totally turning the chorm on. She gives me a hug and she air-kisses me on both cheeks and goes, 'Congrats. You'd an amazing game,' and I go, 'Thanks,' even though I know she knows fock-all about rugby. She's there, 'Sorcha said she's SO sorry she couldn't come; she's up to her eyes organising this Lenten fast,' and I go, 'It's cool, she texted me,' but Aoife ignores me and she's like, 'She is going to be SO thin after it, the bitch.' She takes a sip out of her Ballygowan and I go, 'Aren't you going to introduce me to your friend?' because there's this bird – bit of a babe actually, not *that* unlike Libby off 'Neighbours' – and she's just, like, standing there on the edge of the group, like a spare one. Aoife goes, 'This is my cousin, Cara,' and straight away I'm giving it loads, roysh, playing it Kool AND the Gang, going, 'And where have you been?' as in where have you been all my life?, roysh, but she thinks I mean this after-noon and she goes, 'Me and Aoife took the afternoon off for the ATIM open day. I'm thinking of going there next year too. Then we came here to see Fionn play,' and I go, 'Cool,' and there's, like, two or three min-utes of silence and I'm thinking this bird's got basically fock-all to say for herself. She's crashing and burning here and she doesn't even know it. She goes, 'Em ... you had a good game. How many, er, things did you get?' I go, 'Tries? We're talking three,' and just as I'm saying this, roysh, I notice these two crackers over the far side of the boozer and they're, like, staring over, obviously waiting to get some face time with the man of the moment. This Cara one knows she's losing it, roysh, and just as she's telling me that she hasn't done a tap all year and she SO has to pull her socks up if she's going to pass the Leaving, I go, 'I'm going over here to talk to these honeys.'

So Slick Mick moseys on over, roysh, and he's going, 'Hey,' and they're like, 'Hihoworya?' and one of them, we're talking the one in the pink sleeveless bubble jacket – Polo Sport – she goes, 'Oh my God! you had an amazing game. They wouldn't have won it without you,' and her friend – I'm pretty sure they're Whores on the Shore; kind of know them to see – she goes, 'Ohmygod, they SO wouldn't.' The one in the bubble jacket is definitely the better-looking of the two, roysh, we're talking Joanna – a total ringer for Chloë out of 'Home and Away' – and her friend, who's not bad looking either, says her name's, like, Keelin and that I know her cousin, we're talking Sara Hanley. I'm there, 'Why is that name familiar?' laying it on really smooth, roysh, and she goes, 'She knows you from Irish college last summer,' and I agree with her when she says that Sara's SUCH a cool person, one of the nicest people you could ever meet and one of the few people you could ACTUALLY call a true friend, even though I don't know who the fock she's talking about.

So we're standing there, roysh, chatting away, and all of a sudden this goy comes over, one of the Skerries heads, he's actually one of their second rows, and he's got one of his eyes closed, roysh, and he goes to shake my hand and he's like, 'Put it there, bud,' and I don't know whether he's ripping the piss or not, roysh, but I shake his hand – basically just to let him know I don't hold it against him, being a skobie and everything – and I'm there, 'No hord feelings. What happened to your eye?' and the focking orsehole goes, 'It got poked out by your bird's collar there.' Keelin's got her collar up, oh big swinging mickey. He just, like, bursts out laughing, roysh, then he walks back over to this crowd of CHVs who are also breaking their shites laughing and he tells them that he said it.

Of course there's no way I'm having that, roysh, so I'm straight over there and – this is actually me talking, roysh, nobody told me what to say or whatever – I just go, 'Why are you such a knacker?' but it seems to go over his head, roysh, because he just, like, cracks up laughing in my face. I'm there, 'I know you. You're that Damien O'Connor they were going on about in *The Irish Times* this morning. A stor for the future, my orse.' He laughs in my face again, roysh, then he turns around to his mates – all creamers, of course – and he goes, 'Listen to the way he talks, lads,' and one of them goes, '*Dad, I need five grand for my cor insurance,*' basically trying to take me off.

I don't even know how they got past the bouncers because they're clearly all Ken Ackers. I've got, like, Christian on one side of me now and Oisinn on the other, basically for back-up in case I need it, and I go, 'Stor for the future? The only thing you're going to be doing in the future is dealing drugs. You won't be playing much rugby, unless the Joy has a team, which I seriously doubt.' One of his mates goes, 'Batter the little poshie,' and Oisinn goes, 'The only that's going to be battered tonight is your dinner, chipper scum,' which is almost as good as my line.

I'm there, 'What are you doing here anyway? There's no birds with leggings and hoopy earrings in here,' and Oisinn gives it, 'Yeah, stick to your own side of the city. You never see me out in Tomango's trying to cop off with AJHs on Mickey Tuesday,' which is basically a lie, roysh, but I don't pull him up on it. This Damien tool, roysh, he looks at Oisinn and he goes, 'I'm here because I'm gonna royid your sister,' and I go, 'Well the joke's on you then because Oisinn's sister's a total hound,' and Oisinn nods.

Then the dickhead goes, 'Come on, lads, let's hit the good soyid of town,' and as they're heading out the door, roysh, leaving a trail of, like, fake *Adidas* aftershave after them, I go, 'Yeah, drown your sorrows and then fock off back to the Fleck Republic.'

Joanna shakes her head and she goes, 'I don't know even know how they got in here,' and Keelin's there, 'That's the first time I've ever seen a real sovereign ring. Oh sure, I've seen them on television and in photographs, but never in real life.'

Pretty much everyone's buying me drink all night, roysh, and at one stage I've got, like, six pints in front of me and I'm knocking them back, we're talking double-quick time, and after basically two hours I'm totally horrendufied. Anyway, roysh, we end up in a nightclub that looks vaguely familiar but I'm too shitfaced to recognise which one it is, and the next thing I remember is, like, Joanna and Keelin dragging me out onto the dancefloor for some, I don't know, Backstreet Boys song, maybe 'Backstreet's Back', and I can hordly stand I'm so off my tits. Then it's that 'I Believe I Can Fly' and Joanna, who's obviously decided she's going to try to be with me, is holding me up while we slowdance and then it's 'Two Become One' by the Spice Girls, which Joanna says she SO loves. So I end up throwing the lips on her on the dancefloor, roysh, and it has to be said, she's a pretty amazing wear.

Spinning around in circles is storting to make me feel sick, roysh, so I tell Joanna I have to sit down and I find a seat and end up overhearing Fionn having a borney with Aoife. She's totally hysterical, and we're talking totally here, and I can't make out a word she's saying, but Fionn is, like, trying to hug her and he's going, 'You're not fat. You're SO not fat,' and all of a sudden someone sits down beside me and I turn around, roysh, and it's Simon. He's like, 'You entering Kruffs this year then?' and I'm there, 'Say again,' and he goes, 'Just wondering what you're doing with the mutt,' and he points to Joanna, who is, like, gesturing, I don't know, wildly I suppose, with her hands and telling Keelin and some other bird I know to see from Loreto Foxrock that she is SO going to become a vegetarian, she SO is. I'm there, 'What are you talking about? She's a total honey,' and he goes, 'From a distance maybe. Like Mallin Head to Mizzen Head. In a thick fog,' which I know is total bullshit, roysh, because Simon tried to be with her ages ago but totally crashed and burned. I remind him of this, roysh, and he just, like, smiles and high-fives me and then he focks off.

Anyway, roysh, the night basically flies and at the end of it all the other goys have gone and it's only me, Oisinn, Joanna and Keelin left. Oisinn is with Keelin, as in *with* with, and I'm wondering is he still seeing Amie with an ie, though that would hordly matter to Oisinn, what with him being a total horndog. He must be able to read my mind, roysh, because he puts his orm around my shoulder at one stage and he whispers in my ear, going, 'An erect mickey has no conscience,' which is one of his favourite phrases. The four of us end up in Keelin's house in Monkstown, what with her having a free gaff with her old pair in Chicago for the weekend.

The next morning, roysh, I wake up early and my head is hanging off my shoulders. I'm there going, 'Oh my God, I actually *want* to die,' and we're talking totally here. I try to get dressed without waking Joanna, roysh, but she hears me as I'm, like, putting my shoes on and grabbing a pair of knickers to show the goys later, and she asks me where I'm going. I don't want to lie to the girl, roysh, but I end up telling her that I generally help out at a Simon Community hostel on a Saturday and she tells me that that is SO cool, helping homeless howiyas, and she says she had SUCH an amazing time last night and that I shouldn't worry about you-know-what and she sort of, like, looks at my crotch as she says it, and she says she'd SO love if we could see each other again, roysh, and I tell her I'll give her my number and then I say the first seven numbers that come into my head. She writes it with, like, an eyebrow pencil on the cover of *Image*, which she tells me has a photograph of one of her best friends in it, as if I give two focks. She storts, like, flicking through the pages, roysh, but I tell her I have to go and she, like, blows me a kiss as I'm leaving and I just, like, smile at her.

I have five messages. I don't know who the first one is from but I can pretty much take a guess, roysh, because that song 'Short Dick Man' is blasting out and someone is obviously, like, holding the phone up to the speaker, ha focking ha. The second one is from Eloise. I can hear someone in the background going, 'He's not worth it, Eloise. Don't give him the pleasure,' and then she's going, 'Hello? This is a message for Ross. You're a wanker. An absolute, total wanker,' and she bursts into tears, roysh, and before the phone is put down I hear her friend go, 'I SO knew this wasn't a good idea.' The next message is from Alyson, who also calls me 'an absolute, total wanker.' The fourth is from Sian. She's hammered, but at least she's original. She goes, 'Every girl around thinks you're, like, hot stuff? News flash, Ross. You're, like, a total loser,' and then she goes, 'LO-SER!' The last message is from some bird called Keeva, who I nipped in the rugby club recently and who now wants to know why I stood her up on Friday night and whether I think it's actually funny leaving her standing outside the Hat for, like, an hour and twenty-five minutes and why I haven't returned any of her calls since then and why I seemed so keen before but am now doing a total Chandler on her, whatever the fock that is.

I get the Dorsh to Dun Laoghaire, pick up the *Times* and the *Indo* at the station and, like, read the reports on the game while I wait for the

46A. Tony Ward's got, like, half a page on the match and it's like, 'The schools game is the bedrock of rugby in this country and MAKE NO MISTAKE ABOUT IT the performance by Castlerock College in the second round of the Leinster Schools Senior Cup yesterday was as fine an exhibition of how the game should be played as you are likely to see at any level. This team is simply awesome and the game against Skerries was a particular *tour de force* for young Ross O'Carroll-Kelly, who MARK MY WORDS is an undoubted star of the future.' *The Irish Times* had, like, six paragraphs on the game, which described my kicking as unerring – whether that's good or bad is anyone's guess.

So I get home, roysh, and the old dear doesn't even mention the fact that I didn't come home last night, which pisses me off big-time. She's sitting in the old man's study, roysh, and she's got her focking glasses on, which means she's probably writing to all the local councillors again about this halting site they're building down the road. I walk past and she doesn't even look up, roysh, just goes, 'You'll have to fix your own breakfast, Ross. I have to prepare for tonight's committee meeting.' I'm there, 'You mean Foxrock Against Total Skangers?' and she finally looks up and she takes off her glasses and she goes, 'That is *not* the name of it, Ross, as well you know it isn't.' I go, 'I couldn't give two focks what your anti-halting site group is called,' and she goes, 'We're not *anti* halting site. We just happen to believe it's not appropriate for an area like this,' and I just go, '*What*ever,' and I hit the kitchen.

CHAPTER THREE
'Cheeky and disruptive'

I'm in town with JP, roysh, just picking up a few new threads – a pair of cream G-Star chinos, which I might bring back tomorrow and exchange for Dockers and a light blue Ralph – and we go back to the cor and he's like, 'Going to make a bit of a detour on the way home,' and I go, 'That's Kool and the Gang,' because we drove in in his old man's beamer. So I'm not really paying any attention to where we're going, roysh, but the next thing I look up and I realise we're on DNS, as in De Nort Soyid, and I'm there, 'Have you lost your focking mind?' and he's going, 'Come on, Ross. Think outside the box for once,' which is one of these wanky expressions he's picked up from his old man, who's an estate agent. He drives for, like, ages, roysh, and further and further northside we go. I'm there, 'JP, it's still not too late to turn around,' but it's like the dude's got a death wish.

So anyway, roysh, we eventually pull up in this council housing estate and it's like hell on Earth, roysh, we're talking boarded-up houses, horses eating the grass in people's gardens and fat women in leggings sitting on walls and smoking. And right in the middle of all of this, JP stops the cor and actually gets out. He has lost his focking mind. He walks around to the passenger side and opens my door and he tells me he wants me to drive and I agree, roysh, because I'm thinking, 'At least if I'm in control of the wheel I can get us the fock out of here.'

He goes, 'I want you to drive slowly, Ross. We're talking five miles an hour,' and he winds down the window and as I let down the handbrake, slip her into first and then move off slowly, JP practically climbs out the window – he's standing up with only his legs actually inside the cor – and he storts shouting, 'THE BREADLINE,' at everyone we pass. That focker is going to get himself killed one day.

XXX

It's time to stort seriously love-bombing this French bird, so I meet Fionn in the library and he hands me a pen and an A4 pad. I'm there, 'I was actually hoping you'd write the letter for me,' and he goes, 'She's *your* exchange student,' and I'm there, 'Yeah, and I don't have a word of focking French!' He takes the pen and pad from me and he goes, 'Okay, tell me what you want to say in English and I'll write it out in French for you.' I'm there, 'Hey, I owe you one, Fionn. Roysh, what kind of shit do these French birds like to hear?' and he goes, 'It's not a case of ... Look, it's about letting her know who you are, and where you are in your life right now, and why you decided to become involved in the exchange programme. Answer me honestly, Ross, what do you hope to get out of this,' and I look at him, roysh, like he's got ten heads or something and I go, 'My Nat King.' He goes, 'Okay, be maybe a *little* less honest. What do you want her to think you want out of it?' and I go, 'Improve my French, blah blah blah,' and he's there, 'Good. But let's stort off by telling her a bit about you.'

My favourite subject. I'm there, 'I play rugby,' and he goes, 'Let's stort with your name. Je *m'appelle Ross O'Carroll-Kelly et j'habite a Foxrock.* Okay, what else?' I go, 'I can bench-press ...' and he's like, 'Ross, she doesn't want to know how much you can focking bench-press. Fock's

sake ... it's just the relevant stuff. Okay. *Je joue au rugby et je suis un outhalf.*
Je joue pour Castlerock College, c'est mon école. What about your family?' I go,
'My old man's a dickhead.' He puts the pen down and he goes, 'Ross,
I'm talking about how many brothers and sisters you have. You can't
say ...' and I'm there, 'Fionn, if she's going to be staying in my gaff, she's
going to find out pretty quickly that he's the biggest tool who's ever
lived. I don't want her walking out after one day saying I didn't let her
know what to expect.' He just, like, nods, roysh, and he goes, *'Je n'ai pas
des frères ou des soeurs et mon père est un ... homme inhabituel.* What would you
like to do when you leave school?'

I go, 'Probably play rugby,' and he's there, 'Ross, you *do* realise that if
this girl isn't into rugby, you're up Shit Creek.' I go, 'What'll I put then?
Hey, put bank manager. Birds love that shit,' and he storts writing again
and he goes, *'J'ai plusiers films pornographiques,'* and I'm there, 'Good,' and
he's like, *'Je voudrais coucher avec toi,'* and I'm like, 'What the fock's that?'
and he goes, 'My favourite subjects are Physics, Mathematics, History
and Geography,' and I'm there, 'This is good. Make me out to be some
kind of intellectual.' He goes, *'J'aime regarder les hommes le faire et j'adore ton
derriere.* I am a member of many societies at school and also do a great
deal of charity work in my spare time.'

I'm there, 'Fionn, you're, like, a genius, my man.' And he gets me to
sign it, roysh, then he goes, 'Well, it's not exactly Rimbeau, but I think
she'll get the general idea of what you're like.'

I don't believe it. By the end of March I'm going to be having hot sex
with some frog bird. I take the letter off him, high-five the dude, then
fock-off to get some nosebag.

XXX

I'm sitting there watching telly, roysh, trying to chillax, when all of a sudden the two focking muppets arrive in. The old dear goes, 'Feet off the table, Ross,' and I just, like, give her a look and she knows better than to say it again. The old man goes, 'Actually, we'd like a bit of a word, if we might,' and I ignore him and he goes, 'Would you mind lowering down the volume on the television?' and I throw my eyes up to heaven and switch the thing off altogether and I go, 'Satisfied now?'

The old man's like, 'It's about this parent-teacher meeting, quote-unquote, we went to today.' I'm there, 'What about it?' and he's like, 'Well, you've got seven teachers, Ross, and ... three of them have never heard of you.' I'm there, 'So?' and he's like, 'So? Ross, it's the end of February in your Leaving Certificate year and three of your teachers couldn't pick you out of a police line-up. You've never sat any of their exams, submitted any of their coursework or attended any of their classes, from what they can see.'

I'm there, 'I'm sure there's a point to all of this, is there?' and of course he hasn't a bog what to say to that. The old dear gets in on the act then. She's going, 'The four teachers who *did* remember you didn't have very nice things to say about you either. Rude, hostile, uncommunicative and arrogant, they said.' The old man goes, 'I told them. I said, "He didn't pick any of those bad habits up at home. It wouldn't be tolerated".'

I'm there, 'Is that it?' and they don't know what to say. I turn on the telly again and I go, 'Make yourselves useful and get the dinner ready. At least *pretend* to be proper parents.'

XXX

HEY FIONN
HEARD YOU TRIED TO BAIL
INTO SOME WHORE ON THE SHORE
LAST NIGHT AND CRASHED
AND BURNED !!
Ross

XXX

What's dirty, brown and ugly and hangs off the side of a satellite dish? The answer is a council house, roysh, and I've already heard it before but I couldn't be orsed telling Kenny, this total tosspot who Sorcha insisted we share a table with, just because she's in Amnesty with his bird, Helena – a total moonpig, before you ask. Helena's telling Sorcha that the media are OH! MY! GOD! totally ignoring what's going on in Rwanda, we're talking four years on from the genocide, with thousands of unarmed civilians being extrajudicially executed by government soldiers – 'It's like, HELLO?' – while almost 150,000 people detained in connection with the 1994 genocide are being held without, like, trial. She goes, 'I'm not even going to *stort* on the thousands of refugees forcibly returned to Burundi. It's like, do NOT even go there.' Sorcha's saying that President Pasteur Bizimungu SO should be indicted for war crimes if half of what she's read on the Internet is true. She's there, 'It's like, OH! MY! GOD!' but I'm not really listening, roysh, I'm giving the old mince pies to Amanda, this total lasher who's, like, second year Orts.

And of course it's not long before Sorcha cops it. She goes, 'Your chicken's getting cold, Ross,' but I just, like, blank her and keep staring. All week, roysh, I've been listening to Sorcha and her friends going on about this bird Amanda Cooper and how she was going to be wearing the famous Liz Hurley dress – *that* dress, the black Versace one with the safety pins – to the Orts ball. I heard Sophie and Chloë telling Sorcha that each pin cost OH! MY! GOD! eighty sheets. Now I know why everyone was so freaked out about it, roysh, because there isn't a goy in the room who can keep his eyes off her, and that's saying something considering the scenario that's here.

Have to say, roysh, Sorcha's looking pretty hot herself. She's wearing this, like, blue backless ball gown, I suppose you'd call it, and whenever anyone, like, compliments her on it she mentions that it's an Amanda Wakeley and then she goes, 'And do you like the shoes? Red or Dead.' I've pretty much stolen the show in my Ralph Lauren tux, which I borrowed from JP's brother, Greg – must get my own for when I'm in UCD myself – and one of those, like, novelty shirts, which is white, roysh, but has, like, cartoon characters on the sleeves. Sorcha has an eppo when I take my jacket off at the table, we're talking total Knicker-fit City here, giving it, 'Oh my God, oh my God, I am SO embarrassed.'

Oisinn is also here, roysh, with Rebecca, this friend of his sister, who's, like, first year Engineering, and he's also wearing a novelty shirt, though he's sitting at a different table.

The skivvies come to collect the food and I notice, roysh, that none of the birds at our table have, like, touched theirs and I hear the waitress – bit of an oul' one really – muttering under her breath about what a terrible waste of food it is and all of a sudden, roysh, this Helena one, at the top of her voice, goes, 'If you've got something to say, say it out loud,' basically like a teacher would say if he, like, copped you whispering to someone down the back of the class. The bird's there, 'I'm just saying, it's a terrible waste of food.' Helena goes, 'Your point being?' and old biddy's like, 'You cheeky little madam. There's young children starving in Africa,' and Helena's there, 'I doubt if they'd be interested in your Chicken Supreme.'

I have to say, roysh, I know this one works in the service industry and everything, but she doesn't deserve this. As she's walking away, roysh, Helena goes, 'Excuse me,' and when she turns around Helena's there, 'You see this girl here?' and she, like, points at Sorcha. 'Her father is Edmund Lalor. Of Edmund Lalor and Portners. He has all of his conferences in this hotel. He basically spends a fortune here. If you want to keep your job, I'd advise you to learn some manners,' and I'm about to stort clapping, roysh, as in *that told her,* but all of a sudden, roysh, Sorcha jumps up out of her seat and goes, 'How DARE you?' and I'm thinking, 'Okay, let's just see how this one plays out.' She's there, 'How dare you sit there pontificating about the terrible injustices happening in countries you've never been to and will never go to, then treat someone less fortunate than you in that way. You shallow, supercilious BITCH!' and she gets up and storms off to the jacks.

And it's at times like that, roysh, that I remember why it is I still love Sorcha, if that doesn't sound too gay. She has, like, principles, if that's the right word. She always stands up for what she believes in. Sometimes I wish I was more like her. Helena goes, 'What's *her* focking problem?' and I can feel everyone at the table just, like, staring at me, roysh, and I can't help it, I just shrug my shoulders and in a sort of, like, sneer, I go, 'Time of the month,' and everyone laughs and I hate myself for not having guts like she's got.

It turns out, roysh, that this bloke Kenny's a bit of a rugby head and he asks me if I've thought much about what club I'll sign with when I leave Castlerock and I tell him I haven't given it much thought, at the moment my main focus is on the Senior Cup and nothing else. He goes, 'The word is you guys have got a kick-ass team this year,' and I nod and go, 'Totally,' just as the dessert arrives. Only one bird at our table wants profiteroles – I think she's called Kerry – but just as she sinks her spoon into one, Helena goes, 'A moment on the lips, a lifetime on the hips,' and some other bird at the table who I don't know gives it, 'What you eat today, you wear tomorrow,' and she ends up eating one spoonful, then pushing the bowl away and lighting up a Marlboro Light.

I'm bored off my tits at this stage, roysh, and I'm casing the place to see can I spot Amanda Cooper, maybe bail in there, and I see her, roysh, on her own up at the bor and I decide it's time to give her the pleasure of my company. I'm straight up to her, roysh – fock, she's beautiful – and I go, 'Hey, babes,' and she just, like, looks at me, bit of a filthy if the truth be told. I'm there, 'Your dress is amazing,' and she throws her eyes up to heaven, like it's the fiftieth time she's heard that tonight, which it probably is. I'm there, 'Can I get you a drink?' and she's like, 'You're not going to come up with *one* original line, are you?' 'Out of the corner of my eye, roysh, I cop Erika, who came with some tool who's supposed to own his own yacht, and she's got this, like, smirk on her face, a real superior look, her usual look, and she's obviously loving watching me crash and burn. The borman comes over and Amanda asks him for a Coors Light, roysh, and she doesn't ask me if I want a drink. I go, 'Suppose I *better* lay off the sauce. Big game in a week's time. I play rugby, in case you didn't know.'

The next thing, roysh, I feel this, like, tap on my shoulder and I turn around and it's this total honey, and when I say total I mean totally to-tal, we're talking Teri Hatcher here, a dead-ringer. Of course Mister Shit Cool here goes, 'Hey, no fighting over me, girls. Play nicely,' as, like, a joke, and this Teri Hatcher one, who turns out to be Amanda's best friend, goes, 'Sorry, we're not interested in ...' and she looks me up and down and goes, 'schoolboys.' I'm there, 'No? Not even a member of the Castlerock College S?' but even as I'm saying it, roysh, I realise that it means basically fock-all to these birds. They're in, like, college. They're out of my league. Amanda goes, 'Run away back to your little rugby groupies,' and she turns her back to me and – total mare – I have to face the old walk of shame back to the table, where everyone's been watching me.

Oisinn comes over and he's like, 'I saw it, but I don't believe it. Was that a mission abort?' and I go, 'She's a focking lesbian,' and he laughs and we both high-five each other. That's when, roysh, out of the cor-ner of my eye, I notice that Sorcha's back from the jacks – course she is, that was half a focking hour ago – and she's basically chatting to this complete tool over the other side of the room and even from where I'm sitting, roysh, I can see that the goy is hanging out of her. This, like, jealousy, I suppose you could call it, just takes over me, roysh, and I'm straight over there and I can hear the goy going, 'Mure-ngezi is a lawyer who, for want of a better word, *disappeared* in Kigali in January. The Government ... Sorry, can we help you?' I don't know how long I was staring at him, but it must have been ages. I just ignore him, roysh, and I'm there, 'Sorcha, can I talk to you? *Alone*,' and she ignores me, roysh, so I grab her by the hand and pull her up and I'm just about to drag her away when this goy – glasses and this stupid focking quiff – he stands up and he's there, 'Hey, you are SO out of

order,' and I'm going, 'Do you want me to deck you?' and Sorcha's like, 'Stop it, you two! Paul, I'm really sorry about this, but I have to have a word with Ross,' and he's gone, 'Hey, don't sweat it, Sorcha. I'm right here if you need me,' like he's going to sort me out if I step out of line, and I'm thinking, 'Yeah, roysh.'

Sorcha is NOT a happy camper. *She* ends up dragging *me* to a table where nobody's sitting and she storts giving it, 'WHAT is your problem?' I'm there, 'Who's that tosser?' and she goes, 'His name happens to be Paul. And he's a really good friend of mine.' I'm there, 'There's something about him I don't like. I just don't want to see you get hurt, Sorcha.' She goes, 'I asked you a question, Ross.' It's only then that I notice how hammered she is. She's always been a total wuss when it comes to drink and she's only had, like, three bottles of Miller and she's already off her face. I'm like, 'What question?' and she goes, 'I asked you what your problem was with me talking to Paul.' I know the answer she's looking for and I give it to her. I'm there, 'I suppose I was, like, jealous.'

She goes, 'But we're not going out together anymore. You dumped me, remember?' I go, 'You were the one who broke it off,' and she's like, 'HELLO? Because you kissed, like, my best friend? I don't THINK I was being unreasonable.' I'm there, 'It was a mistake, Sorcha. I really miss you. Especially your friendship.' She goes, 'Bullshit! Ross, you didn't even stick up for me earlier when I had that row with Helena,' and I'm there, 'You should have heard me giving out yords to her when you were gone,' and she looks at me, roysh, like she knows I'm lying and she goes, 'You didn't even come after me to see was I alroysh.' I'm like, 'That's because ...' but I can't even look her in the eye, roysh, and I go, 'That's because ... because ... because I'm scum, Sorcha. You know it and everyone knows it,' and I can feel my eyes storting to, like, fill up and I'm hoping Oisinn hasn't copped me, roysh, but then suddenly the next thing I know Sorcha's thrown the lips on me and it's, like, amazing. 'A Million Love Songs Later' comes on – Take That or some shit – and we stop wearing the face off each other and Sorcha goes, 'Let's go upstairs.' I'm like, 'Where?' and she goes, 'I've booked a room in the hotel.'

I'm there, TOUCHDOWN! though I didn't say it, roysh, just thought it. I'm there, 'Okay, Sorcha, but only if this is what you really want.' She stops, roysh, just as we reach the elevator and she goes, 'It is what I want. But I am SO warning you, Ross, you better not mess me about this time. I don't want any of that rubbish you came out with before about wanting your freedom and not wanting to be chained down. If you still have commitment issues I want to hear about them now, as in this moment. I don't want you doing a Chandler on me again.'

I'm trying to remember if it was Keeva or Sian who said that to me the other day. We reach the third floor and the lift doors open. We find the room and as she pushes the key cord in the door she turns around to me and she's just like, 'It's a copy, by the way,' and I'm there, 'What is?' and she goes, 'Amanda Cooper's dress. It's not a real Versace. Her aunt is a dressmaker.'

XXX

We're all looking forward to kicking some serious St Mary's orse, roysh, but it's like the game is never going to come around. Doesn't matter what you're doing, roysh, it's there in the back of your mind the whole time. There's a place in the semi-finals of the Leinster Schools Cup up for grabs and no one needs to be reminded of the stakes. I'm in the gym at lunchtime with Christian – just working on basic strength really – and he tells me he's been pretty hord to live with the past couple of weeks, he's been snapping at his old pair and he's really going to make it up to them when all of this is over. I tell him I've probably been a bit short with mine as well the last couple of days, believe it or not, but once we get through Friday, then the semi-final and then the final, I can hopefully spend a bit of time with them and let them know what a couple of penises I really think they are.

Not that they've any interest in me or my life. It's still nothing but Foxrock Against Total Skangers at the moment. Meeting councillors and writing protest letters and trying to find someone in this day and age who's prepared to accept bribes. The old man was on the news last week, shouting his mouth off and making a total tit of himself outside the Dáil, going, 'What's wrong with my money? It was good enough for you last year.'

Christian tells me his old pair are having a lot of borneys lately, and we're talking MAJOR borneys here. I think his old man's a bit of a swordsman and his old dear is sick of him not coming home, or finding other women's numbers in his Davy Crocket. I tell him everything will work out, roysh, but only because it's the first thing that comes into my head and he nods and says, 'I know. I mean, it wasn't always hearts and flowers for Han and Leia, was it?'

I'm there, 'What have we got this afternoon?' and he goes, 'English. We're supposed to have *Waiting for Godot* read for today. Did you ...' and he realises it's a stupid question before he's even asked it. I go, 'Why don't me and you fock off for the afternoon, hit your gaff and watch the three *Star Wars* movies back-to-back,' and his face just completely lights up, roysh, and he goes, 'Like the old days,' and I'm there, 'Yeah, just like the old days.'

XXX

Fehily tells us that we are just three steps away from greatness. He goes, 'And pay heed, my children, to the significance of that holiest of holy integers. *Three* parts to the Blesséd Trinity. The Resurrection happened on the *third* day. But, oh, it is solemnly I tell thee that the path thou shall tread tomorrow is uneven and treacherous. St Mary's are a formidable enemy. Did the Good Lord himself not say before He crossed the Sea of Galilee, "Beware the team with the strong, mobile pack". But this is a battle we must win.'

He goes, 'And so, in all due modesty, I have just one more thing to say to my opponents – I have taken up the challenge of many democratic adversaries and up to now I have always emerged the victor from the conflict. I do not believe that this struggle is being carried on under different conditions. That is to say, the relation of the forces involved is exactly the same as before. In any case I am grateful to Providence that this struggle, having become inevitable, broke out in my lifetime and at a time when I still feel young and vigorous. Just now I am feeling particularly vigorous. Spring is coming, the spring which we all welcome. The season is approaching in which one can measure forces. I know that, although they realise the terrible hardships of the struggle, millions of German soldiers are at this moment thinking exactly the same thing ...'

XXX

An inappropriate gesture is what *The Irish Times* said I made to the crowd during the match and I'm there, 'An inappropriate gesture? HELLO? I just gave them the focking finger,' and it wasn't, like, inappropriate either. The crowd were giving me major stick all through the game, roysh, and we are talking MAJOR here. Mary's were a lot tougher than we thought, roysh, and I had a bit of a mare with my kicking, missing seven out of my twelve kicks. And of course their crowd, roysh, were loving it until Christian blocked down a drop-goal attempt about five minutes from the end, roysh, the ball fell to me and I pegged it seventy yords down the other end to score. Just threw the ball up in the air after that, roysh, ran over to their supporters and gave them the finger, as in who's in the focking semi-final now?

So I get up Saturday morning, roysh and the old man is on to *The Irish Times* sports desk and he's basically giving out yords, fair focks, tool and all as he is. He's going, 'Your representative said my son made an inappropriate gesture but made no reference whatever to the level of provocation he was subjected to,' but he's obviously getting nowhere with the goy on the other end of the phone, roysh, because the old man's going, 'It's quite evident from your coverage that you care nothing for the schools game. It strikes me that Mister Tony Ward Esquire from your main rivals is the only rugby writer in the country who appreciates the seriousness of it. I mean, where the HELL was Gerry Thornley on Friday?' There was this, like, silence, roysh, then the old man totally exploded, going, 'WELL GET HIM BACK FROM PARIS! WHO GIVES TWO FIGS ABOUT THE FIVE NATIONS?' and he finishes off by reminding the goy how much money he spends on, like, advertising in the paper every year and then he, like, slams down the phone.

XXX

It's Monday morning, roysh, and we've all been given the day off school today because we're, like, totally wrecked after the last few weeks. The training has been pretty intense, it has to be said, we're talking before school, at lunchtime and then after school as well, and weekends on top of that, so we're all focked at this stage. Anyway, roysh, because we all have the day off, me and goys decided to do something together, as a team, we're talking for morale? So we decide to head out to see the Irish team train, roysh. JP's had an offer to play for the Greystones under-19s next season, so it's an excuse to go out and check out the set-up and the facilities and shit.

There were six messages when I checked my phone this morning. Joanna rang to see how I was and to say she understood why I hadn't been in touch, that I must have been, like, SO focused on beating St Mary's and she wished me luck against the Gick in the semi-final and then she said that I'm capable of doing anything I want to in life as long as I put my mind to it, the focking sap. Then she said she'd, like, see me on Thursday afternoon, whatever the fock that means. The second and third calls were from Sorcha, who said she needed to speak to me about something and it was totally urgent and I feel a little bit bad for focking her around again. The fourth call was at ten o'clock last night and it was someone – again – playing 'Short Dick Man' down the phone, focking hilarious as it is. Zara and – this girl's a fool for love – Alyson, both phoned to say they saw *The Irish Times* on Saturday and they both wondered if I was alroysh and if I needed someone to talk to, blah blah blah.

I meet the goys at Blackrock Dorsh station and we're having the crack. Oisinn and Simon are on the other side of the platform, chatting up these two birds from Pill Hill, or *pretending* to, because they're both mingers and the goys are, like, totally ripping the piss out of them, Oisinn's giving it, 'This is the time of year when we turn our attention to who we're bringing to the debs. And I want you girls to know, you're candidates.' Of course the two birds are gagging for them, roysh, and we're all giving it, 'WE WILL, WE WILL ROCK YOU ...' across the platform, totally ripping the piss as well.

Of course the goys end up nearly missing the Dorsh, roysh, because they're so, I don't know, engrossed, if that's the right word, in talking to the two skobes that they don't notice the train coming and they have to peg it up the steps and over the bridge and they make it just before the doors close. It's, like, high-fives all round. Oisinn goes, 'I swear to God that girl was wearing *Blue Stratos*,' and we all break our holes laughing. Then it's, like, high-fives all around, roysh, and then of course the goys break into a chorus of, 'WE'VE GOT ROSS O'CARROLL-KELLY ON OUR TEAM, WE'VE GOT THE BEST TEAM IN THE LAND,' and this old goy, roysh, who gets on at Sandycove, he turns around and he goes, 'Excuse me. There are other people on this train. Would you mind keeping your voices down?' and quick as a flash, roysh, I'm like, 'Fock off back to Jurassic Pork,' and Simon calls him an old fort and when the train stops at Dalkey, roysh, the goy gets out and goes up to have a word with the driver, who obviously couldn't give two focks, roysh, because the next thing we know the train is moving off and the old tosser is just left standing on the platform, looking totally pissed off, and we're all there giving him the finger through the window, going, 'Yyyeeeaaahhh!'

We stop at Killiney, roysh, and JP jumps up all of a sudden and goes, 'Hey, Ross. There's Sorcha,' and I look over the other side of the platform and she's there with Aoife and they're obviously heading into town. Oisinn says it must be colder than he thought because Aoife's seems to be wearing two jumpers around her waist instead of her usual one, and we all crack up of course, but then we stop, roysh, because we remember that Fionn broke up with her not so long ago and Oisinn turns around to him and goes, 'Hey, no offence, man,' and Fionn pushes his glasses up on his nose and goes, 'Hey, it's cool.' They don't notice us looking at them for ages, roysh. Sorcha takes off her scrunchy, shakes her hair loose, smoothes it back into a ponytail, puts it back in the scrunchy, then pulls four or five stands of hair loose. Aoife looks pretty crap, it has to be said. She's lost basically shitloads of weight. She has a bottle of Evian in her hand and she storts scanning our train to see if she knows anyone on it. When she cops us, roysh, she waves and then she, like, nudges Sorcha and I can see her mouth the words, 'OH! MY! GOD! there's Ross,' and Sorcha, who's putting on lip balm, sort of, like, squints her eyes and when she cops me she makes the shape of a phone with her hand, as if to say, 'Ring me,' and she looks majorly pissed off, which is no surprise I suppose because, despite my promise that this time things would be different, I haven't returned any of her calls since the night we were together at the Orts Ball, and all the goys are giving it, 'Whoa! Who's in the bad books?' and then they're going, 'Leg-end! Leg-end! Leg-end!'

We get off the Dorsh in Bray, roysh, and we're waiting for the 184 to Greystones when all of a sudden this bird comes over to us – a Virgin on the Rocks – and she walks straight up to JP and goes, 'You're JP Conroy, aren't you?' and JP's there, 'The one and only. You're Lisa, right?' but she doesn't answer, roysh, just goes, 'You've been telling people you were with me,' looking seriously focked off. JP's there, 'Shurley shome mishtake,' trying to, like, defuse the situation with a bit of Sean Connery. She's having none of it. She goes, 'You told Esme McConville's brother that you were with me two weeks ago in the rugby club and that I've been gagging for you for ages,' and JP, roysh, he doesn't handle the situation very well, he ends up going, 'You HAVE been gagging for me for ages,' and she just, like, flips the lid, calls him an orsehole and, like, slaps him across the face. Then she storms off, roysh, and we're all there cracking our shits laughing, and JP is as well, fair focks to him. He's going, 'The girl's got it bad for me.'

One side of his face is still red when we get on the bus.

XXX

I text Erika, roysh, and it's like, **Wud u lik 2go4 a drnk?**

And she's there,

I'd rather be boiled alive in my own spit.

Which I take as a no.

XXX

I'm having a few cans in JP's gaff the other night and we're both bored, roysh, and I still haven't heard from this French one – Fionn probably told her I was a focking transvestite in that letter, for all I know – so I end up sort of, like, taking it out on him by ringing his gaff. I know he's not home, roysh, because he said he was going back to school to study after training, so I ring his number and his old man answers and I put on this, like, voice and I'm going, 'Hello. Am I speaking with Fionn's father?' and he's like, 'You most certainly are. And if it's about that book on the nitrogen cycle, it's my fault. He asked me to return it today and I just pure clear forgot. And what, pray tell, is the fine?'

I have to put my hand over my focking mouth so he doesn't hear me laughing. He's like, 'Hello? Is anyone there?' I'm going, 'Hello, sorry. No, I'm not calling from the library. I'm the father of, em, Jeff, who's Fionn's, shall we say, friend. And not to put too fine a point on it, I'm a bit worried.' JP's in the kitchen, listening in on the other line. Fionn's old man goes, 'Worried?' and I go, 'I'm worried, yes, that they might be a little bit more than friends, if you get my vibe.' He just goes, 'Oh, wonderful. That's great news. Andrea, come and hear.' I'm like, 'Did you say great news? They both disappear up to Jeff's bedroom at six o'clock every night and they stay up there for hours on end and you think that's wonderful?'

He goes, 'It's another world, I know. Andrea and I are really embracing it. The Internet's a wonderful resource. All sorts of sites that would open your eyes.' I'm there, 'But do you not think this kind of behaviour is wrong?' and he's like, 'Only according to social conventions.' I'm laying it on good and proper now. I go, 'Just because you don't mind your son going to hell,' and he turns around, roysh – real snotty now – and he goes, 'Do NOT quote the Bible at me. Our gay son is a gift from God! Good day to *you*, sir,' and he hangs up and I swear to God, roysh, me and JP laugh for the next three hours.

XXX

I finally get this letter back from Clementine, roysh, and it's all,

> Dear Ross,
>
> It was very pleasure to receiving your letter, the photograph of you in your rugby clothes and as well the newspaper writings about some of your matches. You must to be a very excellent player at rugby if it is to believed what the man Tony Ward writes about you.
>
> I am eighteen years of old also and I am in school also and will to do my last year exams in the summer times. My hobbies are to play the racquetball, to do the drawing, to dance, to collect the fancy paper and to play the clarinet. Also I like very much the music of George Michael. And I like too to meet the new people.
>
> It is with my mother and my father that I live in an apartment in Paris and I have two sisters which are Marie-France et Claudette. They are working at being the solicitors. When I am completed, I like very much to do the

fashion designing. I like very much to work for Calvin Klein, but it is a dream!

I like very much also to go to Ireland to visit you. You appear like a very nice boy and I think something nice can happen for us. I would like very much to come to Ireland and get to know you very nice, you understand?

Write again to me in a very soon time. It is nice to be getting the letters.

Love, Clementine x x x

So of course I hop in the old dear's cor and I'm straight down to Fionn's gaff, roysh, to find out my next move, him knowing more about the French and what they're into than me. I ring the bell and it's Ned Flanders who answers the door and he's going, 'Well lookie here, it's Ross. Hey, Andrea, Ross has come to visit. Wonderful,' and it's, like, hooray, get out the focking trumpets. So I'm brought into the kitchen and I'm asked if I'd like a glass of pomegranate juice, whatever the fock that is, and I say no and then Fionn's old dear sort of, like, winks at me, and she goes, 'No announcement yet,' and his old man's there, putting on the kettle, going, 'Give him time, Andrea.'

And she goes, 'It's not like there haven't been ... signs. Shall I show him, darling?' and the old man's there, 'Yes, but *be* careful. He'll be down those stairs any minute.' She goes to the kitchen door and looks up the stairs, roysh, and then closes the door, pegs it across the kitchen and opens this drawer. She goes, 'Lots of things have been arriving for him in the post. And we've found other *things* lying around his room. There's been a lot of magazines. Lifestyle tips and all the different positions these people can *do it* in. And the various toys. All very educational.'

The old man goes, 'I've told her she shouldn't be nosing around in there but she insists,' and she's like, 'Ewan, I'm taking an interest in my son. Anyway, Ross, the other day I was rummaging around in his sock drawer when I found this,' and she drops this brochure for the Mazda MX5 onto the breakfast counter. I'd completely forgotten I'd slipped it in there. Don't know how I kept a straight face, roysh, but I just go, 'It's worse than we thought,' and the next thing we hear Fionn coming down the stairs, roysh, so she lashes it back in the drawer and we crack on that we were talking about something else.

Fionn goes, 'Heard you coming in, Ross. Sorry, I was—' and quick as a flash I'm there, 'Trying to decide what to wear?' but it goes totally over his head. I'm there, 'I got a letter back from this French exchange hotty. Want you to have a look at it,' and we excuse ourselves from the proud parents and go into the sitting-room. I pull out the letter, roysh, open it up and hand it to Fionn. I'm like, 'Tell me what she's saying.' He sits down with it, roysh, reads about two lines, turns it over, then looks at the front again and goes, 'Ross, this is in English,' and I'm like, 'No shit, Sherlock.' He goes, 'Well, you can see what she's saying yourself. She likes racquetball and George Michael and ...' I'm there, 'Yeah, but I thought you'd be able to read between the lines, pick up the vibes. These French women are dirty bitches,' and he goes, 'Ross, there are no *doubles entendres* in this. She's interested in you. End of story. Why don't you write another letter to her?'

And I whip a pen and a piece of paper out of the pocket of my Henri Lloyd and I go, 'No, why don't YOU write another letter to her? You know what they're after, these French girls.' He sits there thinking for a few seconds, tapping the pen off the side of his glasses, then he goes, 'Romance. Okay, she's coming to Ireland to practice her English for her summer exams. But the possibility of falling in love gives it an extra *frisson*.' Him and his big words. He goes, 'You're going to romance this girl,' and he storts writing. I'm there 'Make sure she knows she's on for it,' and he's like, 'Leave the phraseology to me, Ross. You want to tell her that when you wake up in the morning her photograph illuminates your day. *Je voudrais coucher avec ta mère et ton père et tes soeurs.* And what about a bit of *Je voudrais caresser tes jambes*.' I'm there, 'What's that? No, keep writing,' and he goes, 'It means, I have never felt this way before. Is it really possible to fall in love with an image? *J'adore les grands hommes.* I am counting the days until you arrive. *Je voudrais manger ton visage.*

He finishes it, roysh, sticks it in an envelope and gives it to me to post. Oh yes, some hot French loving is winging my way.

XXX

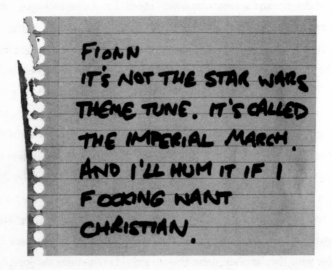

✗✗✗

If the truth be told, roysh, I'm a little bit worried about my kicking so I stay behind for an extra half an hour after lunch to practice, just booting ball after ball between the posts from different angles. Anyway, roysh, where all of this is going is that I ended up being half an hour late for, like, double History, roysh, and it has to be said that tosser Crabtree's not exactly a happy camper when I decide to, like, show my face. The first thing he says to me, roysh, real sarcastic as well, he goes, 'You're late,' and of course I'm there, 'No shit, Sherlock,' giving him the same amount of attitude back. Everyone breaks their shites laughing. I sit down, roysh, and check in my bag to see do I even have my History book with me. He's not going to let it go though. He's there, 'Have you an explanation, boy. One you would care to share with me and perhaps your little band of cheerleaders down there in the back row?' I just, like, shrug my shoulders and I go, 'I was practicing my kicking,' trying my best to keep my cool with the focker. He goes, 'And too busy, no doubt, to consider more cerebral matters, such as the causes of the First World War, yes?' I'm there, 'What are you going on about?' He goes, 'You were to have learned this off by rote for today, boy.' I don't like the way he says that word. It's sort of, like, *boy.* He goes, 'What were the causes of the First World War?'

I sort of, like, lean back on the chair, roysh, with just the two back legs on the ground, which I know he hates, and I go, 'I don't think you understand. I'm on the S,' but he's straight down my throat, roysh, going, 'I don't care if you're the grand wizard in the Jessop County Clavern of the White Knights of the Ku Klux Klan. Answer the question.' I shrug my shoulders again, roysh, and I go, 'Well, I wouldn't exactly say Hitler helped,' and everyone in the class cracks their holes laughing and

I actually think they're laughing *with* me until Crabtree goes at the top of his voice, 'WRONG WAR, YOU IMBECILE!' and I'm looking at him thinking, You are SO totalled for that. He goes, 'That's the problem with you and your rugby friends. Too fixated on what's between your legs and no interest at all in what's between your ears. You are *still* the only one in the class who hasn't presented to me details of your special topic, so I have no other option but to choose one for you.' I'm just there, 'Enjoy the moment, orsehole.' He goes, 'The life and times of Gavrilo Princip. You know who Gavrilo Princip is, I presume?' and I go, 'I'm not focking stupid,' even though I haven't a bog and I'm, like, shitting it in case he calls my bluff and asks me who she is. Then it turns out to be a bloke. He goes, 'The Life and Times of Gavrilo Princip. Who was he? Where did he come from? His involvement with the Ujedinjenje ili Smrt and the opposition movement to Austro-Hungarian rule in the Balkans. The events, if any, that informed his political view in the lead-up to the events in Sarajevo in June 1914 as the great colonial powers of the late nineteenth and early twentieth century slid inexorably towards war. I want a full and detailed proposal on my desk at nine o'clock – no, seven-thirty – in the morning, also listing five reasons, based on European history, why you considered that this topic merited special study and naming all the sources you intend to consult for your information. That's all.'

That's all? No *please* or *thank you* or anything, but I don't pull him up on it, roysh, I'm there just staring at him, with that big focking smug look on his face, and I'm thinking, Oh my God, you are SO sacked it's not funny.

So when the class is over, roysh, I head up to Fehily's study and I tell him pretty much what happened and he goes totally ballistic. He's there, 'Do you mean to tell me that a member of the Castlerock College Senior Cup team was treated disdainfully by a member of the teaching staff?' I go, 'That's exactly what happened, Father,' and he's there, 'Well, I am NOT prepared to stand by and allow this to happen in MY school,' and he storms off, roysh, down to the staffroom and, according to a couple of fifth years who happened to be standing outside – one of them being a cousin of Fionn's – Crabtree ends up getting the balls chewed off him, we're talking the bollocking of a lifetime here. Half an hour later, roysh, I'm called out of Maths and Fehily turns around to me and goes, 'How far do you want to push this, Ross?' I'm there, 'What do you mean?' and he goes, 'Well, to my mind this is an open-and-shut case of gross misconduct. I can dismiss him immediately or suspend him pending a disciplinary hearing, or I can ...' and I'm there, 'No, it's cool. A simple apology from him will do. In front of the rest of the class, of course.' He goes, 'Oh, you'll get your apology, make no mistake about that. I'm just so very sorry it happened. We can't have members of our Senior Cup team made to look small by the hired hands. In the Year of the Eagle, of all years!'

CHAPTER FOUR
'Refuses to listen'

I'm walking down the corridor, roysh, and I cop this poster on the wall outside the drama room and it's only then, roysh, that I realise what Joanna meant when she said in her message that she'd see me Thursday afternoon. Turns out we're doing a production of *My Fair Lady* with the old Whores on the Shore and they're actually coming to the school today for, like, auditions. Of course straight away I'm going, 'Oh my God, I am SO going to rip the piss out of this.' I try to drum up a bit of crew for it, roysh, but Simon and Oisinn say they're going to the gym and Fionn's going to the library, the steamer, though JP and Christian are John B – JP because he wants to get talking to Gemma, who's, like, head girl and Christian because he fancies the orse off this bird Diardra, who's captain of the hockey team. He was with her once in the rugby club.

So two-thirty arrives, roysh, and everyone's packed into the assembly hall. Me and the goys wait upstairs in the library to see them arrive. Picture the scene, roysh, we're talking me, Christian and JP, each of us with a pair of binoculars, which I pegged home to get at lunchtime, and we're standing up on a table, looking out the window, watching them get out of their bus, pointing out the ones we've been with, or the ones we could have if we'd basically wanted them. JP goes, 'Diardra Lewsey. Nice rack. My compliments on your choice, Christian,' and Christian's there, 'Thank you, Obi Wan.' I'm there, 'Look at that goys. Four-in-a-row. Alicia what's-her-name, Carol Bennett, Ann Marie Taylor and that bird who goes to the School of Music. Plays the clarinet. I've had all four of them,' and JP's there, 'That's an accumulator,' and I crack up laughing and I high-five the dude. Then he goes, 'Christian, is that that bird you were with at Emma McNally's eighteenth?' and he's there, 'I think it is.' JP's there, 'She's a lot easier on the eye now, no offence to you, of course,' and I go, 'That's got to be fake tan,' and Christian goes, 'No, she goes to the Seychelles for a week with her old pair in January every year.'

I spot Gemma, roysh, a total lasher, no arguments there, a little bit like Angelina Jolie if you asked me to describe her, and I wouldn't mind bailing in there myself if JP wasn't a mate. He goes, 'Look at her, Ross. Look at the way she holds herself. Beautiful, and she knows it,' and then he storts going, 'Go girl, go girl ...' The two boys, roysh, it's like I've taught them fock-all over the years, they both hop down off the table and stort pegging it for the door and I call them back and I'm there, 'What's the focking rush?' JP goes, 'What's the rush? It's feeding time, Ross,' and I'm there, 'Goys, you must have learned something from the maestro here over the years. You don't want to look too Roy, do you?' and the goys – focking clueless, it has to be said – are there just looking at me. I go, 'Give it ten minutes. Let everyone sit down and get comfortable. Then – BANG! – we walk in. More impact.'

Which is exactly what happens, roysh. Ten minutes into the auditions, everything's really quiet, roysh – because they're basically knobs, the kind of people who go to these things – and all of sudden the doors swing open and in walk our three heroes, giving it loads, and we are talking totally here. The place is focking jammers and you can see all the birds, roysh, looking around as if to say, 'OH! MY! GOD! Who are they?' except they know who we are, roysh, because to them, being with a member of the Castlerock College Senior Cup team is even more important than the Leaving. They know it and we know it.

Old Battleaxe Kennealy, the drama teacher, she sees the three studs arriving, roysh, and she goes, 'Glad you lads could make it. Nice to see some of our boys are interested in the dramatic arts,' ripping the piss really, she's sound like that. All of the girls are cracking up laughing, roysh, and all of the blokes – nerds and benders most of them, Fionn will be raging he missed it – they're bulling, roysh, because suddenly the chances of them scoring any of the old Collars Up Knickers Down brigade have, like, gone out the window. Ms Kennealy – I actually think she has a thing for me – she tells us to come up and sit in the front row, which we don't mind, roysh, and we walk up, throwing serious shapes, like three male models on the focking catwalk, every set of mince pies in the place glued to us.

So anyway, roysh, Ms Kennealy asks for volunteers to, like, sing a scale and then to sing 'Amazing Grace' while she accompanies them on the piano, I suppose just to sort out the ones who actually want to be in the musical from those who are here to scope the scenario. So after a few minutes, roysh, Christian turns around to me and he goes, 'Ross, there's that bird you were with. What was her name ... Joanna?' I'm looking around me. He goes, 'Nine o'clock. Second row back, third from the left. She's wearing a pink scorf,' and I turn around, very subtly of course, and I go, 'I remember her. She's practically stalking me. Rings my phone all the time. Text messages, the lot.' JP goes,

'Bunny-boiler, huh? I thought you said she looks like Chloë out of 'Home and Away',' and I'm there, 'She does,' waiting for the punchline of course and JP turns around, has another look and goes, 'She looks more like focking Alf,' and he cracks up laughing to himself.

Of course Ms Kennealy knows the three boys in the front row are basically pulling the orse out of the whole thing, so she turns around to us, roysh, and she's there, 'Up you come, boys,' and we're there looking at each other going, '*Hello?*' She goes, 'Let's hear what sweet voices you have. Come on, up.' The goys are giving it, 'Oh my God, get me out of here,' but I turn around to them and I'm like, 'What are you, a pair of wusses? This'll be SOME crack.' So up we go, roysh – all the birds giving it loads, clapping, cheering, the whole bit – and Kennealy's there, 'Choose a song, boys. I'll accompany you on the piano.' Of course, JP, roysh, he's well up for it now. He's giving it, '*Laaahhh ...*' as if he's trying to find the right note and she's going, '*Laaahhh ...*' with him and whacking various, I don't know, keys on the piano to try to, like, find the note he's singing. After, like, half a minute of *laaahhhing*, JP all of a sudden breaks into, '*You can reach, but you can't grab it,*' and of course that's me and Christian's cue. We're going, '*You can't hold it, control it, you can't bag it.*' And we sing the whole of 'Discothèque', roysh, me looking straight at Ms Kennealy when we sing the line, '*You just can't get enough of that lovie dovie stuff*', to give her a thrill more than anything else, wouldn't say she gets much, like, action.

Of course, we go down like – what is it Oisinn says? – a Northside bird in a barrel full of mickeys. *But tonight, tonight, tonight. BOOM CHA. BOOM CHA. DISCOTHÈQUE.*' The whole crowd goes ballistic and I turn to JP and I go, 'We can have anyone we want now,' and JP nods and goes, 'It's an all-night buffet, goys.' We take a bow and stroll back to our seats and even Ms Kennealy's clapping and going, 'Excellent. Excellent. You might not be what we're looking for for *My Fair Lady*, but I'll see if I can think of a role for you ...'

Now it's just a case of sitting back and waiting for the bullshit to end. Up on the stage, roysh, it's all lah-de-dah, the whole song-and-dance routine, and after about an hour or so, they've found twenty or thirty people knobby enough to want to be in it. So when it's all over, roysh, me and the two boys stort working the hall, moving from group of girls to group of girls, like we're holding auditions of our own. Me and Christian end up talking to these two birds, one of which – Jill – has been giving him the once-over all afternoon. She's actually a total honey, the absolute spit of Janeane Garafalo. Her mate, roysh, I didn't think she was the Fred West when I saw her first, but up close she has a boat race like Gabrielle Anwar, and I tell her my name's Ross and she goes, 'I know,' and I'm there, 'Do *you* have a name?' and she goes, 'OH MY GOD! I am SO embarrassed. It's Evy. Short for, like, Evelyn?' and I'm there, 'It's an amazing name,' really laying it on thick. I'm sort of, like, eavesdropping on Christian's conversation as well, roysh, making sure he doesn't fock things up by saying 'May the Force be with you' in the first ten seconds, but the goy is playing it like Steve Silvermint for once. Jill's going, 'I saw your picture in *The Irish Times* last week,' because they'd a shot of him scoring our first try. She's there, 'I don't know anything about the rules of the game, but I know it was supposed to be a totally amazing try as well,' and I'm thinking, Don't say, 'Thanks, Princess,' but he doesn't, roysh, he just goes, 'I wish I'd had somebody to dedicate it to,' and the poor girl's knees nearly go from under her, the sap.

Evy's giving me loads at the same time, roysh, it's all, 'You go to the

Institute on a Friday night, don't you?' and, 'Do you not remember being introduced to me one night in Annabel's,' really coming on to me and eventually, roysh, totally out of the blue she goes, 'You were with Joanna Mulhall, weren't you?' and I'm there, 'Word gets out fast,' and she's like, 'Only because she told, like, the whole world.' Jill's ears have pricked up at this. Evy goes, 'I'm not being, like, a bitch or anything, but nobody could believe it when they heard you were actually *with* that girl. She's really nice and everything, but she's a bit of a—' Jill butts in, roysh, and she goes, 'A bit of a Wendel.' I'm there, 'A what?' and Evy makes an L shape with her thumb and, like, forefinger and she goes, 'LO-SER!' and Jill goes, 'Careful, Evy. She's over there.'

I turn around, roysh, and there she is, sort of, like, hanging around the outskirts, like a stale smell. Of course I make the mistake of making eye contact with her, which she takes as her cue to come over. She's there, 'Hi,' and the two girls are going, 'Hi, Joanna,' and Evy's giving it, 'OH! MY! GOD! Your hair is SO amazing,' even though she's actually ripping the piss, roysh, and when she's not looking Evy does that L thing behind her back again, which I have to admit is pretty funny.

Joanna says she is SO sorry we've been, like, missing each other lately and she says I never seem to have my mobile switched on, unless I'm screening calls, which is understandable because OH! MY! GOD! she's been pretty much doing the same thing herself, what with helping to organise the Debs and the whole drama over her CAO application and then netball as well. I'm there, '*What*ever,' and I can hear Evy and Jill sniggering, roysh. She goes, 'Em, I was wondering, if you're not doing anything, would you like to come out on Saturday night? It's my eighteenth and a few of us are ...' Straight away, roysh, I'm there, 'No,' and Evy actually laughs out loud, being a total bitch, which I like. But

Joanna, roysh, she cracks on she doesn't hear it and she tries to get out with her, like, dignity intact, if that's the right word. She goes, 'I understand. You're probably trying to focus on your game and ...' but I'm like, 'No, YOU don't understand. I was with you ONCE. A focking beer goggles job. I've no interest in you. You're a focking sap. I've no interest. Now fock off,' and she just, like, bursts into tears, roysh, and runs out of the place and one of her friends runs out after her and Evy goes, 'Well, someone had to tell the silly little girl,' and Jill's there, 'What a total retord,' but Christian doesn't look happy with me, roysh, it's like he thinks I went too far.

Anyway, we head off to find JP, roysh, and we spend the next half an hour working the room, just basically collecting mobile numbers off birds and then Jill and Evy come up to us and say they're heading off and me and Christian, roysh, we ask them if they're, like, doing anything later on, if they maybe fancy going for a few scoops, nothing too mad. Jill says she has no clothes with her and there's no way she's going all the way out to, like, Greystones and then heading back into town, but Evy says they can go to her gaff in Blackrock and she can borrow clothes from her and Jill goes, 'Cool. As long as it's your black Prada shirt,' and Evy goes, 'Eh, no,' and the two of them crack up laughing. Evy says she is SO going to wear that pink camisole top she got from Warehouse and then she phones her old dear, roysh, and asks her to come and collect them. Me and Christian tell them we'll see them later, and as we're heading off I hear Evy say to Jill that she doesn't want to be a bitch or anything, but she cannot BELIEVE how much weight Cliona Curran has put on.

XXX

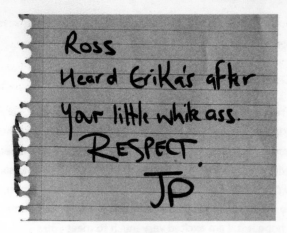

Ross
Heard Erika's after
your little white ass.
RESPECT.
JP

✗✗✗

I walk into History, we're talking ten minutes late, and Crabtree's going, 'What we'll deal with today is the reaction in the Dáil and in the country to the Anglo-Irish Treaty from the moment of its signing on the sixth of December 1921 right up to the outbreak of the Civil War.' He sees me, roysh, and he goes, 'Oh hello, Ross. Great to see you. Sit anywhere you like,' and I just, like, saunter down the back of the class, roysh, flop down on a chair and put my feet up on the desk. He cops this but knows better than to say anything. He goes, 'Em, now, in yesterday's class we discussed the controversial Oath of Allegiance,' and I'm like, 'Em, excuse me,' and he stops talking and he looks at me and I go, 'I think you've got something you'd like to say to me?' He goes, 'Em, yes, class, I'd just like to, em, apologise to Ross for the way I spoke to him here in class a couple of days ago. It was wrong of me and I'm, em, sorry.' I'm there, 'Louder,' and he's like, 'SORRY,' and then I go, 'Proceed.'

✗✗✗

I get another letter from Clementine and it's pretty clear, roysh, that she's gagging for me.

> **Dear Ross,**
>
> I received your letter just today and it make me very, very happy. I am love you too. I am think about you every time and it make me happy that I come to Ireland and meet with you. I will go to Ireland on 21 March arriving at six o'clock in the evening times. Is it possible please for you to meet with me at the airport and car me to your home? I hope it is. I am excited very much to meet you.
>
> **A lot of love, Clementine x x x**

I show it to Fionn down the back of, like, Maths and he writes this amazing reply, full of all this romantic shit, and it's like, '*Oui, je t'aime – oh oui, je t'aime. Moi non plus. Oh, mon amour. Comme la vague irrésolue. Je vais, je vais et je viens.*' Meaning, 'You are the first thing I think about in the morning and the last thing I think about at night.' Then it's, '*Entre tes reins. Je vais et je viens, entre tes reins et je me retiens. Je t'aime, je t'aime. Oh oui, je t'aime. Moi non plus, oh mon amour,*' which is obviously, 'I am counting the days until you come to Ireland. Thinking about you makes my mind race and my hort beat faster. You are my world. If you're passing through duty free on the way over, would you grab a couple of slabs of Brie for my mate Fionn's old dear.' Then it's, '*L'amour physique est sans issue. Je vais, je vais et je viens, entres tes reins. Je vais et je viens, je me retiens, non! Maintenant viens ...*' which is basically, 'I'll see you at the airport on March twenty-first.'

After class, roysh, I think about asking Fionn the French for, 'Make sure to bring some sexy lingerie,' but it'd probably spoil the whole romantic vibe.

XXX

I wouldn't have bothered sitting my driving test at all, roysh, except the old man said he'd buy me a black Golf GTI with alloys – we're talking the ultimate babe magnet here – if I managed to get my full licence, and of course Oisinn comes up with the bright idea, roysh, for me to do it in some bogger county where it's supposed to be, like, easier to pass. So anyway, roysh, I ended up applying to do it in Wicklow, of all places, and there was no way I was waiting twelve months for it to come up, so I got Dick Features to write me a letter saying I worked for him and needed the cor for my job, bullshit, bullshit, bullshit.

So the day of the test, roysh, all the goys decide to come down to Wicklow with me, supposedly to offer moral support, but basically to go on the lash down in the focking wilds and score some complete randomers. We check into The Grand in Wicklow Town, roysh, and the goys are already on the beers when I head out for the test at, like, one o'clock and they're all giving it, 'Kick ass, Ross,' and, 'We'll have one ready for you when you get back,' which is all, like, positive stuff to hear.

So there I am, sitting in the test centre in the town – had my inoculations and everything – and I'm waiting for my name to be called, and eventually this old fort comes out, roysh, and tells me to follow him into this little, like, room, where he asks to see my provisional licence and then storts asking me these totally dumb-ass questions. He's there, 'How do you know when you are approaching a pedestrian crossing at night?' and I'm going, 'You just, like, keep your eyes open for, like, people,' and I can tell he doesn't like that. They don't like people who make it basically sound simple because of course that does them out of a job. He goes, 'No, no, what I'm asking you is how would you know you are approaching one when it's dark,' and I'm there, 'I've already answered your question. Anyway, we're in the middle of Bogland. How many pedestrian crossings do you see in an average day down here?'

He just, like, stares me out of it, roysh, like he's trying to make out whether I'm serious or not, then he tells me to follow him outside and we get into my cor – well, the old man's Lexus – and he tells me to drive the way I normally would, which means he definitely has it in for me and wants me to fail. Before I put the key in, like, the ignition, I ask one question, roysh, and the dude flies off the handle. I'm like, 'Do you mind if I put a few sounds on?' and he goes, 'WILL YOU PLEASE JUST START THE CAR!' and I'm thinking, I am SO going to report this focker if he fails me.

We've been driving for, like, ten minutes, roysh, and I have to say I'm doing fairly alroysh until he asks me to do a turnaround on this, like, country lane. I'm there, 'HELLO? It's a bit narrow, isn't it?' and he's going, 'Please proceed with the manoeuvre.' A lot of these goys see you're driving a cor that's going to attract birds and they're jealous, roysh, and they want to keep you off the roads, which is portly the reason I lose the rag with him then. I'm there, 'Are you deaf or something? I said it's too narrow.' He goes, 'What would you do if you were in a situation where you HAD to turn around on this road?' and I'm there, 'I'd do what any focking normal person would do. I'd find, like, a driveway or something to turn into,' but he just can't leave it, roysh, he's going, 'What if there was no driveway? What if there were roadworks here and the road ahead was closed? What would you do then?' It's enough basically to wreck anyone's head so eventually I lose the rag with him and go, 'How often do you think I come down here? I'm only doing the test here because it's supposed to be a piece of piss. That was according to Oisinn. He's totalled when I see him.'

I decide to let it rest then, roysh, and put the whole thing behind me and I have to say I end up actually driving really well for the next, like, fifteen minutes. We're on the way back to the test centre, roysh, when my mobile rings and it's, like, JP. From the noise in the background, the goys are already half horrendufied. I'm there, 'Yo, JP. Not a good time, my man,' and he's like, 'You're still doing it, then?' and I'm there, 'Affirmative.' He's like, 'How goes it?' and I'm there, 'Reasonably confident,' and he goes, 'I'll get the borman to stick a pint of Ken on for you. Here, before I go, you will never guess who Oisinn was with in the Sugar Club the other night?' and I hear this big, like, roar from the goys. He goes, 'Esme. As in Esme O'Halloran?' and I'm like, 'As in second year Commerce UCD, plays hockey for Pembroke Esme O'Halloran?' and he goes, 'The self-same,' and I'm like, 'The focker. He knows *I* liked her.'

The next thing, roysh, I stort losing the signal, which is no surprise considering we're in the middle of focking *Deliverance* Country. I'm there, 'Can you hear me? JP, can you hear me?' and I snap the phone shut, roysh, and I turn to the tester and I go, 'Fock, I lost him.' The goy – OH my God, he SO has it in for me – he just goes, 'Will you bloody well concentrate on the road. Do you know how close you came to hitting that blue Micra back there?' and straight away I go, 'No way, José. I had plenty of room to overtake him. You better not fail me on that,' but he doesn't answer me.

Back at the test centre, though, he comes straight out with it. He's there, 'The bad news for you is that you haven't been successful,' and

I'm there, 'Was it the Micra, or was it that cow we hit? Because if it was the cow, I have to say I don't think he was badly injured,' but he just blanks me and storts filling in this piece of paper with, like, twenty or thirty things on it that I'm supposed to have done wrong. He hands it to me and I read it and then I tell him he's a tool and walk out.

'The goys are all at the bor when I arrive back. JP goes, 'How the FOCK did you not pass?' and I'm there, 'I don't know. They must have to fail x amount of people per day. It's the only explanation,' and Christian goes, 'Never mind, young Skywalker. Get this into you,' and he puts, like, a pint of Ken in front of me, which I knock back in, like, three gulps, then call up another.

By six o'clock, roysh, I'm as shit-faced as the rest of them and that's when we decide to hit one of the local battle cruisers, which turns out to be like the one out of *Star Wars*, the focking Wookie Bar or whatever it's called, except, as Fionn points out, the clientele in here are even uglier. Of course the whole place just goes silent the second we walk in the door, roysh, everyone stops talking and the music – 'Stand By Your Man', for fock's sake – just stops as though someone, like, pulled the plug on the jukebox. Everyone's just, like, staring at us. The men all look like they want to kick seven shades out of us and the women, if you could call them that, are looking us up and down and they're obviously thinking, Raw meat, happy days.

The state of them, though. The cardinal sin for birds with fat orses is wearing leather trousers, roysh, and let's just say there's a lot of focking cardinal sinners in there. How some of them managed to squeeze into them in the first place is, like, a mystery to me. They must, like, butter their legs or something.

I'm not making this up, roysh, but there's an actual bloke dressed up like a focking cowboy. He's got, like, a Stetson on and cowboy boots with actual spurs on them. And tight jeans. Anyone who's not wearing leather trousers is wearing tight jeans.

JP shouts, 'Five pints of your finest Heineken, innkeeper,' and the borman just, like, stares at him, roysh, like he's trying to make up his mind whether he should serve him or shoot him. Then he storts, like, pulling the pints and that's taken as a sign that we've been accepted, the music comes back on and everyone storts, like, talking again.

The Wicklow accent's focked-up, sort of goes up and down. 'So *what* has *yiz* down *in* Wickli?' this voice beside me goes. I stare at the person it comes from, looking for an Adam's apple, and there isn't one, roysh, so I take it for granted that it's a woman but with a moustache. I'm like, 'Sitting my driving test. Oisinn over there said it was easier to pass if you sit it in Bogsville. Full of shit, he is.'

I take a look over my shoulder, roysh, and three or four of the *lawculs* have taken Fionn's glasses off him and they're examining them like, I don't know, a bunch of aliens who've dropped out of space and have never seen a pair of glasses before. One of them goes, 'What *do* you *need* them *for?*' and Fionn goes, 'Reading, for storters,' and the four of them repeat the word and then, like, laugh and one of them goes, 'It's *reading* now, is *it?*'

Then I hear JP shouting, 'THE BREADLINE!' and I'm suddenly thinking there's no way we're getting out of here alive.

I go to get the round in, roysh, and I can feel someone lifting up the back of my Henri Lloyd sailing jacket, and of course at first I'm thinking some bogger's trying to, like, pickpocket me. But I turn around, roysh, and the bird with the moustache goes, 'Sorry, *just* having *a* look *at* your *arse.* It's *not* bad, *Sally,*' and suddenly there's this other bird behind me having a scope.

I'm probably the soberest out of the lot of us, roysh, so it falls to me to tell the goys that we're in serious danger of being killed here, but Christian is, like, locked in conversation behind me with these two guys who look like they're out of some American trailer pork and they're finding out the very subtle differences between the regular TIE fighter and Vader's model. Oisinn is – wait for it! – wearing the face off quite possibly the most hideous-looking bird in Wicklow, and that's saying something given the competition. Fionn is still trying to persuade his new mates to give him his glasses back and JP is raising a toast with a couple more locals who he's got shouting, 'THE BREADLINE!' with him, not realising they're taking the piss out of themselves.

I turn back and out of the corner of my eye, roysh, I can see the bird with the moustache trying to get her wedding ring off. I look at her and she smiles at me. She has two teeth. Another shout of 'THE BREADLINE!' goes up. Now I am very scared.

XXX

I've got, like, four new messages, roysh. Keeva says she's SO sorry for flipping out in her last message, that I must think she is OHMYGOD! SUCH a psycho and that I probably already have enough on my plate, what with the semi-final coming up, but when it's over maybe we could go for a drink, or to the cinema or something, that *Jerry Maguire* is supposed to be OHMYGOD! SO amazing, and then she says thanks for the advice that night on what song they should do for the graduation and that they've actually decided to do 'One Moment in Time' by, like, Whitney Houston, which wasn't her choice, it was Jade's, as in Rotary Club Jade, who is SUCH a lickorse that Miss Holohan would ACTUALLY take her word over the word of the deputy head girl, we're talking,

HELLO? Sorcha rang twice to say she needs to speak to me urgently and will I get my finger out of my orse and return her calls. And Oisinn rang to say he wants to meet up – as captain of the S – and have a chat about the game against the Gick, which is only, like, ten days away now.

I ring him back, roysh, and we arrange to go for, like, a sauna out in Riverview. His old man's a member. So I hop out of the sack, have a shower and grab a glass of orange juice while I'm deciding what to wear. I go for the old All Blacks jersey, black O'Neill's tracksuit bottoms and the old brown Dubes, but then I'm thinking, roysh, that maybe me and Oisinn will end up hitting town for a few scoops later on and I don't want to have to come back home, so I change into my navy Armani mock turtleneck, my tan G-Star deckpants, Dubes and my navy Henri Lloyd and, not being big-headed or anything, but I look shit-hot.

Meet Oisinn in the place. He high-fives me and we hit the bor, order a couple of Cokes, bit early to go on the batter. He asks me if I heard about Aoife, roysh, and I'm there, 'No,' and he says she totally flipped out in the rugby club on Friday night, storted going totally ballistic, telling Fionn he was this, that and the other. I'm there, 'That girl has totally lost it since Fionn red-corded her,' and he goes, 'She lost it long ago, Ross. That's why Fionn got rid. She was wrecking his head. She's very focked up. Sorcha's very worried about her.' I'm there, 'Sorcha? Must be why she's ringing me constantly. Needs a shoulder to cry on, if you know what I mean,' and Oisinn laughs and high-fives me and tells me I'm the man, which I have to say I am.

We hit the sauna then and Oisinn gives me this big major pep talk, which I really need at the moment. He reminds me how important the game against the Gick is, not just for the goys, roysh, but for the school and for the school's name, and he tells me how much is riding on my kicking. He goes, 'If you think about the S as one big machine and all of the players as, like, cogs, you are the most vital cog of all. So much depends on those two- and three-pointers, Ross,' and I'm going, 'I know, I know,' and he's like, 'I just wanted to make sure you're focused on your game, that the old pair, teachers, whatever, aren't on your case about, like, homework and whatever?' I'm there, 'Everything's Kool and the Gang, Oisinn,' and he high-fives me.

It's actually good to talk, though. We head off for a couple of frames of snooker then and Oisinn tells me he ended up snipping Wendy O'Neill on Friday night, as in second year Commerce in UCD – as in, 'She looks like Liv Tyler,' – which is a bit of a surprise really because he usually goes for mingers. He goes, 'I couldn't believe what she was wearing, Ross. It was a delightful fusion of vanity rose, fuschia and butterfly orchid – that much is true. But it had another, subtle, almost unspoken quality that captured the mood of a woman who will never accept second best.' I crack on that I know what he's talking about. I'm there, 'Is it going anywhere?' and he's there, 'She asked me to go to the Comm Ball with her, but, I don't know, I don't really want to get involved in that whole heavy relationship scene while we're still in the Cup,' and suddenly I feel guilty about hitting the old sauce so hord in the last few weeks. He has to pick his sister up from horse-riding, roysh, so he tells me he'll see me in school tomorrow and we high-five each other and, like, say our goodbyes.

XXX

I'm hopping into the cor, roysh – the old dear's Micra, SO focking embarrassing – and the next thing my phone rings and like a focking spa I end up answering it without checking my caller ID and who is it only Sorcha, and we're talking MAJOR hostility coming down the line here. It's like, 'Why haven't you returned any of my calls?' and I'm there, 'Chill out, babes,' and she's going, 'WHY HAVEN'T YOU PHONED ME, ROSS?' and I'm sorry, roysh, but this HAD to be said, so I just go, 'In case it's escaped your attention, we're not ACTUALLY going out with each other anymore,' and that storts her off, the old waterworks, and I'm thinking, Uh-oh! The Reds must be playing at home, because she always gets a bit, I don't know, emotional when she's got the painters in. She's there, 'You are SUCH an orsehole, you know that?' and I'm going, 'You don't OWN me, Sorcha. You might WISH you did, but, sadly for you, you don't.'

She goes, 'I told you there was something I needed to talk to you about and it was urgent. And you couldn't even be orsed ringing me back?' and I'm giving it, 'What is it? Make it quick, I've got a date tonight,' which is actually bullshit. She's there, 'HELLO? I CAN'T tell you over the phone. Call out to the house,' and I'm going, 'Like I said, I've something on. I'll call out during the week if I get a chance,' and she totally flips then. She goes, 'If you're not here by seven o'clock tonight, Ross, I'll say what I have to say to you in front of everyone in Annabel's. I'll make a TOTAL show of you, Ross, and I mean TOTAL,' and I know Sorcha long enough to know she's not bluffing, so I tell her I'll be out to her at about a quarter-past seven, just so she doesn't think she's getting her way completely.

It's only when she hangs up, roysh, that I remember that it's, like, our anniversary tomorrow, which she insists on celebrating, despite the fact that we've broken up, and the reason she's probably so keen to get me up to her gaff is that she's got, like, a present for me and I'm hoping that if it's aftershave it's, like, *Hugo Boss*. On my way home, roysh, I stop off in Stillorgan – mickey *marbh*, as the goys call it – and get a cord for her, then I go back to the gaff, roysh, go to the fridge and grab this massive box of Leonidas that the old dear got from one of the neighbours to thank her for her work with the old Foxrock Against Total Knackers group, the stupid bitch that she is. I tear off the message, write some shite on Sorcha's cord about being the only one who has ever truly loved her, then I go upstairs to get ready. I'm thinking about changing into the black Sonetti sweater that she really likes, roysh, and the Hugo Boss loafers she bought me for my birthday, but I don't want to look like I'm making too much of an effort; I'm pretty sure this one's in the bag.

I stick the cord and the chocolates inside my jacket, roysh, and I'm on the way down the stairs when – FOCKING great – the old pair walk in the door. The old dear goes, 'We've just had afternoon tea with Dermot and Angela,' who are, like, these orsehole friends of theirs from Sandymount. I'm there, 'Like I care.' She doesn't know what to say then so she goes, 'A girl called Suzanne phoned when you were out. Sounds like a lovely girl. Turns out her mother plays tennis in Monkstown. She wants you to ring her back today. After six, she said, because she's got hockey.' I'm just there, '*What*ever,' giving her focking daggers. Lainey focking Keogh.

The old man goes, 'Come on and have some coffee with your old dad and your old mum,' trying to get in with me. He's there, 'We're going to pop open that lovely box of chocolates that Helen bought your mother for her work with that Halting Sites Where They're Appropriate group of ours.' I go, 'The chocolates are gone,' and the old dear's there, 'Gone? Wherever have they gone, Ross?' I'm there, 'I'm giving them to a bird. I'd have bought a box myself but you two are too focking scabby to give me any decent pocket money.' The old man goes, 'A hundred pounds a week should be plenty for ...' but I hold up my hand in front of his face and I go, 'Talk to the hand.' I check the old Lionel in the mirror, roysh, probably needs a cut, and the old man's still moaning, going, 'That's a pity. We were rather looking forward to having one,' and the old dear's there, 'Oh, well,' and it's like, hint-hint, roysh, so to end all arguments I turn around to the old dear and I look her up and down and I go, 'Do you really think you need any more chocolate?' which shuts the two of them up.

Then I go, 'I'm out of here,' and the old man's like, 'Where are you going?' and of course I'm there, 'Sorcha's gaff. Are you focking stupid?' He goes, 'Just wondered how you were getting there,' and I'm like, 'I'm focking swimming, of course. You *are* stupid. I'm taking your car.' He sorts of, like, blows through his lips then and he goes, 'We've been through this before, Kicker. The roads around Killiney are far too narrow for the Lexus. Why not take your mother's?' I just give one of my dagger looks. I'm there, 'The spa-mobile? I am SO not arriving at Sorcha's gaff in a Micra,' and that's, like, my final word on the subject, roysh. He knows I've already taken the keys. He goes, 'Okay, well take the Lexus,' as if he has a focking choice, and he goes, 'but maybe drive it to Dun Laoghaire and perhaps get the train the rest of the way?'

AS IF!

I drive straight out to Sorcha's gaff – this amazing pad on the Vico Road – and her old pair obviously aren't home, roysh, because the only cor in the driveway is Aoife's, this convertible Merc, which is, like, shit-hot. I'm wondering what the fock she's doing in the house, roysh, but I guess she's probably giving Sorcha some last-minute advice on how to play it cool, make him work for whatever he gets, blahdy blahdy blah.

So I ring the bell, roysh, and it's, like, Aoife who answers, still not looking the George Best it has to be said, and I'm wondering is that the pink and white cheesecloth Tommy I bought Sorcha for, like, Christmas. She looks me up and down, roysh, and she goes, 'I don't even know why she's bothering to talk to you. You're an orsehole,' and I'm thinking she's obviously got some kind of problem with me, so I just go, 'Fock you, you fat bitch,' not because she is, roysh – she'd need to walk around in the shower to get wet – but because I know it's what'll really hurt her, roysh, and the second I've said it I regret it, but it's too late to apologise because she, like, pushes me out of the way and jumps into her cor.

I go into the house and Sorcha's, like, standing at the door of the kitchen. I go, 'Hey, Sorcha,' and she holds up a bag of popcorn and goes, 'Aoife forgot these. I'll text her if she doesn't come back.'

I can't help but notice, roysh, that she's wearing a white airtex with the collar up, blue O'Neill's tracksuit bottoms and a small bit of make-up – what is it they say? – thinly but carefully applied. The whole look – the clean white T-shirt, the bare feet and the, I suppose, understated use of foundation – they're the sign of a girl trying to look well without it looking like she's made an effort. Apparently this is, like, a trade secret among birds, but I overheard Sorcha telling Sophie about it in Kiely's one night. I go, 'Are your parents in?' and she doesn't answer. I go, 'Are they out for the night?' wondering if it'll have to be a quickie. She goes, 'They're *actually* in the Cayman Islands. Not that it's, like, any of your business.' I'm there, 'Tribunal shit, I presume? Yeah, my old man's got some loose ends he needs to sort out as well,' still playing it super-cool.

She goes, 'Don't pretend that you actually care,' and I'm there, 'I DO care, Sorcha. I care more than you'll ever know,' which is a bit gay, I know. I go, 'I really miss your friendship,' laying it on the line that I want to keep this, I don't know, plutonic, and making her do some of the spadework for a change. She goes, 'Do NOT go there, Ross. Do not EVEN go there.'

So I go to hand her the cord, roysh, and the chocolates and I go, 'I bought these for you. Happy Anniversary,' but she just turns away, roysh, and she walks out of the room and I'm left there wondering whether she's turned on the old waterworks, so I leave the cord on the table and the Leonidas – it's the big box as well, the ungrateful wagon – and I follow her into the sitting-room to try to offer her a bit of, like, I don't know, comfort. She's sitting on the sofa, roysh, and though the tears haven't arrived yet, they're in the focking post. She turns on MTV and I sit down beside her and she jumps up, roysh, like some total skobe has just porked himself down beside her on the bus with a six-pack of Dutch Gold, and she goes, 'Stay away from me! You make my flesh crawl!' and she moves over to one of the ormchairs and that's when I realise, roysh, that there's more than the usual playing-hard-to-get vibe going down here.

So we end up sitting there for ages, roysh, neither of us saying anything and All Saints come on and it's, like, 'Never Ever', and I'm about to ask her – to break the ice more than anything – which one Robbie Williams is throwing it into, when all of a sudden she goes, 'I heard you were with Evy Stapleton?' I'm there, 'Who?' and she just looks at me as if to say, you know damn well who. I go, 'Who told you?' and she's like, 'Word gets around,' and then she goes, 'So does she, I hear,' and she's all, like, pleased with herself. I go, 'You know her?' and she goes, 'I used to play tennis with her sister. She's an orsehole as well.' I'm there, 'I'm only *seeing* her,' not knowing why I'm suddenly explaining myself to her.

She gives me this sort of, like, pitying smile. She goes, 'You know she was with Gavin Cullen in the PoD on Saturday night?'

I just, like, shrug my shoulders, like, I couldn't GIVE a shit, which I couldn't if the truth be known. Then I go, 'Have you got a problem with me being with her?' knowing she has, roysh. She's there, 'I just can't believe you've, like, lowered your standards, that's all.'

Not being a wanker or anything, roysh, but I've been here for the best part of, like, half an hour, roysh, and there's not a sniff of a score, and I'm getting a bit tired of the whole Frigid Bridget scene so I'm thinking of hitting the road. As, like, a porting shot, roysh, I turn around to her and I go, 'Look, Sorcha. You're gonna have to get over *us*. We ended up being with each other at the Orts Ball – big swinging mickey. It was For One Night Only. There's no additional perform-ances. You need to get over that fact. I can be with whoever I want,' and I'm just wondering, roysh, whether I've been a bit too hord and focked up my chances of a bit of the other, when all of a sudden she turns around to me and she goes, 'I'm pregnant.'

I can feel, like, my whole body go cold, roysh, all of a sudden. I can hear, like, the blood flowing in my ears, and it must be ages before I say anything because by the time I snap out of, like, the trance, Sorcha's changed the channel and now she's watching 'Porty of Five', and finally I go, 'You're WHAT?'

She goes, 'I'm pregnant, Ross. As in, *pregnant*?' I'm there, 'How?' and she's like, 'I know you're on the senior rugby team, Ross, and you probably haven't got your teeth into the biology syllabus yet, but I'm pretty sure you know the basics.' I'm there, 'But you said you were on the Jack and ... on the pill.' She goes, 'I *am* on the pill. But even with the pill, there's still an outside chance.'

I just, like, put my head in my hands and I go, 'Oh MY God, this is SO unfair.' She looks at me, roysh, and she's there, 'It might have been a thousand-to-one shot, but it's happened and it's a fact now.' I keep shaking my head. *Pregnant.* I can't take it in. I go, 'How come you're so, like, calm about it?' and she's there, 'I've had a couple of weeks to come to terms with it.' I go, 'Have you told your olds?' and she's like, 'Not yet.' I'm there, 'Thank fock for that. The fewer people know about this the better.' She looks at me like I'm focking Baghdad and she goes, 'HELLO? I think it's going to become a bit obvious after a while, don't you?' I'm there, 'Hold on. You're not actually thinking of HAVING it? Tell me you're not thinking of having it.' She goes, 'I'm going to have it, Ross. I'm having it.' I don't know what to say. I am SO not ready for this. I go, 'What about college?' and she's like, 'I can defer for a year,' and I'm like, 'Look, Sorcha, have you actually even thought that maybe *I* don't want to have a baby. I'm still only, like, eighteen?' and she's giving it, 'It's MY choice and my mind is made up.'

And of course I end up saying something I shouldn't have, roysh. I go, 'How do you know it's mine anyway?' and she goes totally ballistic, roysh, and we're talking totally here, giving it, 'BECAUSE I DO NOT SLEEP AROUND! BECAUSE I AM NOT SOME ... SLAPPER! I AM NOT EVY STAPLETON! THAT'S HOW I KNOW!' and then I make the mistake of going, 'Hey, take a chill pill,' which doesn't go down well either, it's fair to say, because she ends up slapping me across the face, roysh, and I have to hug her and tell her to, like, calm down and then I remind her that she's got, like, the baby to think about now.

When she stops having an eppo, roysh, I go, 'Whatever you decide, Sorcha, we'll deal with whatever we have to face together,' and she is SO not happy with that. She goes, 'We'll *what?*' and before I get a chance to answer she goes, 'Ross, I'm only telling you this because Aoife said you had a right to know. When this baby's born you're not going to have anything to do with it. I'm going to raise it myself.' I go, 'If that's what you want,' and she's like, 'It is. Now I want you to go.' I'm there, 'I'm not leaving you while you're this upset,' and she loses it again and goes, 'GET OUT OF MY FOCKING HOUSE!' which I do.

My head's, like, totally wrecked as I go out and get into the cor. I stort her up and just, like, drive, not even knowing where the fock I'm going. Sorcha's old pair are going to go spare when they find out, and I'm wondering how I'm going to tell mine.

I'm not even looking at the road at this stage, roysh, and I end up taking this narrow right bend at about, like, forty and at the last minute I notice this, like, Peugeot coming in the opposite direction and I have to, like, swerve to avoid it and I end up smacking into a wall. The goy in the Peugeot doesn't even stop, the tosspot, and I get out to check the damage. I've focking totalled the cor. The whole front of it is, like, wrecked and we are talking totally here. Of course I'm never going to hear the end of this from the old man, the penis.

The next thing this dickhead pulls up in a Ford Mondeo, this old fort who can't keep his nose out of other people's business, and he winds down his window and goes, 'That's some bang you've taken there.' There's focking steam coming from the bonnet. I'm like, 'No shit, Sherlock.' He goes, 'You'd want to be careful on these roads. Very narrow, you see. Probably a bit too narrow for a car like that.'

CHAPTER FIVE
'Academic application non-existent'

My head is focking fried. Just can't come to terms with what Sorcha told me. I'm not ready to be someone's father. Me with, like, a baby? It's like, I don't *think* so. But for some reason, roysh, everywhere I go, there's, like, reminders. Every time I open a magazine or turn on the television or get on a bus it's like,

THERE'S NO MILDER WIPE THAN A JOHNSON'S BABY WIPE

and it's,

HiPP TODDLER RUSKS – GROWING UP NEVER TASTED SO GOOD

and it's,

INFACOL RELIEVES INFANT COLIC AND GRIPING PAIN.

And if it's not that it's,

SMA MEETS THE NEEDS OF EVERY LITTLE CHARACTER

Or,

PERSIL NON-BIO – FIRST CHOICE FOR BABY'S SKIN

Or it's,

CAPTURE THOSE MAGICAL MOMENTS WITH YOUR LITTLE TREASURES WITH KODAK.

It's everywhere. And it's going to be SO, like, hord for me to concentrate on my rugby.

XXX

Evy sends me a text and it's just like, **ASSHOLE!**

XXX

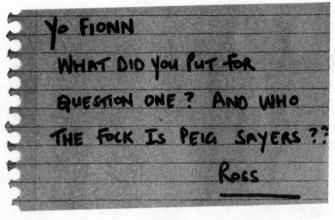

Yo FIONN

WHAT DID YOU PUT FOR

QUESTION ONE? AND WHO

THE FOCK IS PEIG SAYERS??

Ross

XXX

Us and the Gick: we've got, like, history. And we're talking a *lot* of history here. They've put us out of the Cup loads of times down through the years and there's always a bit of, like, needle between us. They basically think they're great, roysh, because, I don't know, some Taoiseach or some other tool went there, which basically means nothing, roysh, although Castlerock has never really produced anyone, unless you count people like my old man, which I don't.

Anyway, roysh, the last time Castlerock actually won the Leinster Schools Senior Cup was, like, twenty-five years ago, roysh, and it was the Gick they beat in the final, so Fehily has arranged for one of the stors of that team to come back and give us a bit of a talk, just for, like, inspiration.

So we're all sitting there, roysh, in the assembly hall, and Fehily's up there going, 'I want to introduce to you a man whose name is synonymous with success. In his day he was probably one of the finest rugby players of his age anywhere in the land. Now he is better known as one of this city's leading captains of industry ...'

Fionn leans over to me and goes, 'Tony O'Reilly didn't go to Castlerock, did he?' and I'm there, 'Don't think so,' pretending that I know who the fock Tony O'Reilly is. Fehily goes, 'He was the very foundation of the famous Castlerock pack in that unforgettable Cup-winning year. And it's no surprise that he should have gone on to make his living from, well, bricks and mortar. Yes, boys, I have great pleasure in introducing to you ... Edward Conroy of Hook, Lyon and Sinker Estate Agents in Donnybrook.'

Everyone claps. It's JP's old man. Out he comes, roysh, big Ned Kelly on him, and this giant turd of a cigar clamped between his teeth, which he's lighting as he's waddling out into the middle of the stage. As the clapping dies down, JP shouts, 'LEGEND,' ripping the piss, or at least I *hope* he's ripping the piss. Then he goes, 'THE BREADLINE!'

His old man just, like, raises his hand, as if to say, Enough, and then he goes, 'A lot can happen in twenty-five years. The first day I walked through the doors of this school was the year that man walked on the moon. The Vietnam War was still going on. Lennon and McCartney were still talking. And the price of a bribe to allow you to build something anywhere you bloody well liked was as little as twelve old pounds, and I can see you all looking at me in disbelief but that's what it was. Twenty-five years is a long time. But all the same, it's gone in the blink of an eye.

'There's not a day goes by that I don't think about the chaps, the ones I was proud to soldier alongside. Paddy Pemberton. Johnny Gilchrist with his dazzling runs on the wing. Lugs Lane. Roddy Allen. Sadly, we lost them all. Paddy signed for Blackrock the following season. Johnny and Lugs went down to Shannon, and Roddy – old Slaphead Allen – he fell on hard times and ended up playing League of Ireland soccer, Lord have pity on him.

'But they, like me, will never forget what it meant to win this school's first, and only, Schools Senior Cup. Castlerock's record since then, I am ashamed to say, is much the same as the houses I sell every day of the week – shit. That's not to put too fine a point on it. Terrible quality. You wouldn't put your worst enemy in some of the homes I sell to young newly-weds every day of the week.

'But that's beside the point. The actual point is that this school has waited twenty-five long and lean years for a team like this to come along. And if that makes you feel special, then that is understandable because special is what you are. In you – it makes me very proud to say – I see echoes of the last great Castlerock side.'

He notices that his cigar has gone out, roysh, and he takes out his lighter and gets it going again. He goes, 'I'm gonna make you kids an offer,' and I can see Fehily suddenly looking up, all interested. He's there, 'You're two games away from glory. Win them ... and I'll rent you the entire top floor of the best hotel in the city. For a weekend. Penthouse suites, boys. And ladies. Lots of very compliant ladies. Broads,' I can see Fehily running his finger across his throat, basically telling him to shut the fock up. He goes, 'I know people in this town. One phone call and – once it's illegal – I can have it for you in half an hour. I ring my man and pretty soon you're all going to think you're

Hugh Heffner. That's right. Take three or four into the Jacuzzi with you. Plenty for everyone. Fill your boots.

'That place in the final is yours. Don't let Terenure – of all schools – keep you from your destiny.'

XXX

I left eight messages on Sorcha's phone today and sent her six texts, but she won't return any of my calls. I just think we should, like, talk. I know now I was a bit, I don't know, hasty saying she shouldn't have the baby. I've had a bit of time to think about it and I think I'm ready to do the roysh thing. That's the only reason I'm so, like, desperate to talk to her. She told Sophie that I've turned into a total stalker and said she's thinking of changing her number.

XXX

It would not be an exaggeration to say that I am totally kacking it when Oisinn stands up to, like, make his speech, roysh, and I realise that having breakfast at the school this morning was SO not a good idea. We're all, like, SO nervous, roysh, that we can't keep anything down. JP is in trap one and Simon is in trap two, borfing their chicken and pasta back up, and Sooty is down on his hands and knees, roysh, slapping the floor and shouting underneath the gap in the bottom of the door, 'Cough it up, lads. Cough it up. Nerves are good. It's a matter of channelling that energy. Channel it, lads.'

Oisinn stands up, roysh, and he goes, 'Coach is roysh. Nerves are a good thing. This is a huge game. Gerry Thornley is out there today, which I think shows just how high the stakes are. Nerves show that you know it too. Terenure are a great side. You don't make it to the semi-finals of the Leinster Schools Senior Cup without being a great side. There are no soft touches left in the competition now. But we're so close, goys. We're so close now that we can almost smell it. So let's see off these orseholes today and make sure that it's us who's at Lansdowne Road on St Patrick's Day.'

After that, roysh, we all just shout out this big cheer and we all stort high-fiving and hugging each other. We go through the usual, like, rituals I suppose you could call them, to try and, like, psyche ourselves up. Oisinn's there, 'Okay, I want ten now, goys,' and we all count to ten. It's like, 'One, two, three, four,' blah blah blah. Then he goes, 'C. A. S. T. L. E. R. O. C. K,' basically spelling out the name of the school, roysh, and we give it, 'CASTLEROCK!' and then he's like, 'Pick the spuds,' and we all have to get down and pretend we're picking potatoes, roysh, and then it might be, 'Pull the chain,' and you basically all have to do the actions. It's all about morale and teamwork and shit. Of course by the end of this the goys are all going totally apeshit, kicking the walls and, like, punching the lockers, but I'm just sitting there with my towel over my head, trying my best to focus on my game.

Donnybrook is, like, jammers. We run out, roysh, and the crowd are, like, SO up for this game and even before it storts, roysh, they're giving it, 'ATTACK! ATTACK! ATTACK-ATTACK-ATTACK!' which is basically what they want us to do from the off. And it's what we end up doing. There's only, like, five minutes gone when Fionn – blind focker and all as he is – slices through a gap and gets over for a try, which The Master here converts. But then things stort to go wrong, roysh, when Simon goes and gets himself red-corded. There's a ruck, roysh, and he ends up stamping on the goy's head – I mean, the focker was offside – but his ear was pretty much hanging off and to be honest he made the most of it. Twenty or thirty stitches and it would have been back on, and even if the worst came to the worst you can get, like, prosthetic ones, if that's the word. But no, the referee totally over-reacts and sends Simon off and we're all there shaking our heads, wondering whether the rumours are true that the referee went to Terenure himself and that his nephew is actually Jonathan Palmer-Hall, their captain who, I don't think I've mentioned yet, is a complete tool who tried to be with Sorcha once and who hates me and the two are probably connected.

But Simon, roysh, is SO vital to our pack that once he's off, Terenure end up basically riding us. They score, like, three tries in the next fifteen minutes, roysh, and we are, like, SO lucky to be only 32-28 behind in the last five minutes, thanks, it must be said, to my kicking. So anyway, roysh, there's only a few minutes to go and they're murdering us down our end, looking for another try to, like, seal it, and our supporters are giving it, 'DE-FENCE! DE-FENCE! DE-FENCE!' but all of a sudden, roysh, one of their goys drops the ball and it lands roysh in front of me and I just, like, boot it and it must travel, like, forty yords down the field. But it stays in play, roysh, and I bomb it down the field after it, but who's pegging it beside me only this Jonathan wanker and we're, like, neck and neck, roysh, and I'm going, 'You haven't got the pace,' to him and I'm psyching him out of it. I'm there, 'Your legs are gone. You're never gonna make it, Jonathan,' and I get to the ball about a second before him, roysh, and give it another boot, which takes it just over the line and I dive on top of it, just as the dickhead lands on top of me. It's 33-32 to us and it's, like, game over. I just, like, push him off me, roysh, and I go, 'I said you didn't have the pace. On your knees and worship me.'

When the goys arrive at the other end of the field to, like, congratulate me, I'm still, like, sitting on the ground and I'm, like, holding the ball above my head and all the goys just, like, dive on top of me and eventually the referee – he's definitely Gick – he tells us he's adding on at the end any time we waste. But it doesn't matter how much he adds, roysh, it won't be enough because I add the points and we end up holding out for the last few minutes and after getting basically pissed on for most of the match we end up in the final. Unfair, I know, but fock them, they're Gick.

When the final whistle blows, roysh, all our fans invade the pitch. There's, like, four or five hundred from our school, then there's birds from, like, everywhere, we're talking Mounties, Alex, Whores on the Shore, the Virgin Megastore. I even saw one or two from Dogfood Manor – God loves a trier. So anyway, roysh, the whole crowd picks me up and they're, like, carrying me on their shoulders going, 'ONE ROSS O'CARROLL-KELLY, THERE'S ONLY ONE ROSS O'CARROLL-KELLY ...' and it takes me, like, half an hour to get off the field and back to the dressing-room. And of course who's waiting there when I do only Dick Features and that slimeball mate of his, looking a right pair of tools in their sheepskin coats and their trilby hats. Wankers, basically. The old man goes, 'Cometh the hour, cometh the man. Hennessy here said it, Ross. You're a big-game player. And he's Clongowes. So coming from him, it means something.' Hennessy goes, 'To survive as you did with your backs to the wall for so long and still to have the self-belief and the will to win that you showed ...' but I just ignore him, roysh, and I turn around to the old man and I go, 'Give me three hundred bills.' He goes, 'Three hundred? Em ...' like he thinks it's too much, the focking tightorse. I'm there, 'HELLO? I want to get hammered,' and he goes, 'You can get drunk on a lot less than three hundred pounds, Ross,' and I go, 'Well then I'm going to get VERY hammered.' He whips out this massive wad and he peels me off three hundred bills, and looking at how much money is in his hand, roysh, I wish I'd asked him for five hundred. Then I walk off.

As I'm going into the dressing-room, roysh, who do I bump into only Jonathan what's-his-face, who's on his way out. He's just finished with the niceties, the losing captain congratulating the winning team, saying he enjoyed the match and wishing the rest of the goys best of luck in the final. He sees me, roysh, and he goes to shake my hand – he ACTUALLY goes to shake my hand – but I just, like, pull away from him and stand there with my orms up over my head in sort of, like, triumph I suppose. He just, like, shakes his head, roysh, and he goes, 'You got lucky.'

Of course, I just smile at him and I'm there, 'No, I got the ball.'

XXX

Melanie is this slapper from Pill Hill who I was with two weeks ago, roysh, and she's left, like, a message on my mobile that's kind of, like, struck a raw nerve, if that's the right expression. It was left on Thursday night, roysh, in between two more of those 'Short Dick Man' ones that basically aren't funny anymore. Anyway, she says I'm, like, an orsehole for not ringing her and at least telling her I didn't want to see her again and that I don't give a fock about anyone's feelings except my own and that one day I'll meet someone who I really care about and they'll treat me like shit and then I'll know how it feels. And she's crying as she's saying this, roysh, and then I stort crying as well because I know she's basically roysh and it's already happened. This Sorcha situation is on my mind the whole time

If the truth be told, of course, the only reason I want her is because I know she doesn't want me and it's, like, wrecking my head at this stage. She won't, like, return my calls or anything. I thought she might ring after the game, especially after the stuff Gerry Thornley wrote about my performance – a star is born, blah blah blah – but she probably didn't even read it.

I make up my mind, roysh, to go and see her. It's, like, Saturday morning, which means she'll be, like, working in her old dear's shop – boutique, she calls it – out in the Merrion Shopping Centre. So I lash on my white Henri Lloyd, which I know she likes, roysh, and my bottle-green Timberland fleece, and I drive out there. I hang around outside for, like, ten or fifteen minutes, roysh, looking into the shop, obviously not wanting her old dear to see me, just in case Sorcha's, like, spilled the beans. It doesn't look like Sorcha's actually working today because I can see her old dear and her cousin, Clara, who's, like, first year International Commerce with French in UCD, but there's no sign of Sorcha. I'm about to head off, roysh, when I hear this voice behind him and it's like, 'OH MY GOD! *What* are you doing here?' and I turn around and it's, like, her and she's holding, like, three takeaway coffees, probably cappuccinos, because it's pretty much all she ever drinks.

I'm there, 'Sorcha, we have things to talk about,' and she's like, 'It's too late for talking,' and I'm going, 'I just came out to see how you've been?' She's there, 'As if you give a damn,' and I go, 'I do, honey,' and I'm trying to get a sly look at her stomach, roysh, to see if it's, like, storted to show yet, but her eye contact is, like, pretty intense, roysh, and I know I'm going to get sussed. Probably a bit early for her to be showing anyway.

I tell her she's looking well and she goes, '*What*ever,' and I ignore this and tell her I was a bit scared to go into the shop and face her old dear and she goes, 'Boutique. And I don't blame you.' I go, 'You haven't told her yet?' and she goes, 'With all she has on her plate at the moment? I don't THINK so,' and I ask her if her old man's still in the whatever-you-call-it islands and if she misses him and she goes, 'He HAPPENS to be there on business. Mum could end up losing the boutique, you know.'

I go, 'Sorry, I didn't realise ... how are you coping with ... I mean ...' and she goes, 'The baby? You can say the word, Ross. Actually, I'm not even thinking about it. I've got too much on my plate right now. The Leaving is, like, twelve weeks away and I'm SO far behind. Then there's this petition I'm doing for Amnesty to try to stop all these executions without trial in Rwanda – whatever she did or didn't do, time is running out for Virginie Mukankusi. And this whole Aoife situation is, like ...' and I go, 'I know, she doesn't look well,' and she goes, 'What the fock do you care?' and I go, 'I do care,' and she's there, 'You don't care about anyone but yourself, Ross. And that is why I don't want you having any-thing to do with this baby. You're an orsehole. And I don't want MY baby having an orsehole for a father.'

I look into her eyes and I know she means it. I search for something to say, roysh, something – anything – that might change her mind, but all I can think to say is, 'Did you hear we're in the final?' and she looks at me, roysh, as if she's just wiped me off the sole of her shoe and she goes, 'Grow up, Ross.'

Then she looks me up and down and says it again. She goes, 'Just GROW up.'

XXX

The old dear's left one of her birds' magazines on the table in the sitting-room, roysh, and I just sort of, like, pick it up and flick through it and I swear to God, every page I open has something to do with babies and pregnancy. It's either,

DO YOU BELIEVE IN SEX AFTER CHILDBIRTH? – FROM EARTH MOTHER TO SEX KITTEN WITH THESE TEN EASY TIPS

Or it's,

HOME FROM HOME – BEHIND THE SCENES OF A NATURAL BIRTHING WARD

And if it's not that it's,

NOTHING BUT THE TOOTH – SURVIVING THE AGONIES OF YOUR BABY'S TEETHING.

XXX

I've better things to be doing than listening to the old man crapping on about nothing, but when he calls me into the sitting-room, roysh, I make the mistake of actually going in. He's there, 'Ah, Kicker, there you are,' and I'm like, 'This better be important.' He goes, 'Well, I just thought, you know, big game tomorrow – big with a capital B, of course – St Michael's in the Schools Cup final and so forth, I just thought ...' and I'm there, 'Any chance of you getting to the point before I need to shave again?' which I have to say I'm pretty pleased with.

He goes, 'It's just, I wondered if you'd like to sit down with your old dad and watch a video. It's Ireland beating Scotland 21-12 to win the Triple Crown. Lansdowne Road, how are you? Twentieth of February 1982, thank you very much indeed. God, I remember it like it was yesterday. You wouldn't, of course, but we sat and watched it together. You must have been all of eighteen months old. We were in the old house then. Glenageary, quote-unquote.'

He's there, 'The tickets. Rare as hen's teeth, they were. Myself and Hennessy – he was doing his devilling that year if memory serves – we got our hands on a couple. Morning of the match, you got an attack of colic. Cried all day. Well, your mother felt one of her world-famous migraines coming on and she took to the bed. So I rang Hennessy and I said, 'Cockers' – because that's what we called him at school; Coghlan and so forth – I said, 'Cockers, I've got an emergency at home and it's one with a capital E. So you're going to have to tell Ciaran Fitzgerald and Hugo McNeill and old Ginger McLaughlin that they're going to have to do it without me.

And do it, they did. Ollie Campbell. Magnificent. Kicked twenty-one points that day. Six penalties and a drop goal. A record points haul for the master technician. Talk about grace under pressure. Five steps backwards, up and down on his toes and then – WALLOP – another one in your eye, so-called Scotland.

And you know what the oddest thing was? You stopped crying. There wasn't a peep out of you for the entire match. You just sat there, mesmerised by the great man. I knew then you were going to be a kicker. Your mother came downstairs not long after the final whistle. Said she was feeling a bit better. She had some work to do on some campaign or other. I think it was Travellers then as well. It was houses they were after in those days, but that's by the by. We'd just bought our first video recorder – they were new at the time – and I taped the game. Your mother asked me why on Earth I'd bothered recording a game I'd just watched. And I remember – it's like it happened yesterday – taking the tape out of the machine and telling her, "This, Fionnuala, is history."

So that night, Hennessy and I arranged to meet for a couple of celebratory brandies in the Shelbourne, which was where the Ireland players were staying. And I remember saying to him that night, I said, "Hennessy, that little lad of ours, he sat silently throughout that match today, transfixed by the performance of the great man. He's an outhalf, Hennessy, I can feel it." And I said to him, "Mark my words, he'll go on to play for Castlerock. And the night before the schools cup final, I'll pull out that tape and we'll sit down together, as father and son, and we'll relive the match that started it all." So what do you say, Kicker?' and he slaps the sofa cushion beside him to try to get me to sit down.

I go, 'I'd rather stick pins in my eyes.'

XXX

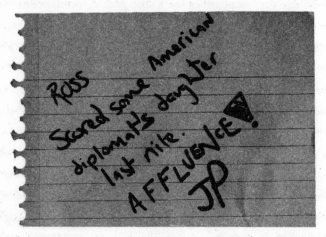

Ross
Scored some American
diplomat's daughter
last nite.
AFFLUENCE!
JP

XXX

JP goes, 'Of course there is one major incentive for us to win tomorrow,' and we're all, like, totally clueless of course, and he goes, 'We'll all get a kiss off Oisinn's old dear,' and we're all, like, 'Yyyeeaahh!' The mother of the winning captain always gets to present the cup, roysh, and Oisinn's old dear is a total yummy-mummy. Oisinn takes this well, of course. He's giving it, 'No tongues, goys, I mean it,' and we all crack our holes laughing. Then JP leads us all into a chorus of, 'We're rich – and we know we are, we're rich – and we know we are ...' which is sort of, like, *his* song and at the end he storts shouting, 'THE BREADLINE!' over and over again and we're all cracking up. I have to say, roysh, staying over in the school dorms tonight was a really good idea, just to, like, boost morale and stuff.

Oisinn – you've got to admire his focus, roysh – goes back to his perfume catalogue, learning off all the shit about some new range or other, which he says keeps him from worrying about tomorrow. But of course I've got, like, Sorcha and the baby to do that. Christian knows that something's up, roysh. I know he's away with the, I don't know, Ewoks half the time, but he's actually good at sussing out when something's wrong. He catches my eye, roysh, and sort of, like, gestures at me to follow him outside, which I do and we go into the kitchen and straight away he goes, 'What's she done now?'

Of course I'm going, 'Who?' but there's no fooling this goy. He's there, 'Ross, did you know you've got two looks when someone's pissing you off – one for when it's Sorcha, the other when it's someone else.' There's no point in beating around the bush. I have to tell someone. Might as well be my best friend. I go, 'She's pregnant, Christian,' and even saying it makes my whole body go weak. He's there, 'PREGNANT? And you're the ...' I'm like, 'Father. I can say it now. Couldn't at first. I wanted her to have ... well, you know. It was just a shock, I suppose. But now I've actually storted to like the idea. Me and Sorcha and our little, I suppose, baby. Okay, it's not like I expected things to be but – Fock it - the old man will give us the money for a house.'

Christian goes, 'But I take it Sorcha wants nothing to do with you?' and I'm there, 'I don't blame her because of the way I, like, reacted. But it was just shock, Christian. My whole life was being turned upside down and ...' He goes, 'Have you ever thought that hers was too?' I look at him. He's there, 'All the things she was looking forward to after school – college, travelling, a social life, a life full stop – they've gone, Ross. And for what? Half an hour of passion?' He's being a bit generous there, but I just nod. He goes, 'I'm saying this to you as your best friend, Ross. Don't be too hord on her. What you're going through is probably only a quarter of what she's going through. Give her time. She'll come round.'

I love talking to Christian. I go, 'I've barely been able to think about anyone else. I've got that French bird coming next week. Haven't even got excited about that.' He goes, 'Ross, there's only one thing you should be focusing on right now and that's tomorrow's game. You don't need me to tell you how much the team relies on your kicking. If you're not roysh, then the rest of us aren't either. All these other things, Ross, they'll sort themselves out. Things have a way of working out for the best. You just need to focus on the here and now.'

I give the goy a hug, roysh, a really long one. Then he looks at me and he goes, 'You, a father. I can't believe it myself.'

Inside the dorm we can hear JP shouting, 'THE BREADLINE!' again and we both crack up. Then Christian goes, 'You must rest, Skywalker. You've had a long day.'

CHAPTER SIX
'Usually the ringleader whenever there's trouble'

Fehily says that education can go to blazes so long as a boy can outjump his peers in a lineout, punch his weight in the scrum, or kick a three-pointer from an obtuse angle deep in injury time. He's giving us our final pep talk before, like, the final. He's going, 'Books, education, learning – these things have their place in the life of young men, of course. But not in yours. Because you are the élite. You don't ask a pure-bred stallion to drag a cart uphill into town and similarly we here at Castlerock would never conceive of encumbering such fine athletic specimens as yourselves with such fripperies as schoolwork. The reproductive system of the earthworm, the fixed rhyming schemes of a Shakespearean sonnet and the principle industries of the Benelux countries should not matter a jot to you. Iambic pentameter, chlorophyll, Maginot Line, hypotenuse – such terms should have no relevance to your lives.'

Oisinn, roysh, he turns around to me and goes, 'Iambic what?' and I'm there, 'Don't ask me. I haven't been in Maths since, like, Christmas.'

Fehily goes, 'Your lives begin today. None of you know where you're going to be in ten years' time. But verily, I say unto thee, that you will always look back on this day and remember exactly where you were this afternoon. You can see your lives stretching out in front of you. Many of you will go on to play rugby for clubs and form new allegiances. A good number of you will meet a fellow at your new club who will get you a highly paid yet unfulfilling job that requires you to wear a suit – perhaps in a bank or some other such financial institution – where you'll open envelopes for fifty or sixty thousand pounds a year. Others will discover that the inability to spell the word lager is no hindrance to getting a job as a rep for a major brewing company if they happen to sponsor your team. Some of you will go on to manage your father's businesses.

'I think the point I'm trying to make here is that whatever you do and whatever you achieve in life you will always be Rock boys. Always remember where you're from. Did Jesus not utter those self-same words to His friends in the Garden of Gethsemane as he prepared to meet His Father?

'We don't have funny handshakes. There's no bizarre ceremonial rituals here. But we *are* a brotherhood. A fraternity. Call it what you will. But wherever you find yourselves in the world, and irrespective of what trouble you find yourselves in, all you need to do is make a call and you shall have succour, the same kind Jesus had as he prayed among the olive trees before going off to face his death, because you are Rock and Rock isn't merely the name of a school. It's an institution. A way of life. And it is underpinned by rugby and rugby – as the Good Lord told our friend from Cyrene as they carried the cross up to Calvary – is the very essence of brotherhood.'

I'm basically bawling here, roysh, and I have a sly look around and I notice that that isn't a dry eye in the place. He goes, 'From blood, authority of personality, and a fighting spirit springs that value which alone entitles a people to look around with glad hope, and that alone is also the condition for the life which men then desire ... It is not for seats in Parliament that we fight. But we win seats in Parliament in order that one day we may be able to liberate the German people. Do not write on your banners the word 'Victory': today that word shall be uttered for the last time. Strike through the word 'Victory' and write once more in its place the word which suits us better – the word 'Fight'.'

It's, like, totally amazing stuff, roysh, and we all suddenly burst into a chorus of 'Castlerock Above All Others', roysh, with Fehily just standing there with, like, his hands on his hips, nodding his head. Then when we're finished, roysh, he comes down to us and he shakes hands with every single one of us. Until, that is, he comes to me. He holds his hand out, roysh, but I don't shake it. I just hold mine up and he cops what I'm at, roysh, and he just, like, high-fives me. It's a totally unreal moment.

We arrive at Lansdowne Road about, like, half an hour before kick-off and the noise is already totally deafening. All our goys are up in the West Stand, roysh, singing all the Rock songs and we can actually hear them from the dressing-room as Sooty gives us a last minute bit of advice. Basically he tells us the things we already know, roysh, that Michael's haven't been in the final for, like, ten thousand years but they have a great team this year, wankers or not, and they are really going to be up for it. He tells us it's time to kick ass.

The butterflies are, like, SO bad as we leave the dressing-room and the roar of the crowd gets louder. We're standing there in the tunnel, roysh, and Christian turns around to me and goes, 'I have a bad feeling about this,' which is something Han Solo or some other goy says, and I go, 'The Force will be with us today,' and he turns around and he high-fives me and it's a great moment. Fionn looks at me and he goes, 'Ross, I know we don't always see eye to eye, but I'm proud to count you among my friends. I'd die for you out there on the field, you know that,' and I hug him and for a couple of seconds I actually regret sending that bunch of pink roses to his house with a cord saying, 'All the best, Ducky, from all the boys in The George,' with six or seven big kisses underneath it.

So there we are, standing in the tunnel, roysh, and out come the Michael's heads and they queue up beside us and I'm not sure if it's my imagination, roysh, but they are big fockers and very fit looking and I wouldn't say I'm alone in wondering whether we should have gone totally off the sauce this year. Some of them I recognise from Kiely's, the M1 and The Bailey, some of them I don't, all in their faggy jerseys. But they're actually very focking focused, roysh, so focused that it's actually, like, scary? They're not even looking at us, they're just, like, staring straight ahead, cracking on that the opposition don't even matter to them, that they're only concentrating on *their* game. So to ruffle their feathers, roysh, I turn around to their tighthead prop – I think his name's Risteard, a no-neck focker – and I go, 'You're a faggot,' and he turns his head to the roysh and he looks at me and goes, 'Repeat that, please.' I go, 'I said, you're a faggot,' and he turns his head again and it's like he's, like, weighing up what I've said, roysh, trying to decide what to do, then all of a sudden he takes a swing at me. Christian jumps straight in front of me, roysh, and he goes, 'You deck him and you're going to have to deck me first,' which I don't think would present much of a challenge for this goy – he's a focking animal – but then Fionn gets in on the act and then Oisinn and a couple of their goys as well and there's a bit of pushing and shoving in the tunnel, roysh, before a gang of stewards come and break us up and the referee tells us all to calm down and don't let the tension of the occasion spoil our enjoyment of the game.

We're told it's time to go and I turn around to the goy again and I'm like, 'Bent as a rusty nail,' and Oisinn goes, 'Let's kick FOCKING orse,' and then we run out onto the field and you can hordly hear yourself think, the noise is so loud. We head, naturally enough, for the South Terrace end of the ground and it's all, like, black and red striped shirts and the crowd stort chanting my name and I'm wondering whether Sorcha's in there somewhere and – this sounds bent, roysh – but if our little baby is kicking with excitement inside her. I can feel my eyes stort to water and I actually think I'm going to burst into tears, roysh, so I try to do what Christian says and just blank it out.

It's actually a bit of a relief, roysh, when the game storts, but you can tell that both sides are kacking it. It's full of, like, handling errors, turn-overs, blah blah blah. Eunan's giving me shit ball and I end up giving Fionn a couple of hospital passes. JP's knocked on three times under, like, high balls and if it wasn't for Christian tearing them aport out wide and Simon and Oisinn kicking orse up front, we'd actually be behind.

The closest we get to a try, roysh, is when Christian sells their defence an unbelievable dummy and it looks like he's in. He's actually in the air, roysh, about to touch down, when one of their goys appears out of nowhere and drags one of his legs into touch and it's disallowed. We all call the referee a cheat, even though we know he's roysh. Basically, the first half turns out to be a penalty contest between me and their kicker, don't know the goy's name, but I know he sometimes drinks in the Wicked Wolf and he was with Sorcha's friend Sophie at Amie with an ie's eighteenth birthday porty. I get the upper hand, kicking four penalties from six, and we end up leading, like, 12-9 at half-time.

But it's hord-going, roysh. Oisinn has, like, a black eye – Risteard's revenge – and Simon's ribs are pretty badly bashed up and Sooty actually wants to, like, substitute the dude, but he just goes, 'I'll die before I'll go off injured.' The dressing-room is like a focking casualty ward, but hearing Simon say that, roysh, gives us basically the strength to go out there in the second half and go at them again.

Our supporters are giving it loads, roysh, fair focks to them because the match is probably kack to watch from a spectator's point of view. There's very little ball-in-hand stuff, it's all boot and rucks and solid defence. Twenty minutes into the second half, roysh, and the scores are still the same when one of their goys – a total penis who I'm pretty sure is Alyson with a y's brother – he kicks this big, long garryowen for their goys to chase onto, but JP's standing where he should be, roysh, and there's no wind, so he should catch it no problem, but I don't know what happens, he must, like, take his eye off the ball, and when he goes to catch it, it hits off his, like, forerorm and spills onto the ground, and one of their goys – can't even see who it is, but there were enough of them there – jumps on it and they've scored the first try of the game. And of course they stort celebrating like they've won the focking thing already.

They miss the conversion, roysh, but even though we're only, like, two points behind, it's going to be hord now, because they're going to defend like their lives depend on it and in a close game like this it's unlikely that you're going to get a lot of tries, unless they're from mistakes. It's, like, backs to the wall time for them. This Risteard goy, I have to say it, roysh, he's having a focking stormer, the wanker, and he's obviously targeted me as the main danger man because he walks up to me, roysh, during a break in the play and he goes, 'I am going to cream you the next time you get the ball,' and I just, like, laugh in his face, pretending it's not, like, affecting me and shit, but as I go to run off he's there, 'Tell your friends not to pass to you. Seriously, next time you get the ball, you're going to see who's a faggot.'

I'm actually not intimidated, it that's the word, but about twenty seconds later, Eunan pulls the ball out of a ruck and takes half the focking day to give it to me and when he does it's, like, another hospital pass and Risteard – I swear to fock, I've never seen a goy that size move so fast – he comes from nowhere and just, like, clotheslines me. I am smack bang out of it for what must be a couple of minutes, roysh, and even when I come around I must have, like, concoction, if that's the roysh word, because my vision's blurry and I can only just make out the voices of the goys, standing over me, asking am I alroysh. It takes a few minutes before my head clears and the goys help me to my feet and before Oisinn has a chance to say anything to me, roysh, I go, 'I'm playing on, Oisinn. Don't want any arguments.'

But Michael's are unbelievable, roysh. It's, like, attack attack attack from us, roysh, but we can't get any nearer than ten metres from their line no matter what we do, and the goys are getting, like, frustrated. Oisinn decks their second row with the blond hair and luckily, roysh, the ref doesn't see it. The clock is winding down. Then the time's up. We're into whatever the dude's adding on, roysh, and we're still two points behind and ten metres from the line but we just can't make any more ground. And then suddenly, roysh, there's a ruck and Oisinn ends up on the ground and the goy that he decked, roysh, he can't help himself. He sees Oisinn lying there and WHACK! he stamps on the back of Oisinn's leg and you can hear this, like, TWANG, roysh, and it's his hamstring snapping, it's actually the sound of his hamstring snapping, and the ref blows for a penalty for us and it's, like, roysh in front of the posts, we're talking three minutes into, like, injury time, and all our goys are already celebrating. It's probably the last kick of the game.

But Oisinn is focked, roysh, They bring a stretcher on and, like, cart him off, but before he goes he says he wants to talk to me, so the St John's Ambulance dudes carry him over to me and he sits up on the stretcher and he grabs me by the back of the neck, roysh, and he puts his forehead up against mine and he goes, 'This is the most important kick of your life, Ross. You don't need me to tell you what it means. Now kick ass,' and I go, 'It's in the bag ... Captain,' and he's giving it, 'You the man, Ross! You the man!'

So I place the ball, roysh, run my hand through my hair, blow hord, take five steps backwards and four to the left, run my hand through my hair again, do a little dance on the spot and then ... It's silent, roysh, but then I hear something, a voice shouting and without looking, roysh, I know it's that Risteard dickhead and he's there, 'Hey, Ross. I was with Sorcha in The Queen's on Friday night,' and suddenly I can feel all the blood in my body go cold. My mind is, like, gone. I'm suddenly thinking about Sorcha and I'm thinking about what a good person she is and I'm thinking about our little child growing inside her and I'm thinking about that big focking ape with his hands all over her ... all over her stomach and his tongue in her mouth and ... and ... and ...

It must be, like, ages that I'm standing there, roysh, because when I snap out of it everyone's just, like, staring at me, wondering what the fock's wrong. I look at Christian, who's standing there with his eyes closed, probably trying to use The Force to get it through the posts. JP and Fionn are turned around, not able to, like, watch. Oisinn is sitting up on the stretcher on the sideline, waiting for me to knock this over so he can go to the hospital knowing he's got a Schools Cup medal.

And I'm still thinking about Sorcha and I just run at the ball and boot it and suddenly the noise returns and it's all, like, groans and I watch the ball as it sails high and wide of the posts.

The ref blows up straight away and the Michael's goys go mental. I just fall to my knees and then flat on my face and I lie there, roysh, with my nose in the ground, bawling my eyes out and all the goys – we're talking Christian, JP, Fionn – they're all coming over and telling me that it's not my fault, but it's not what I want to hear roysh now. I'm there going, 'I focked up. I focked it up for everyone,' and they're going, 'AS IF! We wouldn't even be here today, Ross, if it wasn't for you.'

Not being big-headed or anything, roysh, but it's actually pretty brave of me to go up with the goys to collect my medal, because my first instinct is to get the fock out of there as quick as I can. But I go up, roysh, and I collect it and Mary McAleese is there, 'You had a very good game,' and it's obvious she doesn't recognise me as the tool who threw the game away and I just go, 'Kool and the Gang,' and I trudge down the steps, wishing the ground would just, like, open up and swallow me.

I walk back out onto the field, roysh, and it's been invaded by Michael's heads and hundreds of birds, most of whom were cheering for us two hours ago but are now fans of the other side. I see Keeva and Sian and Evy and they're all, like, hanging out of the Michael's goys and Keeva sees me and makes an L shape with her finger and thumb and she mouths the word 'LO-SER' at me and I know she's roysh. Then we have to stand there and watch those dickheads go up and collect the Cup and we're all totally bulling.

I walk off the field, roysh, and Christian has his orm around me and I tell him I'm, like, really sorry for focking things up for everyone and he tells me not to be stupid, we lost it over the full eighty minutes and not on the one mistake I made in the entire match, and it's nice to hear even if it is total bullshit. I'm about to go into the dressing-room, roysh, but who's standing at the mouth of the tunnel only Orse Face himself. He's on the focking mobile, roysh, with the old dear standing beside him, hanging off his orm, six baby seals on her back, and when he sees me he goes, 'Hold on a second, Hennessy. Bad luck, Ross. Even Ollie Campbell had his bad days,' and then he goes back to his big focking chat, so I just walk roysh over to him, roysh, and stand roysh in front of him and give him the finger.

We go back to the dressing-room and it's like the world is about to end. Everyone has their heads in their hands. There's, like, tears, the whole lot. I ask Simon what he's going to do now, roysh, and he just, like, shrugs his shoulders and goes, 'Repeat, I suppose,' and I'm like, 'Again? Simon, they're going to suss sooner or later that you're over-age,' and he's like, 'I'm not leaving school until I get a winner's medal,' and I have to admire that. Then he goes, 'By the way, you're coming to my twenty-first on Friday night, aren't you?' and I'm like, 'I am SO there.'

The next thing, roysh, Fehily comes in and I'm expecting him to give us the kind of speech we usually get from him, sort of, like, uplifting and shit, telling us we did the school proud, that the Year of the Eagle will be forever remembered in the school, blah blah blah. But no. He walks in and he tells us that now that we're out of the Cup we'd better knuckle down and study because the mocks stort in, like, two weeks. Then he focks off.

But before he reaches the door, he turns around and he goes, 'Ross?' and I'm there, 'Yeah?' and he's like, 'Have that special topic report Mister Crabtree asked you for on his desk first thing on Monday morning.'

XXX

It's the day after the match and I haven't even looked at the papers to read the reports. I can guess the gist of them: Ross O'Carroll-Kelly Blows His Big Moment. I need to escape the old man and his, 'You'll play for Ireland by the time you're twenty,' bullshit and the old dear with her, 'I feel terribly sad for June (who's, like, Oisinn's old dear) because she was so looking forward to presenting the Cup; she bought a lovely new outfit,' and then all the goys ringing me to see if I'm okay and Ryle Nugent ringing me wondering if I'd like to share with the nation just what was going through my mind when I took that kick, and to be honest, I couldn't even begin to explain.

So I get the fock out of there. I grab two hundred sheets from the old man's safe and hit town for the day. So there I am, roysh, and I'm in the Stephen's Green Shopping Centre and something – I don't know what – just *something* drags me up to the mother and baby section on the first floor. There I am, standing on the escalator, roysh, not knowing what the fock I'm doing, but it takes me up and up, and all of a sudden it suddenly plonks me in the middle of this whole new world.

It's, like, Strollers and harnesses and sleepsuits and sterilisers and Moses baskets. It's EasiRiders and highchairs and baby monitors and potties and those gates that you put at the end of the stairs to stop babies snotting themselves. There's car seats and door bouncers. There's safety socket covers and bouncing cradles. And there's tiny pairs of booties and mittens and these little bibs with, like, Winnie the Pooh and Noddy and Tractor Tom and Boo and Bob the Builder and Fimbles on them. And this bird comes over to me, roysh, and she obviously works there, and she asks me if she can help me in any way, and then she asks me if I need to sit down because I realise that I've got, like, tears streaming down my face. I tell her I'm fine and she tells me not to worry because lots of men find walking into a baby store for the first time an incredibly emotional experience and that sometimes she feels more like a counsellor than a sales assistant. She asks me how far away is the big day and I count back the weeks to the Orts Ball and I tell her seven months. I wipe my eyes and she tells me that if I need any help to call her.

I wander around some more and I look at this Montreal Cot, which costs £129.99 and it's got a three-position base and teething rails that help protect delicate new teeth. Then I check out these freaky-looking things that turn out to be called breast pumps and it says on the box, roysh, that they enable mothers to express and store their breast milk quickly and discreetly for later use, and I put it down quickly in case anyone cops me and thinks I'm a perv. Then I look at the new Powertrack 360, a pushchair with a revolving front wheel that allows greater manoeuvrability in tight corners and a powerful disc brake that operates from the handlebor.

Then this woman walks by, roysh, and she's carrying her baby and I'm just, like, entranced by it, if that's the word. I look at its little fingers with its tiny nails. And the blond hair and the big blue eyes and this huge smile and I can feel myself storting to fill up again so I head for the escalator and just before I step onto it, roysh, the shop assistant I was talking to earlier goes, 'Excuse me, sir,' and she hands me this book and she's there, 'A little gift from us – the best of luck,' and on the front of the book it says, *Celtic Names for Children.*

XXX

The old man asks me where I'm going, roysh, and I am SO tempted to go, 'Who the fock are you? Bergerac?' but I don't, roysh, I try to be nice, I just go, 'The focking airport.' He's like, 'The airport? You're not flying somewhere are you?' I just, like, throw my eyes up to heaven and I go, 'We've got a French exchange student coming.' The old dear looks up from her speech for tonight's Foxrock Against Total Skangers EGM. She's there, 'Ross, you never told us ...' and I'm there, 'I'm telling you now, aren't I?' The only thing the old man can think to say is, 'I hope he likes his rugby, that's all I can say, because you know me and you once we get talking ...' I'm there, 'It's actually a *she*.' The old dear's still looking at me over the top of her glasses. She goes, 'Oh! Well I'd better air out one of the spare rooms, put some fresh sheets on the ...' and I'm like, 'No need. She's staying in my bedroom,' and the old man – I can't believe how slow he is on the uptake sometimes – he goes, 'But, where are *you* going to sleep?' I'm there, 'Do I have to draw you a focking picture?'

Probably sounds a bit, I don't know, rude I suppose. But I lost us the Schools Cup. I've lost Sorcha and our baby. I DESERVE some action with a French honey. So I lash on the old *cK One*, grab the Lexus – the old man's had the damage fixed – and I hit the airport. I check myself out in the rearview mirror – shit-hot – before I mosey on down to the Arrivals gates and even though I'm, like, pretty early, roysh, it's a bit odd that none of the other French Club geeks seem to be here yet. The plane's arriving in, like, half an hour. I try to get Fionn on his mobile, but it just, like, rings out.

I go to the bookshop on the Departures level and buy an A4 pad and a thick black morker. I grab a cup of coffee and I make this, like, sign and it's like,

with a few love horts around it, and then I think it looks a bit, I don't know, gay, so I crumple it up and make another sign and it's like,

and I then I end up putting the horts back on it. I check the time, knock back my coffee and peg it down to the gate. The Nerd Herd still aren't here and I wonder have I got the wrong date. I check Clementine's letter and no, the date's roysh. I check the flight details on the monitor and it is the roysh one and I see that it's landed. She's probably, like, waiting for her luggage as we speak. There better be a French maid's uniform in there somewhere, although you can get them on Capel Street.

I try Fionn's phone one last time but it's still, like, ringing out, then I just remind myself, 'Forget the focking Anorak Pack. Plough your own furrow, Ross.' So I'm standing there, roysh, holding up my little sign and all of a sudden there's this, like, little fat bloke standing roysh in front of me. Of course I'm there, 'Would you mind getting the fock out of the way. I happen to be waiting for someone,' and he goes, 'You are Ross, yes?' and I swear to God, at that moment, roysh, I just felt every hair on my body stand on end. It's, like, suddenly everything is clear to me. Fionn's stitched me up. He goes, 'Hello. I am Clement. I like it very nice to be here,' and he gives me a hug. Oh for FOCK'S sake, he's even got leopardskin suitcases. I don't say anything, roysh, I'm just, like, staring roysh through him.

He goes, 'You have big arms from playing of the rugby, yes?' and I go, 'Don't focking touch me. You wait here. We're talking five minutes. *Capisce?*' and I turn around and peg it up the escalator and on the way up, roysh, I try Fionn's phone again and this time he answers. I go, 'You are focking totalled.' He's there, 'I take it you've met Clement,' and I'm like, 'I hoped you'd at least *pretend* it was a mix-up. Who the FOCK is he?' Fionn goes, 'Well, I found his details on one of those lonely horts websites for gay men ...' I'm there, 'Yeah, I bet you spend a lot of time looking at those,' and he goes, 'I'm not the one who was standing in Arrivals five minutes ago waiting for his boyfriend to arrive. The love horts were a nice touch, by the way.' I flip the lid then. I'm there, 'You were actually, like, watching me?' and he goes, 'We all watched it – me, JP, Oisinn, Simon. I didn't tell Christian because I couldn't be sure he wouldn't tell you,' and I'm like, 'He *would* have told me. Because he's a *real* friend,' and then I'm like, 'Where the fock are you now?'

He goes, 'We're all still down here on the Arrivals level. Your boyfriend looks a bit upset, Ross. Probably thinks you didn't mean all those things you said in your letters,' and I'm there, 'I bet that was all benny talk as well, wasn't it? And where did you get that picture, the bird who looked like Natalie Imbruglia?' and he goes – real focking smort, roysh – he goes, 'Brace yourself, Ross. That *was* a picture of Natalie Imbruglia,' and I can hear all the goys cracking their holes in the background.

I'm there, 'Where are you? I want to meet you face to face,' and he's there, 'Ross, you've spent the last few months trying to convince my parents that I'm gay. Do you have any idea what it's been like living in my house? Asparagus and risotto for every meal. My old dear asking me for my opinion on nail varnish. My old man leaving Elton John CDs lying around my room.' Actually that was me, but I say nothing. He goes, 'And despite all the essays I've written for you in the past, all the homework I let you cog from me, all the exams that I coached you through, you forgot one important fact, Ross. I'm cleverer than you.'

I don't say anything. He storts laughing, roysh, and he goes, 'You should have seen your face when it dawned on you. I laughed so much I almost dropped the video camera.' I'm there, 'HOLY FOCK, you were actually *filming* it?' and he goes, 'That was actually Oisinn's idea. It was just one of those Kodak moments, Ross. You want to be able to enjoy it time and time again. And there were a lot of people who couldn't be here today who want to enjoy the moment of your humiliation too.' I go, 'What am I supposed to do with ... What is his focking name?' He goes, 'His name is Clement, Ross. Probably calls himself Clementine when he's camping it up. We're all still downstairs, Ross. I'll tell you something, he does not look happy. But do you know what's really funny in all of this? Clementine is actually the name of a fruit,' and he hangs up.

I ask this bird who passes me by in an Aer Lingus uniform where you can buy, like, a ticket to France and she points me in the direction of the Air France desk. I'm straight up to the desk, roysh, and I pull out the old man's credit cord, which I liberated from his wallet this morning, and I ask when is the next flight to, like, France. She says there's one seat left on the three o'clock to Paris and I tell her I'll take it. Five minutes later, roysh, she hands me the ticket and I'm back down the escalators to Arrivals, where Clementine, or whatever the fock he's called, is sitting there with a big face on him.

He sees me and his face lights up. I'm looking over my shoulder for the goys, but the place is, like, jammers and I can't see them anywhere. I don't give a fock as long as they get what I'm going to do on camera. He goes, 'Ross, there is no problem, I hope,' and I'm there, 'Only the fact that you're a focking bloke.' He goes, '*Je ne comp* ... I do not understand. You tell me you like to stroke my legs and you say you like to eat my face.' I'm there, 'I SO didn't say that,' and he goes, 'I bring some pornographic film as a gift for you, but the man at the, how you say, custom, he take them from me and he say I am lucky this time to be let go with just a warning.' I'm there, 'Can you get this into your thick skull, *ní mé* interested,' but it's in one ear and out the other. He goes, 'You say you like to do things with my sisters and my ... my family and I think perhaps this boy is a little, eh, *malade* – how to say – sick, yes? But I cannot get you out of my head. I like to watch the men doing it as well,' and I just lose it. I'm there, 'I never wrote any of that shit. It was a SO-CALLED mate of mine, basically ripping the piss. He set me up. You were SUPPOSED to be a bird.' He reaches into his bag, roysh, and – FOCKING! HELL! – he pulls out this big mass of, like, wires, roysh, with little pads on the end of them, obviously for blokes who are into, like, frying each other's nuts, and he goes, 'We have some amusement, yes?' and the whole focking airport is staring at us at this stage. He goes, '*Bzzz, bzzz,*' basically shaking the focking things in my face and making a buzzing sound, and I just throw the ticket at him and he bends down, picks it up and looks at it. He goes, 'This is ... I do not understand,' and I'm like, 'Understand this, then, you focking gimp. Check-in opened ten minutes ago,' and as I'm walking away, roysh, I look over my shoulder and I go, '*Bon voyage*,' which is basically French, roysh, for have a good trip, *adios* and Goodnight, Vienna.

XXX

I very nearly didn't go to Simon's twenty-first, roysh, but Christian basically talked me into it.

Emer says she SO has to change her mobile, roysh, because it's, like, SO last year and Sadbh reminds her that her old man only bought it for her, like, two months ago and Emer goes, 'Yeah but it only stores, like, forty numbers,' and Sadbh goes, 'Sorry, Miss Popularity,' and it reminds me that I must check my messages. But not yet. I'm actually thinking of trying to bail into Emer, this bird who's, like, sixth year Loreto on the Green and SO like Alicia Silverstone they might as well be, like, sisters. She's looking around the room now and she takes a sip of her vodka, soda and lime, sort of, like, screws up her face and goes, 'Why did Simon have to have it in the tennis club of all places?' Sadbh shakes her head and goes, 'OH! MY! GOD! I know. I do *not* need a reminder of how much I've let my game go since I storted going out with Alex.'

Fionn is over talking to Oisinn and JP. He waves over to me and I wave back, roysh, cracking on that everything's alroysh between us. He can wait. I've got a long memory. Actually, I don't. What I'm saying is, I'll bide my time. Even when all those orseholes I've never even clapped eyes on before come over and stort singing, 'Oh my darling Clementine' under their breath, I just go, 'Congratulations, you're the first one to think of that,' basically not rising to the bait.

Emer is going, 'It's not that, Sadbh. It's just that if it was in, like, a pub, you wouldn't have so many kiddy-nippers. I mean, Fiona Manning's little sister is here and she's, like, drinking? HELLO? Fake ID or what?' Emer mentions then that Fiona Manning got – OH! MY! GOD! – SO drunk and ended up making SUCH a fool of herself in the rugby club on Friday night and she ended up being with Jonathan Flood, who's, like, best friends with Adam Brannigan, who she was going out with for two years.

Anyway, engrossed as I am in all this, roysh, the next thing – I cannot believe my eyes here – Sorcha walks in. I'm like, 'What the FOCK is she doing here?' pretending to be pissed off but, like, secretly delighted. Simon hears me, roysh, and he puts his hand on my shoulder and goes, 'Chill the kacks, Ross. I know you two are finished but Sorcha's still a friend of ours,' and I'm there, 'Hey, I'm cool about it.' So she comes over, roysh, and she just, like, hugs Simon and air-kisses him and goes, 'Hi, happy birthday, are you having a good time?' and then she turns around to Christian and she gives him this big, long hug and tells him that she has SO missed him. She totally ignores me and of course I'm left standing there like a Toblerone, as in out on my own. So she heads over to Sophie and Emma who're over at the bor and I am SO pissed off I follow her, and she's in the middle of telling Sophie about the new black pencil skirt she got from, like, Karen Millen when I grab her by the hand and I go, 'I need a word,' and I drag her off to the side and she's going, 'Ross, what the fock is your problem?' Of course I'm there, 'What is YOUR problem?' and she's like, 'I don't have a problem,' being nice as pie now and she goes, 'How are you?' Of course this totally throws me and I'm there, 'I'm fine but ...' and she goes, 'Sorry about the match. Are you okay about it?' and I'm there, 'It was a bit of a bummer, but I'll survive,' wondering if she read Gerry Thornley's report that said I bottled it. I have to say, roysh, she looks drop-dead gorgeous tonight in this, like, blue satin dress. I go, 'How *are* you, if you know what I mean?' and I look down at her stomach and notice that she still hasn't storted showing yet. She goes, 'Fine. I got a pair of Marco Moreo shoes today for ...' and I decide not to beat around the bush any longer. I put my orm around her waist, roysh, and I go, 'Sorcha, what made losing the Schools final even worse was that I didn't have anyone to, like, talk to about it. That's when I realised how much I missed you.'

But she just, like, peels my hand off her and throws it back to me and she goes, 'Nice try. It might have worked once but I am SO over you now.' I'm there, 'Come on, Sorcha. We've got so much to look forward to. We can have an amazing summer together. And then ...' but she goes, '*Hello?* I'm going away for the summer,' and of course I'm just there, 'WHERE?' realising after I've said it that I'm actually shouting now. She goes, 'The States,' and I'm like, 'THE STATES?' and she goes, 'Calm down, Ross. I told you ages ago I was going to Myrtle Beach to work in my uncle's country club,' and I'm like, 'But what about ... I just presumed the baby would have changed all of that.' She looks at me like I'm off my bin, roysh, and she goes, 'Baby?' I'm there, 'Yeah. *Our* baby,' and she just, like, laughs at me and goes, 'HELLO? I'm not REALLY pregnant, Ross. I just told you that to fock with your head,' and then she just, like, walks off, roysh, leaving me standing there for ages, in total shock.

I walk out into the air and I bump into this bird who I've never met before in my life and she's totally hammered and she says her name is Grainne and she's, like, best friends with Carrie, or *was* best friends with her until Carrie threw herself at me, and the only reason was because she wanted to be with me, blah blah blah. I stort wearing the face off her, roysh, but she's ossified and her breath tastes of vom, so I end up just leaving her propped against the wall and she shouts after me, 'Carrie Fitzpatrick is SUCH a slapper, Ross. You know what we call her? Carrie Fitz Anything.'

I don't even look back, I just keep walking. I walk for an hour. Maybe two. I just, like, lose track of time. It storts raining, roysh, and I hail a Jo and when the driver asks me where I want to go I tell him Dalkey. I haven't seen Aoife since she got out of, like, hospital. I look at my watch, roysh, and it's half-ten and I wonder if her old pair are still up and if they'll let me see her. I ring the bell and her old man comes to the door. My old man plays golf with him the odd time. He goes, 'Ross. It's half-past ten at night ...' and I'm there, 'I just wondered how Aoife was,' and I can tell from the way he's looking at me that he's trying to work out how hammered I am. Then all of a sudden he opens the door wide and tells me I can go up and see her, but for five minutes only. As I'm heading up the stairs, he goes, 'And see can you get her to eat something.'

She's lying on the bed, outside the covers, and she doesn't look at me when I come in and sit down on the hord chair next to her bed. The walls are covered in pictures of Brad Pitt and – weird one – Will Carling. She carries on watching 'Friends', staring at the television without looking like she's actually watching it. Fionn said that a couple of weeks ago her old pair came home from the theatre to find her going through the family album with a scissors, cutting herself out of all the pictures. That's when they knew they had to get her in somewhere. There's a plate of, like, scrambled eggs on a tray on a chair on the other side of the bed. Looks like they're cold. I think of saying something about eating, but who the fock am I? We sit there for about ten minutes without saying anything, roysh, and eventually I turn around and I'm like, 'How long do you have to keep seeing the counsellor?' and she doesn't answer, she just goes, 'Have you got a cigarette?' and I'm there, 'I don't smoke, Aoife. You know that.'

Eventually, I give up trying to get a conversation going and I just sit there staring at the television with her and it's only then that I realise, roysh, how hammered I actually am. I can feel my cheeks all wet, roysh, and I realise that I'm *actually* crying again, like a focking benny or something. I'm like, 'Why are we so focked up, Aoife?' and she goes, 'Do you think Courtney Cox's hair would suit me?' and I can't take any more, so I just, like, get up and as I'm on the way out the door I hear her say, 'Bring cigarettes next time.'

CHAPTER SEVEN
'Poor attendance'

The Leaving Cert? Went pretty well, I thought. We're talking,

ENGLISH-HIGHER LEVEL-PAPER 1

I spent the entire time texting Sorcha, asking her what the fock I did to deserve what she did to me, but she didn't answer. Twice the – whatever you call her – the invigilator sussed me, but before she could get down to me, roysh, I slipped the mobile up my sleeve and when she went, 'Did I see you sending an SMS to someone?' I go, 'I don't even *own* a mobile,' and there's fock-all she can do about it. And I think she looks at my paper and sees that I haven't written a single word and there's, like, half an hour left of the exam, so she knows I couldn't be cheating.

ENGLISH-HIGHER LEVEL-PAPER II

This goes a hell of a lot better than Paper 1. I write my exam number on it and then I copy down the first question. It's like,

I. DRAMA

A. KING LEAR (Shakespeare)

(i) 'In King Lear, Shakespeare presents us with a world of

mental anguish expressed in physical terms.'

Discuss this statement, supporting your answer by quotation from or reference to the play.

<u>OR</u>

(ii) 'Gloucester's sons are far more interesting than the King's daughters.'

Discuss this view, supporting your answer by quotation from or reference to the play.

Then I spend the next two-and-a-half hours, roysh, writing out a list of all the birds I've been with in the past two years, with little stors beside the ones I threw a bone. Not all of them obviously, just the ones I can remember. The list takes up both sides of an A4 sheet and I sort of, like, debate over whether I should tear the page out or leave it in to give whoever's correcting it a thrill. In the end I leave it in and I write,

WHAT I DID IN FIFTH AND SIXTH YEAR:

across the top and JP says he was watching me throughout the exam and he can't believe how much I was writing. And then it was like,

IRISH-HIGHER LEVEL-PAPER I

Didn't even bother opening the question paper. Wrote *Tá*, which is, like, the Irish word for thank you, across every line on the first page of the booklet and it was like,

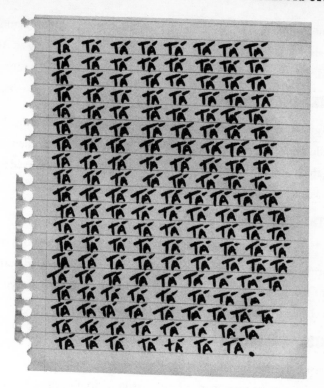

and then did the same on the second page. Halfway down the third page I storted to feel a bit Moby so I stopped and focked off home in time to see 'Home and Away'. And then it was like,

IRISH-HIGHER LEVEL-PAPER II

This was, like, really clever, roysh. I just wrote, 'I have decided not to sit this exam as a protest against the standard of refereeing in this year's Leinster Schools Senior Cup final,' and I try to show it to Christian, roysh, but he just ignores me because he's afraid of being caught. I stay however long it is you have to – half an hour, I think – and I'm back home in time to see the repeat of 'Home and Away' and it's getting to the stage that I can't even look at Isla Fischer without wanting an Allied Irish. The next day it was like,

MATHS-HIGHER LEVEL-PAPER I

Always wondered whether I was cut out for honours Maths, but I needn't have worried. Ruled every page in the booklet and then wrote out the lyrics to 'Sweet Child of Mine'. And after a well-deserved lunch it was like,

MATHS-HIGHER LEVEL-PAPER II

but I think the – what's the word Tony Ward used? – exertions of the morning had storted to take their toll. I was cream-crackered basically but I still found the energy from somewhere to write out the lyrics of 'Smells Like Teen Spirit'. So then it was on to,

HISTORY-HIGHER LEVEL

Got my second wind and used my time wisely, I felt. I just wrote out, like, really smort answers to all the questions. So if it was,

'During the period 1875–1886, Parnell came to dominate Irish politics and built up a strong and tightly disciplined party.' Explain how this came about. (80)

I was like,

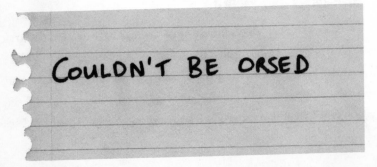

And then if it was like,

Discuss the developments in agriculture and industry in the period 1922–1939. (80)

I was there,

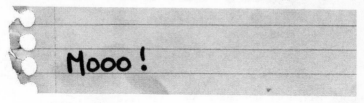

I was cracking my hole throughout the exam. Then, as far as I remember, it was,

FRENCH-HIGHER LEVEL

Bad memories. Didn't write a single word, unless you count the huge set of airbags I drew on the inside cover of the answers booklet. I mean, these correctors have a pretty shit time reading this stuff. Might as well put a smile on their faces. Left after half an hour, but I did much better in,

BIOLOGY-HIGHER LEVEL

when this bluebottle that had been annoying me all focking morning landed on my desk and – how many times has this ever happened to you? – I actually managed to swat the focking thing. SPLAT! Then I borrowed Fionn's ruler – that goy had better watch himself – and used it to smear the fly's guts and brains and whatever else was there all over the first page of my answers booklet. Then at the top of the page I wrote,

THE COMMON BLUEBOTTLE

And then underneath that I put,

DISSECTED THIS MORNING

and then I put, like, arrows pointing to different ports of what was left of him and things like, 'eye' and 'wing' and 'smeg'. Then I close the book over, seal it and hand it up.

Shannon, the character played by Isla Fischer, is having a difficult time of it lately, as do many of the birds who go through Pippa's foster home.

And then it's like,

ART-ORDINARY LEVEL

The hordest subject in the world to fail. If you took a shit in a mug, you could still find some focker who thought it was ort.

Anyway, roysh, the old man asks me how I got on and I go, 'I think I'm going to surprise a few people,' and he claps his hands together, roysh, and he goes, 'Trinity, here we come.' I swear to God, roysh, the sap thinks I'm some kind of misunderstood genius and of course I do nothing to, like, persuade him otherwise, but I *do* manage to persuade him to advance me the thousand sheets he promised me for passing the thing, which is a good job because I ended up failing miserably. JP's claim that you get an automatic pass just for, like, ruling your page and writing your exam number proved a bit wide of the mork. It was, like, *Ross O'Carroll-Kelly, nul points.* Twelve fewer than I kicked in the Schools Cup final, as Fionn pointed out to pretty much everyone.

XXX

To be honest, roysh, at that stage I didn't care. My head was, like, wrecked with everything that had been going on and the summer passed pretty much in a blur. So did the time up to Christmas. I saw little or nothing of the goys. After the Leaving we sort of, like, drifted aport. Happens. I did hear from Christian a lot. He went to Vancouver, where his aunt lives, just for the summer originally but he never came back, although he texted me pretty much every day, just to check I was alroysh and not thinking of doing anything stupid.

I heard that a scout from one of the big design houses – maybe Yves Saint Laurent – had seen Oisinn in action out at the airport and was involved in a catfight with Hugo Boss to sign him up as a rep. JP went to work in his old man's estate agency and was supposed to be doing, like, a morkeshing degree at night. Apparently he talks so much jargon now you need focking subtitles to understand him. Fionn went to UCD to do rocket science. He didn't really, although he probably had the points for it, because he got more than anyone else in the entire country. Had his picture in the papers and everything, and he ended up doing Psychology, which is, like, the mind and shit. He's still a nerd. It said in a notice in *The Irish Times*, roysh, that Simon's wife gave birth to their second child in August, which probably means he's not going back to repeat for a fourth time.

Sorcha went to the States for the summer and is now in, like, UCD doing Orts. She met my old pair in the Frascati Centre and she made sure to tell them she was going out with an amazing goy who's in her year and plays rugby for Blackrock, which makes him an automatic tool in my book. The last time I saw her she was on the 'Six One News' in, like, September or something? It was, like, some student protest or other, roysh, and she was going, 'Four years after the genocide, the Rwandan Government is perpetuating the cycle of violence. We must ensure that Virginie Mukankusi and Deogratias Bizimana did not die in vain. End the executions without trial now.'

She looked amazing.

Erika was rumoured to have married Pierce Brosnan, but it turned out to be total bullshit and she's doing Orts in UCD as well. Aoife got well again and she phoned me once to say she'd never forget the fact that I went to see her when she was ill and she told me I was a very decent person at hort, roysh, and that made me feel good, but then she went, 'Even *if* everyone thinks you're an orsehole,' and that made me feel crap again.

The old pair, of course, remained total dickheads. The council dropped plans for a halting site on our road, roysh, and the old dear became locked in a battle with Dearbhla, one of her friends from tennis, for the chairpersonship of the Foxrock Combined Residents Association, while the old man took most of the summer off to try to get his golf handicap down and became even more of a tool than he already was. Sian never rang again and nor did Alyson, Eloise, Joanna, Keeva, Zara, or Evy.

As for me, I spent most of the time on my own in my room, roysh, or that's how it seemed to me. I couldn't go out for a quiet drink. No matter what battle cruiser I hit, someone, somewhere would stort singing that focking song, 'Oh my darlin', oh my darlin', oh my daaarlin' Clementine ...' So I'd usually end up heading home early and the old pair would be like, 'Not like you to be in before ten o'clock, Ross,' and I'd just flick them the Vs, roysh, or sometimes just give them the finger and go up to my room and watch MTV and think of ways of getting back at Fionn, but I could never come up with anything to top Clementine. In the end I pretty much stopped going out altogether. The old pair were storting to get on my back about doing something with my life, when out of the blue I get a call from Fehily. I recognise his voice straight away. He's there, 'Hello, my child,' and it sends a shiver down my spine.

At first, roysh, I think it's about the damage I did to Crabtree's cor on Rag Day. Thought he might have got, like, I don't know, CCTV footage of me sticking the potato in his exhaust. I'm just about to tell him that he'll have to talk to Hennessy when all of a sudden he goes, 'I'd like you to come to the school, Ross. I have a proposal to put to you,' so I go to grab the keys for the Lexus, roysh, but Bog Breath has already taken it, so I end up having to go in the old dear's Micra, the famous spaz-mobile.

I arrive at the school, roysh, and the first thing I cop is JP's beamer – well, his old man's – outside and I'm there thinking, 'What's going down here?' So I go in, roysh, upstairs and head straight for Fehily's office. His secretary's outside – mad about me – and she goes, 'They're waiting for you,' basically flirting her orse off with me big-time and I'm there, 'Later,' and I go in. I have to say, roysh, I am SO not ready for what I find. The goys are all there. We're talking Oisinn (he's put on weight, impossible as that sounds), JP and Fionn. Oisinn turns around to Fehily and he goes, 'What's the Jackanory? You can tell us now,' and Fehily's there, 'One minute. I want Christian to hear this,' and he picks up the phone. He goes, 'He said he'd wait for the call,' and he dials this number – the dude's still in Vancouver – and he puts him on speakerphone.

Then he stands up and storts pacing the floor going, 'You five boys were part of something special. Something very, very special. You were the kernel, the core, the heart, the root, the essence of a team that brought this school to the brink of something historic and that is why I will believe, as long as there's breath in my body, that you were a gift from the Good Lord Himself.' No arguments there. He goes, 'Unfortunately, the Good Lord has proven something of a miser with regard to this year's gift. The Senior Cup team this year is – not to put too fine a point on it – bloody woegeous. The very words – I think you'll find if you check your scriptures – Jesus himself used to describe Nicodemus's line of patter as he tried to lead him into temptation in the wilderness. I trust you all read about the defeat to Pres Bray in a friendly before Christmas? Tried to stop the papers from publishing it, of course, but to no avail.'

I'm thinking, 'Get to the focking point,' when Fionn – the snake – goes, 'I have a lecture this afternoon, Father ...' and JP's like, 'Yeah, you called this mind-share. Give us the bottom line.' Fehily goes, 'I'm *getting* to the point. I want you boys – all five of you – to come back to the school, with a view to winning ... what is rightfully yours.' Of course all hell breaks loose then. Straight away, roysh, I'm like, 'Repeat the Leaving? Have you TOTALLY lost your mind?' and Fionn's there, 'You want me to drop out of college for the sake of a medal?' and through the speakerphone I can hear Christian going, 'Not for all the Tibanna gas in Cloud City.'

But JP, roysh, he's giving it, 'Just think *in* the box for a moment, goys. Sounds very much to me like there's a highly resourced, precisely targeted results drive going down here,' and Oisinn, the only one in the room who knows what the fock he's talking about, goes, 'I'd just like to say that, for me, not winning a Schools Cup medal is something that's going to haunt me for the rest of my life. Ross, I know you and Fionn have had your differences. But let's not forget that when you played rugby you made the sweetest music together.'

I'm there, 'I'm big enough to put the past behind me if Fionn is. But it's not just him. What about *him*?' and I point at Fehily. Of course *he* looks at me all innocently, cracking on he doesn't know what I'm talking about and I go, 'One day you're telling us we're the chosen ones. We lost one match and everything changed. I ended up having to actually sit the mocks. When I went to you to complain, you said you'd never seen me before in your life.' He goes, 'I was upset, Ross,' and I'm there, '*I* was upset. I missed the penalty that cost us the Cup and for ten months you've let me believe that everyone blamed me,' and he's there, 'I wasn't thinking straight.'

Christian goes, 'What's in it for us?' So much for *all the Tabanna gas in Cloud City*. Fehily goes, 'Apart from an opportunity to mesmerise the crowds again with your fancy footwork?' and Christian goes, 'Eh, yeah,' and JP's there, 'I think the dude wants you to run the numbers, Father. Personally, I think the idea's got core competency, but we all need a bottom line. Ballpark.' Fehily doesn't blink an eyelid, roysh. He goes, 'You'll each be paid five hundred pounds a week. There will be no requirement on you to sit your exams or even to attend classes. In your case, Ross, some of the teachers have asked that you don't. All that is required of you is that you train and play. No more than that.'

Oisinn says he's up for it. JP says we're talking ticks in boxes as far as he's concerned. Fionn takes me by total surprise by saying that he can defer the rest of first year and he tells Fehily to count him in. Then he looks at me, roysh, but I've still got issues here, not knowing whether I could ever, like, trust either Fionn or Fehily again. I'm about to say no, roysh, when all of a sudden Oisinn goes, 'If we do this thing, Father, it's important that you know that I've no interest in being, like, captain again. In fact I'd like to propose that this time Ross leads us,' and straight away, roysh, Fionn goes, 'Seconded,' and I swear to God, roysh, I actually thought I was going to burst out crying there and then. I actually feel like getting up and hugging Fionn – if he wasn't such a queer. And gay as it sounds, roysh, I can't even speak at that moment. Fehily goes, 'Well, Ross? It's down to you. This thing won't work without you, Ross,' and all of a sudden, roysh, I hear Christian's voice coming from practically the other side of the world and he's going, 'You say yes, Ross, and I'm on the next flight home. We're like Chewie and Han, me and you. I'm always by your side.' JP goes, 'Sounds like a strategic fit to me, Ross,' and of course what can I say then, roysh, except, 'Lock up your sisters. The Man is back.'

XXX

Grafton Street is, like, SO packed it's unbelievable, roysh, and I actually shouldn't have bothered my orse agreeing to meet Eimear, this bird I was, like, stringing along for a few weeks because I thought she looked like Calista Flockhart, which she actually doesn't. So much for the light in Annabel's. Anyway, roysh, I ended up accidentally answering the phone to her yesterday, roysh, and being basically too nice for my own good, I found myself agreeing to meet her for lunch in the Powerscourt Townhouse Centre. As it turns out, roysh, she's also meeting some bet-down mate of hers called Tara, who's doing, like, auctioneering somewhere in town and when she finds out I'm repeating in Castlerock she storts that crap of name-dropping people and when it turns out I know them, roysh, she reacts like we're living in, I don't know, China, or some country where there's shitloads of people. She's there, 'OH!

MY! GOD! I can't believe you know Sean Tyner,' and total idiot that I am, roysh, I'm playing along with it, going, 'He's playing in the second row for us this year,' and she's going, 'Is he still going out with Rachel Butler?' and in the end I couldn't be orsed answering her.

I tell the birds I need to drain the lizard and I end up just heading off, hoping Eimear takes some kind of hint from this. I check my phone. I have one new message and it's from Beibhin, who's, like, sixth year Whores on the Shore and who I ended up wearing the face off last week, at Glenageary Dorsh station, believe it or not. Long story, but she was on her way home from violin practice with a couple of her mates, roysh, and I was on my way home from training, and they're all, like, giggling and giving it, 'Are you Ross O'Carroll-Kelly?' and of course one thing leads to another and I end up being with her, although I don't remember giving her my number, roysh, so she must have got it by stalker means. Anyway, in her message, roysh, she says exactly the same thing she said in the one she left yesterday, which is that I mustn't have gotten her last message and she presumes there must be something wrong with my phone or maybe *her* phone and could I ring her later but not after eight because she's got practice again tonight, or if I want to I could meet her outside Pearse Street Dorsh station afterwards, she'll be finished at, like, seven and she'll give me until, like, half-seven to show up and if I didn't she'd presume I wasn't going to, but she hopes I get this message. And I'm thinking, You're the one who's not getting the message, girl.

So I'm heading down Grafton Street, roysh, and who do I bump into only, like, Sorcha and it's actually the first time I've seen her in person since ... well, since all that shit, and I can tell she's not sure what kind of a greeting she's going to get from me, but what can I do, roysh, only give her a huge hug and tell her she looks amazing, which she does. I go, 'Did you have a good time in the States?' and she's there, 'OH! MY! GOD! Martha's Vineyard is, like, SO amazing. If you *ever* get a chance, *Oh my God,* SO go. I mean, we worked, like, really hord, but we went out loads. The social life was, like, really hectic.' I know this is all for my benefit. She goes, 'I came back without a penny to my name, of course. *Oh my God!* I turned into SUCH a pisshead. We nearly got arrested one night. Me, Aoife, Sophie and Claire. You know Claire, my friend from Bray?' I do actually. She was a focking howiya until she met Sorcha through Amnesty or Vegetarians Are Us or one of that shower and suddenly she talks like she's next in line to the focking throne.

I ask whether she wants to go for, like, lunch, seeing as I left the last one I bought on the table in the Powerscourt Centre, and she says she's meeting her old dear outside Pamela Scott's at two and she has, like, an hour to kill. So we hit Fitzer's Café, roysh, and I end up ordering a beef and vegetable stirfry teriyaki and a Coke and Sorcha has a brie and camembert baguette which she doesn't touch, spicy wedges which she picks at and a Diet Coke. She goes, 'I heard you're repeating?' and I'm there, 'Bit of a bummer, but it's a chance to try and put right what happened last year.'

She goes, 'Your mum said you were looking at LBS,' which is a college, roysh, I say *college,* but all the goys say it stands for Loaded But Stupid instead of Leeson Business School. It's, like, six grand a term or something, though at the end you get a degree in morkeshing from the University of, I don't know, Bulgaria or something. I tell Sorcha that that plan fell by the wayside when I heard they had this, like, push on, roysh, to try to get State recognition for it as a legitimate third-level university. And the rumour was that the lecturers wouldn't be giving out the summer exam papers in November, as was the tradition, because they were sick of being treated as a joke by the Department of Education. So suddenly they're not giving out the papers until the end of, like, January, which gave people only, like, five months to go to the library and learn someone else's essay from the previous year off by hort. Sorcha says that sounds SO unfair, but I can tell from the way she says it that she's actually ripping the piss. Anyway, in the meantime the place went bankrupt, so it doesn't matter a fock.

We hordly say anything while we – sorry, I – eat and I realise that, whatever happened last year, I'm actually not over Sorcha yet. I have to prove to myself as well that I could basically still have her if I wanted her, so I turn on the old chorm and stort giving it, 'I've really missed you. Okay, I wasn't exactly an angel while you were away in the States, if you know what I mean, but I did think about you a lot while you were away.'

She thinks about this, roysh, as she takes off her scrunchy, slips it onto her wrist, shakes her head, pulls her hair back into a low ponytail, replaces the scrunchy and pulls four or five strands of hair loose. Then she pushes her food away and takes out her Marlboro Lights and goes, 'Are you seeing anyone?' and the, I don't know, directness of the question sort of, like, throws me. I go, 'Kind of,' and she shakes her head as she plucks a cigarette from the box and goes, 'That was always your problem. You either are or you aren't, Ross,' and I'm there, 'Well, I was sort of seeing this bird – Eimear. Met her in Annabel's,' and I think of her sitting in the Powerscourt Centre, focking steaming when she realises that I've left her with, like, the bill. Sorcha's like, 'Eimear who? As in, what's her second name?' and I'm there, 'You wouldn't know her,' and she goes, 'I bet I do,' and I'm like, 'Eimear O'Neill,' and Sorcha goes, 'Small, thin, straight blond hair? Went to Loreto Foxrock?' and I'm there, 'How do you know her?' and she goes, 'She was on the Irish debating team. She was actually SUCH a good debater.' Like I *give* a shit?

She goes, 'So, you're only, like, seeing her?' and of course I'm there, 'Well, I've been kind of going out with her really,' trying to make her jealous. I'm going, 'I don't know. I'm still searching for *the one*,' and she goes, 'Well, I've found *the one*. I met someone and he's, like, the perfect goy,' and like the fool that I am, roysh, I actually think she's talking about me. I go, 'Oh yeah?' and I'm about to reach over, roysh, to touch her hand when all of a sudden she goes, 'Brandon.' I'm there, 'Who?' and she goes, 'His name's Brandon. Brandon Oakes,' and quick as a flash I've gone, 'Brandon Oakes sounds like a focking retirement home.' She finally lights up her cigarette and she goes, 'Well, he's actually the nicest goy I've ever gone out with. Met him in the States. He has SUCH an amazing body. He plays, like, American football,' and I'm there, 'Hold on, hold on. Can we just rewind a bit? You're telling me that you met this goy in America last summer, we're talking six months ago. And now he's over there and you're over here and you're still, like, going out with the loser?' which I know is out of order the second I've said it. She stubs out her cigarette – she's only had, like, one drag off it – and she goes, '*You're* the loser, Ross,' and she looks at her watch, which is the pink Baby-G I bought her for her birthday last year and she goes, 'My mum is going to go TOTALLY ballistic,' and she gets up and goes, roysh, and it's only when she's gone that I realise that this time it's me who's been left sitting with the bill.

XXX

The old man calls me when I'm passing by his study, roysh, and when I stick my head around the door he looks all pleased with himself. He says he's just been on to *The Irish Times*, roysh, and he's going to be sponsoring their schools rugby coverage and in future they're going to give it, like, two pages. He goes, 'It'll be a bit like their Bulmers Total Golf pages except it'll be called Total Schools Rugby Totally, or some such. We haven't worked out the finer points yet, but isn't it exciting? Hennessy and I are playing golf with Malachy Logan this very afternoon.'

I'm just there, 'Yippee-doo.'

XXX

Fionn's telling us all the difference between the Id and the Ego – fascinating, I don't think – and I go up to get the beers in and while I'm up there, roysh, who sidles up to me only Fionn himself, going, 'No hord feelings,' and I shrug, but I refuse to shake the goy's hand. He goes, 'Ross?' and it all comes out, roysh, I'm there, 'You ruined my focking life,' and he goes, 'You ruined mine. My old pair *still* think I'm a knobber because of you. I could have Linda Evangelista, Claudia Schiffer and Liz Hurley up in my room and they'd be convinced we're just exchanging colouring tips.' I'm there, 'How many copies of that focking video are doing the rounds?' and he goes, 'I only made twelve. I can't take responsibility for any unauthorised copies that are in circulation,' and I'm there, 'Half of focking Dublin has seen it. Him pulling out those electrodes that he wanted to use on my town halls. Total focking strangers have been laughing at me in the street.'

The borman puts the bevvies down on the bor. Fionn goes, 'Why don't we just agree that we both suffered? Look, Ross, we're never going to be bosom buddies, we know that. But when we play rugby together ...' and he sort of, like, lets it hang in the air? I just go, 'Pure magic,' and he repeats what I say, he's like, 'Pure magic.' He goes, 'It's

January. We've got, what, three months together? Three months to work for something that we both want so much. After that we need never look at each other ever again. But the question is, Ross, are you big enough to put our differences aside to win that Cup,' and I think about it for a few seconds, roysh, even though I don't really need to. I just go, 'Let's play rugby,' and we shake on it and then we're back over to the goys with the pints.

JP goes, 'You goys look like you're dovetailing again,' and I'm there, 'We just want to play the beautiful game,' and JP's like, 'Sounds like a win-win situation to me. Oisinn here's just been telling us about his year. Fionn, I know you were doing alroysh scenario-wise in UCD and the Blankers-Koen is wall-to-wall in my game, but I don't know how you're still alive, Oisinn.'

This is all by way of introduction for Oisinn's act. He goes, 'I don't either, Fionn. I ended up having two mobile phones. I'd be selling some bird *Ultraviolet,* or *Escape for Women,* or *Angel.* Bit of seductive chitchat about the smell, sensuous being a key word, couple of squirts and the next thing I knew they were practically begging me for my number. The Motorola was for birds over thirty and the Nokia number was for birds under thirty. You know how it is, some nights you fancy a bit of old and some you want them young. The two were ringing constantly. By Christmas I had the two of them switched off. I'd shagged myself out.'

I tell the goy he's still a legend and Christian says he'll second that and before we know it I'm, like, raising my glass and suggesting a toast to the best team in the land. And whatever did or didn't happen at Dublin Airport is, like, all forgotten now and all I can think about, roysh, is how great it is just, like, catching up with each other again. We're like, 'THE BEST TEAM IN THE LAND ...' and I know that before the night is out, we're going to be looking for a twenty-four-hour garage that sells mince pies.

XXX

Ultra-resistant. Fantasy ribbed. Studded. Lubricated. Luminous. Extra sensitive for her pleasure. Orange. Strawberry. Fruit of the focking forest. I know I've been out of the game for the guts of a year, roysh, but I can't believe how many choices there are nowadays. I drop three pound coins into the slot, roysh, and choose a three-pack of extra-sensitive, gossamer, ribbed ticklers, which sound up to the job. On the way out the door, roysh, I check myself out in the mirror and I have to say I'm looking good tonight and the black eye actually suits me. Then I go back out to Angel, this bird from Clonskeagh who's in, like, first year Law in Portobello.

I ask her if she wants another drink and she says OH! MY! GOD! if she drinks any more there's no way she'll be able to get up for water aerobics in the morning and I go, 'There's only one kind of aerobics you're going to be doing in the morning,' and of course I'm kicking myself for coming across so, I don't, sleazy, roysh, but from the smile on her face, she doesn't seem to mind. Her best friend, Ana with one n, wouldn't mind a shot at the title as well. In fact it was her who tried to get in there first, giving it all, 'Congrats. You had SUCH a good game today.'

We basically hammered CBC Monkstown into the ground in the first round, me, Christian and JP all getting two tries – a brace apiece, as One F in *The Stor* called it – so me and the goys are back in Kiely's living off the glory, roysh, and it's like we've never been away. There must be, like, a hundred, maybe a hundred and fifty birds here and they all want a piece of the focking Dream Team. Like I said, roysh, I've been out of the game a long time and I very nearly make the mistake of taking the first thing that comes along. Ana with one n wants me and I'm actually entertaining serious thoughts of nipping it when I cop Angel, who's like a young Cameron Diaz, and straight away I know that in two hours' time I'm going to be conkers deep in this one.

Ana with one n knows it as well, roysh, because she's resorted basically to being a bitch to Angel and within twenty seconds of me coming back from the can with the jimmie hats she's going, 'I cannot BELIEVE you ate two of those Weight Watchers dinners. That's like, OH! MY! GOD!' and Angel looks at me, roysh, to get my reaction, and of course I couldn't give two focks what she had for dinner, even though I'm going to be tasting it myself soon enough. Angel goes, 'I only ate half of the salmon mornay. It was SO disgusting,' and Ana with one n is there, '*Hello?* That's why I told you to have the chicken in peppercorn sauce in the first place. Instead you had to have, like, two,' and Angel goes, '*What*ever,' and Ana with one n takes her lip balm out of her miniature backpack, gives her a filthy, then focks off to the jacks and when she's gone, roysh, Angel goes, 'I wouldn't mind, but they're MY buckled-back flared jeans she's wearing. You think SHE can afford to shop in Jigsaw? I don't THINK so. Her shoes are from Nine West, but they're the only decent pair she has.'

When she shuts the fock up, I manage to persuade her out onto the dancefloor, roysh, and it's 'Praise You' by Fat Boy Slim and I am giving it absolutely loads. I'm dancing with Angel, roysh, but I'm also flirting my orse off with this bird who Fionn knows from UCD and her name's, like, Rebecca and she's, like, first year Social Science and so like Liz Hurley that you could *actually* be looking at her. So, more to make Angel jealous than anything else, I cruise over beside her and I give it, 'You're a pretty amazing dancer, has to be said,' and she just, like, wiggles her little finger at me, which presumably means she's heard I have, like, a small penis, which I don't.

So then it's back to Angel of course and she obviously hasn't copped what just happened because she goes, 'I'd say that becomes SUCH a pain,' and I'm there, 'What?' and she's like, 'Girls, like, bothering you all the time. Propositioning you and stuff,' and I've gone, 'I'm not exactly fighting *you* off, am I?' and I throw the lips on her. Twenty minutes of deep throat exploration and she's, like, fishing in her bag for her cloakroom ticket and before we know it we're back at her gaff in Clonskeagh, and get this, roysh, she doesn't live with her old pair. They actually *bought* her this gaff so she could study in peace and quiet for the Leaving. We're talking big bucks here.

Much as it pains me to say it, it's ten months since I had my Nat King Cole, roysh, so when she asks me if I want a cup of tea, I don't even answer, I'm just, like, bailing into her, ripping the clothes off her and she's going, 'Be careful, Ross. These combats are Hobo,' but twenty seconds later, roysh, we're both in the raw, on the floor of her sitting-room and she's gagging for me and we're talking seriously gagging here. Five minutes of foreplay – she better not tell anyone or they'll all want that – and I'm ready to do the bould thing but she goes, 'Do you have any protection?' and of course I've got the old Johnny B Goodes in my sky rocket.

So I reach for my chinos, roysh, and I stick my hand in the back pocket and I pull out the little box. And of course I'm there in the dork, roysh, trying to find the little flap in the cellophane that lets you get into the box, but it takes me, like, five minutes and of course I'm worried all this time that the old snake chorming act's gonna fall flat. As it happened, roysh, he held up his end for once. But that's when it all went basically pear-shaped. When I got the cellophane off the packet and tore off the top of the box, what fell out weren't johnnies at all, but – I CAN-NOT FOCKING BELIEVE THIS – a comb and a length of, like, dental floss and a tiny toothbrush and the smallest tube of toothpaste you've ever seen. And of course straight away the performance is over as far as the old pant python is concerned. She looks at all the stuff, roysh, and she storts laughing, not normal laughter, roysh, but evil, Wicked Witch of the West laughter. And I haven't been so humiliated since, well, since Fionn made me look like George Michael trying to pick up some homo at the airport, which is less than a year ago, so I suppose it's not so long. I end up just making my excuses and getting the fock out of there as quick as I can.

XXX

I'm just in from practicing my kicking when Erika rings, and I'm there thinking, to what do I owe this pleasure? But of course I know. Now that I'm on the S again I'm just about worthy of scoring as far as she's concerned and she is SO going to show Sorcha that she could have me if she wanted. She goes, 'I drove past you about half an hour ago. You're not actually looking all that bad. I don't think it's going to be as painful as I thought,' and I go, 'What isn't?' and she's like, '*Puh-lease*. I don't find that Little Boy Lost act the least bit endearing. I'm going to *be* with you, Ross. Not yet. It's still a total no-no for someone like *me* to be with someone like *you*. Especially since I'm in UCD and you're still in school. But if you win this rugby ... thing that you're playing in, you move up a place on the social acceptability scale. I've never been a rugby groupie but I've known Sorcha long enough to know how it works,' and I play it Kool and the Gang, roysh, I really do.

I'm there, 'I'm actually seeing someone at the moment,' which is to-tal bullshit but it doesn't matter, roysh, because she just, like, ignores it totally. She goes, 'I've looked up the fixtures and it seems you're playing Pres Bray tomorrow in Greystones. If you beat them, it's not a terribly big deal. I think I'm going to leave it at least until you reach the final before I'm with you.' I'm like, 'Do I have a say in all this?' and I'm picturing her right now – a total and utter goddess – and I know I don't.

She goes, 'You're going to get the night of passion you've always dreamt of and then we'll see how high and mighty your little girlfriend is,' and I'm about to tell her that Sorcha's not my girlfriend when all of a sudden she goes, 'That's the vet at the door. Orchid's got a twisted testicle,' and when she hangs up, I'm wondering whether she had anything to do with it herself.

XXX

The thing I forgot to mention, roysh, is that Fehily himself is coaching us this year. Sooty got sacked from the school after we lost the final last year, roysh, though not *because* we lost the final. He basically did an interview with the school magazine in which he said that people who live in council houses are paying for the sins of a previous life. Fehily goes, 'Merit as there was in his point, once the Dublin 4 media got their hands on the story, he had no choice but to go.'

I actually don't think Fehily's much of a coach, roysh, but it's like he said, once me and the other goys from last year are firing on all cylinders, the team basically runs itself. As captain, he's also given me a pretty big role in deciding, like, tactics and team selection. To be honest, roysh, he came to me the day before we lashed CBC Monkstown out of it, hands me a blank sheet of paper and asks me what team I'd pick if it were down to me.

Now I'm not the brightest, roysh, but I knew what was going down here. He was basically asking me to pick the team and the first thought that, like, occurred to me was that there were one or two old scores I could settle at the stroke of a pen. I seriously considered dropping Fionn, roysh, but I know the goy's too good a rugby player to leave out, though I'd never admit that to his face. I *do* drop Laurence Leahy, our inside centre who Wardy was bulling up in that morning's *Indo*. Let's see who's a Genuine Star In The Making now. I also end up drop-kicking this tool who plays in our second row, we're talking Rory Smyth. The main, I don't know, stumbling block with him is that he fancies himself as a bit of a ladies' man and had the balls to tell me a couple of weeks ago that New Castlerock – as in the bunch of losers who lost a friendly in Bray before Christmas – would out-score Old Castlerock – as in me and the goys – in the old scenario stakes. The reason he was easy to drop is that he's crap.

Of course he comes to me the morning we played Monkstown, roysh, just after Fehily broke the bad news to him, and he tells me that he's very disappointed not to have even made the bench, and I tell him he needs to keep his head down, lay off the scoops, ease off on the old nights out and keep plugging away. I tell him he's close, so close he can smell it, knowing full well in my mind that as long as I'm picking the team the only chance he has of playing for the school is if he joins the basketball team, which is basically for knobs. He goes, 'Thanks for the advice,' and he focks off, the tool.

The morning of the return game against Pres Bray – which has become a bit of a grudge match – he comes to me again and he goes, 'I want to play today, Ross. When their coach said what he said in the *Bray People*, about Castlerock being a fading power in the Schools Cup competition, I took it personally, because I was one of the players who under-performed that day. You've got to tell Fehily, Ross. I am SO up for this match,' and then Laurence Leahy arrives over and storts throwing in his two-pence worth, giving it, 'We should at least be offered a chance to put things roysh.' I don't know how I don't just, like, crack up laughing in their faces, roysh. Instead, I give them this, like, solemn look and I go, 'This is no time to be taking risks on goys who never delivered in the past. It's a day for men, not boys.' The poor fockers have been breaking their balls in training. I'm there, 'Keep up the hord work, goys, and you never know, maybe you'll make the bench for the quarter-final,' and they go off *actually* looking grateful to me.

Fehily gives us this, like, no-nonsense speech, all about Bray being famous for nothing more than slot machines and inbreeding. 'But last year – owing to the local Presentation College's, it shames me to say it, *victory* over this proud institute of education and social advancement – Bray emerged like an ugly, weeping sore on the face of schools rugby. And this, my children, is the cure.'

He holds up this huge plastic tub, roysh, which it turns out is full of, like, white powder. He goes, 'Fifty milligrams stirred into a glass of water five times a day,' and, almost thinking out loud, roysh, I go, 'Is it creatine or something?' and he's there, 'Creatine is last year's buzz. You don't NEED to know what this is. Just that it works,' and he sends Magahy – the total wanker who coached us as juniors – around the dressing-room, giving us each a tub of the stuff. We all stort, like, pouring it into our water bottles and knocking it back.

Fehily goes, 'What happened before Christmas should shame you all. Yes, there have been some changes since then, some old friends have come back to help us in our hour of need. But even my old friend Matt Talbot never knew the kind of shame that you heaped onto this school by losing to that shower before Christmas. The time for vengeance is at hand.'

He goes, 'First will come honor and then freedom, and from both of these happiness, prosperity, life: in a word, that state of things will return which we Germans perhaps dimly saw before the War, when individuals can once more live with joy in their hearts because life has a meaning and a purpose, because the close of life is then not in itself the end, since there will be an endless chain of generations to follow: man will know that what we create will not sink into Orcus but will pass to his children and to his children's children.'

This is in the dressing-room, roysh, and when he's finished there's no, like, cheering or anything. I just go, 'Come on, goys. Let's go to work,' and we go out there and basically kick ass.

They actually fancy themselves a bit, roysh, obviously got, like, notions about themselves. Their hooker, roysh, William something or other's his name, he comes up to me and he goes, 'Bit sad, isn't it? You lot, I mean, having to leave college to come back and bail out your school,' and without even thinking, roysh, I go, 'This time it's for real,' and he ends up having a mare of a game and couldn't hit a cow's orse with a banjo. We're, like, lording it over them in the lineout and knocking seven shades of shit out of them in the scrum. They hold out for, like, fifteen minutes and then suddenly it's, like, raining tries. Christian scores two absolute crackers. Fionn got one and the Stud Muffin here goes and scores three. After the third, roysh, I shove the ball up my shirt and walk up to this photographer who I think takes the pictures for *The Irish Times* and I stand in front of him and, like, point at myself as if to say, 'Who's the man?'

We're actually ripping the piss at the end, just basically enjoying ourselves while we're waiting for the final whistle, and when it goes, roysh,

I head straight for the press box, roysh, at the side of the field and I go, 'Anyone here from the *Bray People*?' and all the press, roysh, they look up from what they're doing, sort of in, like, shock. One F is obviously on the phone to *The Stor* because he's going, 'Pres Bray ... will remember ... this one ... as fondly ... as a tour of duty ... in 'Nam, full point,' and when he hears what I say he points at the dude behind him, who's like, 'Yes, I'm covering the game for the ...' and I just butt in, roysh, and I go, 'Some fading power, huh?' It must be that powder Fehily gave us that's making me so angry. I'm going, 'You know, by St Patrick's Day you're going to be looking at this team and all we've achieved and you're going to say it was a pleasure to see your team lose to us.'

✕✕✕

I get up, roysh, and the old man's in the kitchen, looking like somebody's pissed on his Corn Flakes. He goes, 'I take it from the equanimity of your mood that you haven't seen it yet?' and I'm there, 'What are you shitting on about now?' He hands me a copy of the paper, roysh, and they've printed the photograph of me with the ball up my shirt and underneath it says, 'Ross O'Carroll-*Kenny* salutes the crowd after scoring his third try in Castlerock's victory over Pres Bray in Greystones yesterday,' and Knob Head picks up the phone and before I can tell him to cop himself on he's giving out yords to some dude on the end of the phone and in the end the goy promises to print a correction. The old man's like, 'I want it on the front page, too. And you can bloody well print the photograph again as well. Otherwise you'll be hearing from my solicitor.'

He slams down the phone and tells me not to worry because Wardy – a *real* journalist – managed to get my name roysh. He's there, 'Wait until you read what he's written about your performance. A cracking prospect. *His* words, Kicker. Not mine.' And as he leafs through the paper to try to find the page, he suddenly stops and he goes, 'A girl called for you this morning. About nine o'clock. Hope you don't mind, I told her you were in bed, recovering from battle. Beibhin she said her name was. Nice girl. Said she'd call you later on your mobile.'

XXX

I'm on the Stillorgan dualler, roysh, and I hit a red light at Cornelscourt, so I check my messages. Some bird called Jennie with an ie rang and said I gave her my number in the rugby club on Sunday night and she hoped I remembered because we were both SO drunk, but she hoped I didn't mind her ringing and she just wondered whether I was, like, doing anything later in the week. Beibhin rang to say that – get this – she read my horoscope in the paper this morning and OH! MY! GOD! she couldn't BELIEVE what it said. Then she storts, like, reading it into the phone, going, '*Hobbies and pastimes bring enjoyment and success.* That's obviously the match against Pres Bray. *But be more prepared to show your softer side. You are about to woo and win the heart of someone close. Prepare yourself for sweet nothings and sentimentalities.* This is the amazing bit. *Strong attractions towards Cancerians*,' and then she lets out this, like, squeal and she goes, 'My birthday's on, like, June twenty-eighth. OH! MY! GOD!' and I'm wondering how focking gone in the head she is that she can believe what Fergus Gibson says and ignore the fact that I've never returned one of her calls since I nipped her that day, the sad bitch.

There's also a message from Angel, who doesn't seem to have been put off by the whole Travel Hygiene Kit incident and wants me to phone her.

The last message is from Sorcha, who says she's SO sorry she hasn't been in touch, roysh, because she's been rushed off her feet with this whole Khemais Ksila situation, which, at a guess, involves some black dude in some shithole of a country who's in the clink for acting the dick and is about to get snotted.

I've a wood on me like a focking broom handle. It must be this stuff we're taking. I lie on my bed, staring at the ceiling, trying to decide whether I should have an Allied Irish or ring Sorcha back.

CHAPTER EIGHT
'A pleasure to have at the school'

Ultan Mac An tSionnaigh is giving me filthies, roysh, and Christian comes over and asks me how I'm feeling and I tell him that I'm about to deck that tosser if he looks me up and down like that again. Christian tells me not to do anything stupid because we need to be calm, roysh, but he knows there's bad blood there, involving, not a bird – unusually enough – but Ultan basically taking my place on the Ireland schools team for the tour of Argentina last summer. I know I focked up in the Schools Cup final, roysh, but the word on the street was that I was still a shoo-in, what with our Junior Cup coach – that tosser Magahy – being on the selection committee. This Ultan orsehole is, like, Belvo. How far did they go in the competition last year? He's obviously repeating as well, roysh, which I'm happy about because he's going to see that I'm basically twice the player I was since I storted taking that white shit, whatever it is.

So I've no need to go losing the rag with the dude. Wardy said in the paper this morning that it's, like, a red letter day for Castlerock College and Belvedere in the Leinster Senior Cup, although I tell the goys, as JP gets ready to boot the ball into the air, that it's actually a kick ass day. Probably sounds a bit weird, roysh, but we're so relaxed that every time there's, like, a lineout in the first fifteen minutes, JP keeps turning around to our crowd behind the goal and conducting the singing, which obviously pisses the Belvo goys off big-style.

At the same time, roysh, nobody's doing anything stupid. The quarter-final of the cup is no place to be taking risks and it's, like, twenty minutes I think before we give away the first penalty of the day with the scores still tied at, like, 0-0. Ultan – what were his parents thinking? – he steps up to take it, roysh, and Stevie focking Wonder would knock this over, that's how easy it is, twenty yords out, a little bit left of centre. Of course that's without Paul McKenna here focking with the dude's mind. I walk up to him, roysh, just as he's taking his five steps backwards – he ripped off his whole technique from me – and I go, 'There's a bit of a wind blowing. Keep it left,' and their prop-for-ward – Gavin's his name, he's going out with one of the Clerkin twins, both lashers – he drags me away, roysh, thinking he's all that *and* your bus fare home. I could have decked him if I'd wanted to and of course Oisinn came steaming in to get him out of my face, but I'd already done the damage I wanted. There's no wind at all, roysh, but I've put the idea in this retord's head that there is and now he can't make up his mind whether it's, like, a bluff, a double-bluff or a double-double-bluff. His head is totally wrecked and he ends up, like, kicking it wide.

Ten minutes later, roysh – it's one of the worst matches I've ever played in – we win a penalty of our own and I have to say, roysh, it's from a pretty difficult position. Of course I'm drinking the Kool-Aid. Forty yords out close to the left-hand touchline? No problem to me. I look around for Ultan and I stort, like, pointing to my eyes, roysh, telling him to watch how the master does it. Then I run my hand through my hair, roysh, blow hord, take five steps backwards, four to the roysh, run my hand through my hair again, do a little jig on the spot and then put the ball over the bor. When he passes me again a few minues later, I go, 'DID YOU SEE HOW IT WAS DONE? DID YOU? WATCH THE MASTER AND LEARN,' and he looks pretty, I don't know, taken aback by how angry I am.

And that's it basically for the first half. We're playing pretty good stuff, roysh, but their defence is, like, SO solid and there's not even a sniff of a try for either side. We go back to the dressing-room and Fehily's, like, pacing the floor, going, 'Now, people of Germany, give us four years and then pass judgement upon us. In accordance with Field Marshal von Hindenburg's command we shall begin now ...' But of course none of us is, like, listening to the dude. Like pretty much everyone else I go straight to my bag, get out my little box of powder, tip a small mountain of the stuff onto the palm of my hand and stort, like, eating it. The thing nearly chokes me, roysh. I'm so keen to get it into me that I forget to take it with water and half of it ends up in my focking lungs. I tip some more straight into my mouth and take a drink straight from the tap. Fehily's going, 'May God Almighty give our work His blessing, strengthen our purpose, and endow us with wisdom and the trust of our people, for we are fighting not for ourselves but for Germany,' but we don't need any half-time pep talks, we're straight back onto the field, so John B to get stuck into Belvo again that we're out there, like, four or five minutes before they've even left the dressing-room.

Ultan Dickhead has had a total mental meltdown, roysh. He misses another penalty early in the second half and – total mortification for the dude – they end up taking him off kicking duties and when they win another, roysh, it's actually their scrumhalf who takes it and he knocks it over from, it has to be said, a difficult angle, despite being a Ginger.

But, like, nothing's going to stop us today, roysh. Ten minutes later we hit them like a steamroller that's gone out of control. It's, like, recycle after recycle and it's, like, relentless if that's the word, and they're focked, you can see it in them, we've got the extra strength. Ball comes to me and I don't even see the three goys in front of me, roysh, just the line and it's, like, twenty yords ahead and I hold the ball to my chest and crash through the tackles and I am not exaggerating, roysh, I take the last five or six steps with a player holding on to either leg and another hanging on to my waist. I get the try and the crowd goes ballistic. I knock over the conversion but we don't really need it.

I'm walking off thinking if that's what I can do on, I don't know, one hundred and fifty milligrams a day, imagine what I could do on three hundred.

XXX

'SHE COULD HAVE LOST HER EYE.' That's what Fehily's saying to us, roysh, at the top of his voice. He's going, 'IT'S DIFFICULT ENOUGH TO BELIEVE THAT CASTLEROCK STUDENTS WOULD BEHAVE IN THIS WAY, BUT MEMBERS OF THE SENIOR RUGBY TEAM?' which we KNOW is total horseshit, roysh, because pelting the birds from Pill Hill with eggs is, like, a tradition at this stage. We actually didn't do it last year, roysh, but there's a few of us sitting around in the common room, bored out of our bins basically, when I turn around to JP and I'm there, 'Let's go yoke the scobes,' and he says he's on for it. What he actually says is, 'I'll take that off-line,' and so we set off for the Home Ec. room, where all the blokes who should have actually been birds are making Rice Krispie cakes and sewing aprons. We storm in, roysh, and JP creates, like, a diversion by shouting, 'SAME-SEX MARRIAGES, HERE WE COME,' and I basically lift a shitload of eggs and when old Bender Bentley, the teacher, tries to stop us we just, like, give him the finger and he knows that because we're on the S there's pretty much fock-all he can do.

So off we go, roysh, and on the way we end up picking up Oisinn and Christian – 'morching into the detention area is not my idea of fun. It's more like ... suicide' – and head down to the convent. It's, like, half-one, roysh, and we spot these three total howiyas coming back from whatever they were doing at lunch, probably shoplifting. So we wait behind these trees, roysh, quiet as a focking mouse, and when they pass by we basically pelt the shit out of them. They're actually in too much shock to run away, roysh, and they're just, like, sitting ducks basically. Anyway, roysh, we leg it, but wouldn't you focking know it, one of the eggs hits one of them in the eye and apparently it's all, like, bloodshot and the nuns – the Little Sisters of Perpetual Sexual Frustration – they have a knicker-fit and end up ringing the school.

Of course Fehily knows straight away who's in the frame, but we all know he's going to do fock-all about it. He goes, 'As you are all members of the senior rugby team and the final is now only four days away, we can put this little episode down to pre-match tension. You won't be punished this time and I'll send this girl a pre-emptive solicitor's letter, just in case she's any notions of looking for damages of some description or other. I'll get Hennessy onto it immediately.' Hennessy's their focking brief! He goes, 'Fiends for compensation, these kinds of people,' and then he, like, gives us a wink and tells us to go in peace.

XXX

'We should open up, like, a pool,' JP goes, 'or a book, or whatever the fock you want to call it, but everyone on the team puts in, like, fifty sheets and whoever ends up scoring her at the debs takes the pot.'

We're basically talking about Miss Roland, the new French teacher, roysh, who actually *does* look like Uma Thurman and, according to a few of the goys who had her in St Columba's, bangs like a barn door in a force ten gale, and whether it's bullshit or not, I'm going to be the one to find out. Oisinn goes, 'This is presuming, of course, that only one of us ends up with her,' and JP's there, 'No it has to be the *first* one to nip her,' and I tell the goys to get with the programme and to forget about the debs because I'm basically going to end up being with her at the Leaving Cert Results Ball at the end of, like, August?

We've just come from, like, Saturday afternoon training, roysh, which was hord, even though none of us is supposed to be on the beer this year. I decide to up my dose of the white stuff to one hundred milligrams five times a day, just to see do I finish training any less wrecked. Anyway, roysh, after training, I – as team captain – suggested we all head out to the driving range in Kilternan, just to, like, beat off the cobwebs and to, like, do something together as a team. And I have to say, roysh, it's one of my better ideas because after a couple of hours everyone's back in the land of the living and having the crack and of course one thing leads to another and before we know it we're in the middle of a session in Johnnie Fox's. I know the semi-final's only, like, a week away, roysh, and I know it's St Mary's, but we really need to cut loose. It's funny but without the distraction of actually having to go to classes, there's that bit much more pressure on us this year because we all know that it's, like, win or bust. This is what I'm telling the goys as I'm knocking back my sixth pint of Ken and suggesting we hit town. The whole gang of us – we're talking Oisinn, Fionn, JP, Christian, the whole crew – we end up in, like, Café en Seine of all places, which is where I tell them that on the night of the Results Ball, roysh, I'm not going to throw the lips on Roland until we hit Buck Whaleys, which is just to, like, lull them into a false sense of security. I've already decided to make my move in the Berkeley Court as soon as we've finished the meal because, according to my information, supplied by a goy I know who claims to have been with her, after two glasses of wine she is literally anybody's.

My mobile phone rings and the caller ID says it's a private number and I answer, roysh, half-expecting to hear the old man's voice. But it's, like, a bird. Very sexy as well. She goes, 'Hey, Ross. It's Jemma with a j.' Forget I said that. I throw my eyes up to heaven and I'm there, 'What a surprise. I don't remember giving you my number,' and she goes, 'I got it from Claire Croft. She's in my furniture restoration class,' and I'm actually not going to ask the obvious question. I haven't a focking clue who Claire Croft is.

But I know who Jemma is. She's a head-wrecker basically. Met her in the M1 a couple of weeks ago and it was, like, the usual story. Her old pair were in Beauvoir-sur-Mer for the week and I ended up giving her the night of her life back in her gaff in Monkstown. Not bad looking and the bod was alroysh. But of course the next morning I was, like, Wile E Coyote, chewing the orm off myself to get out of there without having to give her my number. But she has it now.

She goes, 'I just wanted to get some, like, advice from you. I'm on the organising committee for our debs.' She goes to Our Lady of Perpetual Blob Strop in Templeogue, if anyone's interested. She's there, 'The big argument at the moment is whether we should stort off with, like, a drinks reception in the school itself. Or if we should just have the debs totally away from the school, maybe Powerscourt House,' and I know what she's getting at, roysh, she's basically dropping me bits of bait to see if I'm, like, interested, but of course I'm not biting. I'm there,

'Sorry, Jemma, you're breaking up. Hello? Hello?' and I blow into the phone, then hang up and switch it off.

So three or four vodka and Red Bulls later and we hit Reynords, roysh, and who do I bump into there only Sorcha, who gives me a big hug and tells me she's SO sorry she hasn't been in touch but she's been, like, SO busy and she goes, 'Isn't it SO amazing about Augusto Pinochet being arrested?' and I agree, not having a bog who he is obviously, and she asks me did I sign her e-mail petition and pass it on to someone I knew and I say I did, which is a complete and utter lie.

She's with, like, Sophie and Chloë, roysh, and they're both flirting their orses off with Christian, basically trying to get him to buy them drinks, and he's such a focking soft-horted kind of guy that all of a sudden I feel like telling them to stop taking advantage of him. But Sorcha, roysh, she's got the *Issey Miyake* on and her eyes are locked onto mine and we both know what's going to happen here. She tells me her old dear is opening a new shop – sorry, boutique – in the Powerscourt Townhouse Centre – and that's my cue to move in. It's like all the passion between us has been bottled up for so long and now someone's, like, popped the cork and we're all of a sudden eating the face off each other and I can hear Sophie going, 'I SO knew we shouldn't have come here tonight. It was obvious she wanted to be with him again,' and I can hear Christian going, 'What's wrong with that?' and Chloë going, 'Because he's a bastard basically,' and then Christian going, 'That's my best friend you're talking about,' fair play to the goy.

I don't hear any complaints from Sorcha, though. But I have to say, roysh, once I've nipped her and pretty much satisfied myself that I could have her tonight if I wanted her, I stort to get bored and – this is probably a bad reflection on me – I stort thinking about maybe going on to Lillies, to see if there's any scenario there. Of course Sorcha thinks this is, like, Happy-Ever-After now, which is the thing about her that always frightens me off. She's already going, 'OH! MY! GOD! I can't WAIT to see Erika's face when she hears we're back together,' and then she says she wouldn't mind, like, heading off because she's, like, wrecked after a long week in college, which is basically code for, 'Let's hop on the good foot and do the bould thing.'

Call me a gentleman if you will, roysh, but I don't want it when it's this easy so I go outside with her, intending to walk her, Sophie and Chloë up to the taxi rank then put myself back in the morketplace. So we're all walking up Dawson Street, roysh, me and Sorcha up ahead and Christian lagging behind with the other two, when all of a sudden Sorcha storts all this, like, crying. I nearly end up putting my orm around her she's so upset. She's going, 'OH MY GOD! I'm supposed to be going out with someone. I am SUCH a bitch,' and it's only then that I remember Brandon, or whatever that Septic's name is. I'm there, 'You don't have to tell him,' and she stops crying, pulls a tissue from her sky rocket and storts, like, dabbing at her eyes. She goes, 'No, Ross. It's only fair that he knows about us.' I have to nip this in the bud, roysh, as sensitively as I can, so I go, 'What's all this *us*, Kemosabe?' and that's when she freaks.

Well, first she sort of looks at me all confused for about ten seconds and then she goes, 'You told me you loved me in Reynords.' Actually, I probably did. Heat of the moment, blah blah blah. But then she storts, like, bawling her eyes out, telling me I'm this, that and the other, making a complete orse of herself in front of half of town. She goes, 'Why were you with me if you don't have any feelings for me?' and that's a question I hate birds asking me. The truth is, roysh, I do really have feelings for this girl, but after all that *I'm having a baby* shit last year there's probably a port of me that wants to hurt her and that's the port of me that goes, 'I just wanted to prove to myself that you still want me,' and Sophie, who's caught up with us, tells me to get out of her sight before she does something she'll regret and Chloë tells Sorcha I've always been a bastard to women and she should have known better than to have anything to do with me.

Then me and Christian hit Burger King.

XXX

'Talking about me again?' The old dear nearly craps herself when she sees me, roysh, and she's *actually* going to deny it when the old man stands up and goes, 'Your mother and I are worried about you, Ross,' and of course I'm there, 'That's a first,' which he just ignores. He's like, 'You're quiet, moody, irritable, secretive. You're showing all the classic signs of someone who's – I'm going to have to just come out with this, Fionnuala – on drugs.'

The old dear goes, 'Things have been going missing from the house, Ross. Your father's golf trophy–' and straight away I'm like, '*What* golf trophy?' and I turn to the old man and I go, 'You're shit at golf,' and he's like, 'The one I won in the Pro-Am out in Portmarnock. Playing with Ronan Collins and Christy O'Connor Junior, thank you very much indeed. It's gone, Ross,' and I'm there, 'And you think I stole it to buy drugs? You two are MAJORLY focked up. If you must know, I focked it out the window the night you brought it home. You came in thinking you were so shit-hot, so I thought, 'I'll show the focker.' The old man goes, 'You're missing the point, Ross. The trophy is replaceable. Especially if I keep playing the way I'm playing. We just want to find out what's troubling you lately.'

The old dear's still shovelling food into her face, that's how concerned she is. I just lose the plot, roysh. I'm there, 'Hey, I'm not the
focking criminal in this family, remember? I'm not the one who refuses
to answer the door in case it's a writ. It's not me who jumps six feet in
the air every time the phone rings in case it's the Feds. I'm not the one
who's been to the Cayman Islands so often they're thinking of naming
the new terminal after me.' He goes, 'That's Hennessy's joke, Ross, and
well you know it.'

The old dear goes, 'It's just that we've noticed ...' and I'm like, '*Noticed?* I'm surprised you've noticed anything with your focking cam-
paigns. Ban Poor People from the National Gallery. What are you
focking like?' and she's like, 'There you go again. Over-simplifying
things. That is not what we're about at all. We simply feel that if they're
going to allow schoolchildren in, they should be a bit better behaved
and not let run amok. One morning per week. That's all the girls and I
want,' and I just look at her with total contempt, roysh, and I'm there,
'You and your focking coffee mornings,' and she goes, 'You want me to
catch head-lice off these children, is that it?' and then the waterworks
stort and I have to get the fock out of there. I go, 'When was the last
time either of you knew what I wanted?' and even though I don't know
what I meant by it, it sounded pretty good, it has to be said.

I go upstairs and throw on some new threads – my red and white
striped Polo Sport rugby shirt, my navy Dockers and the old brown
Dubes. I have, like, four voice messages, roysh, but I delete them without even bothering my orse to check who they're from. I head downstairs, roysh, and as I'm opening the front door, the old pair are still,
like, at it. The old man's going, 'You just don't know these days, Fionnuala, it could be these blasted mobile telephones. Electromagnetic

waves and so forth. The atmosphere is full of them. Full, I tell you, with a capital F. I was talking to that Alex Garton at the regatta last week. He's Hennessy's physician, you know? For his sins! Anyway, he said there's so many people using these phones that getting the 46A bus into town now is the equivalent of putting your head in a microwave oven for seven-and-a-half minutes.' She's going, 'I'm not giving him my Micra, Charles,' and he goes, 'No, of course not, darling.'

XXX

Me and the goys are having a few scoops in the M1, but I'm just really, like, bored, and I end up going to the can and snorting a shitload of the magic powder. Then I decide to call out to Sorcha's gaff, not because I regret the way I treated her the other night, roysh, but because I am totally gagging for my end-away and I'm actually storting to believe Fionn, who said he got his cousin, who works in the lab in UCD – another geek obviously – to test the stuff we've been taking and it turns out it's, like, pure focking testosterone, which explains one or two things, like the horn you could use to beat a donkey out of a quarry.

So I hit the Vico Road, roysh, and I know my game plan. I'm going to give it all that, 'I'm really nervous about the game. It's the biggest day of my life. You're the only one who truly understands me and the pressure I'm under,' blah blah blah, basically all the horseshit birds love. So I arrive up at the door, roysh, hit the bell and it's, like, her little sister who answers it, Afric or Orpha or whatever the fock she's called. I'm there, 'Is Sorcha in?' and she goes, 'No, she's at, like, the orthodontist?' and I go, 'Can I come in and wait?' and she goes, 'Sure.'

We go into the sitting-room, roysh, and she's watching MTV and it's, like, Robbie Williams, roysh, and she says she thinks he's, like, SO cool and she asks me did I see him interviewed on 2TV last weekend and I say no and she goes, 'OHMYGOD, he SO cool.' *Stars connecting our fate*, blahby blahdy blah.

She's a total focking airhead, roysh, but she's actually turned into a bit of a honey, although I have to say this is the first time I've ever actually looked at her in that way. No one really pays any attention to little sisters, roysh, and then one day – *whoosh* – they've suddenly got top tens and a great boat race and you're thinking, 'Yeah, I actually would if the opportunity arose.'

She's a Mountie as well, roysh, and I think she must be in, like, fifth year now, because she was definitely in transition year last year, because she did her work experience in my old man's company, although she had a brace on her Taylors and so many Randolph Scotts that she got charged three hundred bills into the cinema last week – this is JP's joke, by the way – because it was three quid a head. Now, though, she's a little focking hortbreaker and unless I'm very much mistaken, roysh, that's the black fur-collared cardigan Sorcha pestered me to buy for her in Morgan when we were, like, going out together. And she's wearing her *Contradiction* as well. I think she's like a young Anna Kournikova.

So I'm there racking my brains, roysh, to come up with a couple of lines that'll get me in there. I'm like, 'You used to play tennis down in Glenageary, didn't you?' and she's like, 'Oh my God, how did you know that?' and quick as a flash – I'm the Kool-Aid dispenser, man – I go, 'I never forget a pretty face.'

Twenty seconds later, roysh, I'm wearing the face off her and she's an amazing kisser and I'm giving her, 'All the time I was with Sorcha, I was actually thinking about you?' thinking we might end up taking this upstairs in a minute, but all of a sudden she pulls away, roysh, and says she has to finish her homework. And I'm there, 'Your homework?' and she goes, 'I'm supposed to be preparing my debate,' and I don't even bother asking her what the topic is, roysh, I just get up off the sofa, head out into the hall and tell her that it's probably best if Sorcha doesn't, like, find out about this. She goes, 'OH! MY! GOD! Sorcha would be SO pissed off if she found out,' and if there was, like, an edge in her voice, roysh, I didn't cop it.

But I get home, roysh, and I swear to God I'm in the door, like, five minutes when the mobile rings and it's, like, Sorcha. Of course I make the mistake of, like, answering it and she's spitting nails. She's going, 'I KNEW YOU WERE A BASTARD, ROSS, BUT I CANNOT *BELIEVE* YOU WOULD DO SOMETHING LIKE THAT,' and I go, 'I don't know what you're talking about,' playing the total innocent. She goes, 'She told me everything, Ross. You were WITH her.' This could still be one of about fifteen birds. She goes, 'My SISTER, Ross.' Fock. She goes, 'I cannot believe either of you would do something like that. She is SUCH a bitch, Ross. She only did it to get at me. Did I really hurt you that much last year that you want to keep doing things like this to me?' but I don't answer, roysh, because I'm actually feeling bad about what I did, weird as it sounds. She tells me I'm a bastard to girls and that she should have listened to Sophie and Chloë and Aoife and even Claire and then, like, the line goes dead.

XXX

All the Mary's crowd are giving it, 'DRUG-GIE, DRUG-GIE, DRUG-GIE,' and Christian comes over to me, roysh, and he tells me not to listen, to stay calm and to stay focused and I think the dude's worried that I'm going to go apeshit or something because of the way I was, like, booting holes in the walls and punching dents in the lockers in the dressing-room, though that was just a sign of how up for this game

I am. The game kicks off and the crowd are still giving it loads, it's all, 'WHERE'S YOUR SYRINGE GONE?' and all that, roysh, but it's a pity their team aren't so clever.

They're actually such a pushover, roysh, that the first half is a bit of an anti-climax. Christian danced right through their defence to score, like, two tries right under the posts in the first, like, eight minutes, roysh, and we were, like, 23-12 up by half-time and already dreaming about March seventeenth at Lansdowne Road. We go back to the dressing-room and Fehily's in there waiting and he goes, 'As Joshua said at half-time in the Battle of Jericho ...' and I just, like, push him out of the way, roysh, and I go, 'Goys, we let this slip last year and we've got to make sure we don't do it again. We owe this to ourselves, goys. Just keep telling yourself, we've earned this,' and we go straight out there again.

And the second half is an even bigger piece of piss. Oisinn and Fionn both get tries, which I also convert, and the Mary's crowd end up, like, taking their frustration out on me, going, 'WHO'S THE JUNKY, WHO'S THE JUNKY, WHO'S THE JUNKY IN THE RED?' meaning me, roysh, but I have the last laugh when I slip two tackles and sell one of their backs an amazing dummy, even if I say so myself, and I get over for a try. Then, roysh, for my celebration, I get down on my hands and knees and stort, like, snorting the white line, which does NOT go down well, but we're in the final, against Newbridge of all schools – crowd of muckers – so I couldn't give two focks.

XXX

It's Fionn who sees the white powder on the front of my jumper, roysh – we're talking my black, vertical ribbed Sonetti – and he storts looking at me suspiciously. I'm there, 'Do you have a problem?' and he pushes his glasses up on his nose and goes, 'No, but you obviously do.' I'm there, 'Are you a doctor or something?' and he's like, 'Let's just say I know enough to know when to stop taking that stuff. You're snorting it now, aren't you?' and I lose the plot then and I make a grab for the goy. But Oisinn hops up, roysh, and he tells me that, captain of the S or not, I'm out of order, in fact I'm BANG out of order and I should go for a walk to, like, sort my head out. I realise, roysh, that everyone in the sixth year common room is, like, staring at me, so I go, 'What the FOCK are you lot looking at,' and I boot the wall and my foot goes right through it and I just, like, walk out.

I must have had, like, seven hundred milligrams of the stuff already today and it's only, like, lunchtime and now my head is throbbing like nobody's business. I need to get some tablets and maybe something else, I don't know what, to try to get me calm because I feel like just ...

So I walk down as far as the Merrion Shopping Centre and go into the chemist. And there I am, roysh, looking through all the various boxes and bottles and tubes, not knowing what the fock I'm really looking for, when all of a sudden I feel this, like, tap on my shoulder. I spin around, roysh, and it's, like, Sorcha. She's there, 'Hi,' and I'm like, 'What are you doing here?' and she's like, 'Working. HELLO?' Her old dear's shop. Of course.

She looks incredible. I blurt it out. Not *that*. I just tell her that her shirt's nice and she tells me it's a Scott Henshall and she tells me it goes really well with the black wool shrug she bought in Morgan that day we went shopping together and I just nod. She goes, 'I heard you played really well against St Mary's. Congrats,' and I'm there, 'It's Newbridge in the final and it's going to be tough, boggers or not,' and she smiles and says I'm probably glad that she's not around this year to fock things up for me again and I don't answer.

She doesn't even mention what happened with her sister. It's like she's blocking it out, roysh, but she says she's SO embarrassed about what happened that other night in town. She's like, 'I can't believe I was actually with you. I met the girls for a quiet drink after hockey practice and we ended up going on the complete lash and, well, I hadn't eaten all day and ...' and I just say, 'It's cool,' and I'm about to ask her whether she told her so-called boyfriend that she was sucking the lips off me last week, but I don't because I wouldn't give her the satisfaction of thinking I GIVE a shit one way or the other.

She goes, 'Preparation H? You haven't got piles, have you?' and I look down at the tube in my hand and I end up going, 'No, I'm in looking for, em, condoms,' and I can see her face drop, roysh, and I pick up five packets of johnnies and then after a few seconds I pick up two more. She goes, 'I heard you were with Angel,' and I'm there, 'What's that got to do with you?' and she goes, 'Nothing, I suppose. Just glad to see you're taking precautions these days,' and she goes off and I swear to God, roysh, she was on the point of bursting into tears.

XXX

I get a text from some bird called Hazel and it's like,

> **hey ross its hazel, just wondring did u realy mean wot u sed last nite cos i ben doin sum tinkin n I tink I feel d same way**

Who the FOCK is Hazel?

XXX

The old dear's sitting at the kitchen table, roysh, reading the National Gallery's response to her suggestion that their staff be armed to deal with, as she put, 'the riff-raff element,' and I take it from her expression, roysh, that they're not exactly Roy on the idea. She's just going, 'Terribly disappointing,' over and over under her breath, the stupid wagon, and when she finally notices that I'm actually in the room, she looks at me over the top of her glasses and she goes, 'Oh, hello, Ross,' and I know straight away that she's after something. She goes, 'The big match, eh? Won't be long now. You must be excited. *I'm* excited,' and I'm there, 'What have *you* got to be excited about?' and she goes, 'Well, I'm the mother of the Castlerock captain. If Castlerock win, I get to present the Cup ...'

HOLY FOCK! I should have thought of this.

She's there, 'Going to go shopping for a dress tomorrow. Andrea's going to come with me. We might try Sorcha's mother's place. See what she has,' and straight away I go, 'There's no point.' She's still looking at me over the top of her glasses. She's like, 'No point, is that what you said?' and I'm there, 'There's fock-all wrong with your hearing, don't worry. The old dear of the winning captain doesn't present the Cup anymore,' which of course is total horseshit. She goes, 'Oh,' and then, 'I'd better ring Andrea,' and then, 'When did they stop it because Oisinn's mother told me ...' and I'm going, 'They stopped it last year. Too many old bags making complete tits of themselves.'

I'll tell everyone she's got, I don't know, some contagious disease or other, and get Christian to ask his old dear, who's actually pretty tasty, to present it to me instead.

XXX

Ana with one n – now there's a voice from the past – she leaves me a message to say she has tickets for the Lighthouse Family if I want to go and I'm wondering does Angel know she's ringing. Then I cop it, roysh, that the two of them have had a row because next there's a message from Angel herself and she says she's SO sorry she hasn't been in touch but Ana with one n is being SUCH a bitch and OH! MY! GOD! I will not BELIEVE the shit she was coming up with this morning, TRYING to make her feel guilty for eating, like, a packet of Hula Hoops, which is, like, three-and-a-half points, we're talking, HELLO? I don't even listen to the full message. I just, like, flush the chain, make sure it's not a floater and then go back to the old scratcher, where Elinor – this total Claire Danes lookalike – is fast asleep beside me. I'm only getting about two hours' kip a night since I storted taking this shit.

Me and JP actually did well last night. He pulled her best mate – as in Melanie – and she must have known a few tricks, roysh, because I could hear him through the walls going, 'QUALITY DRIVEN!' and 'CLIENT FOCUSED!' and that went on for, like, half the night. Have to say, roysh, it was a bit of a blow to the old ego to hear that, especially with me doing it during the ad break in 'Ally McBeal', though Elinor's not gonna complain. For her it's just BEING with Ross O'Carroll-Kelly that matters, nothing more, nothing less.

We're actually in JP's house, roysh, because his old pair are in, like, Chicago for the week, shopping. So there I am, roysh, lying there, actually in the mood for another round of the other, and I'm trying to come up with an excuse to wake Elinor up, when all of a sudden JP bursts into the room, roysh, and he goes, 'ROSS, QUICK! AL AND KAY GUY ARE AT THE DOOR!' and of course I'm like, 'Fock! The ones who caught–' and he's like, 'MICHELLE SMITH! YES! QUICK, EAT

THE EVIDENCE!' so he pegs it back to his room, roysh, and I grab the tub of powder out of my chinos, which are in a ball on the floor, and I stort wolfing it back and washing it down with the bottle of Evian that Elinor left on the bedside locker.

I'm thinking that if they ask to drug-test me, roysh, I'll tell them I'm already the most tested schools rugby player in Leinster and you only have to look at me to know that ... And then I'm thinking, what the FOCK is JP at, telling me to eat this shit if they're going to be asking me for, like, a piss sample? I look up, roysh, and he's standing at the door, cracking his hole laughing. He goes, 'You have to admit, I got you there, Ross.'

XXX

As if I need to be reminded what this match means, roysh, Erika phones me up the night before and she goes, 'What aftershave do you wear?' I'm like, 'Don't I even get a hello?' and she goes, 'Don't wear *Cool Water* or anything by Davidoff if you want to be with me. It's an allergy I have,' and she hangs up.

XXX

'Newbridge are a bunch of total boggers who have no business being in the final of a competition like this.' None of us can disagree with Fehily when he says this. He goes, 'These people are muck savages. Not a laywer's son between them. I don't think any person of sound mind would disagree that their appearance in the final denigrates the entire competition. But ... it is solemnly I tell thee, they came through the various rounds of the competition to get here and the rules are the rules. Until a fairer way can be devised to stop schools from the country from progressing in the competition, we just have to play by the rules, imperfect and all as they are. But you owe it not just to your school but to your class, your people, your way of life, to ensure that every single upper class one of you stands up and makes himself count this afternoon,' and before he has a chance to say anything else, roysh, we're all stamping our feet in the dressing-room and I'm leading us in a chorus of 'Castlerock Above All Others'.

Then we morch out onto the field in single file, roysh, with the cheers of our fans ringing in our ears. Fehily was roysh what he said to Tony Ward in this morning's paper, that the famous Castlerock roar is like having a sixteenth man on the field.

This year, roysh, we've left nothing to chance. We watched, like, videos of Newbridge's quarter-final and semi-final, roysh, and Fehily and me – as captain – went through the various ways in which we thought they were weak.

I've decided, roysh, to give my pre-match speech not in, like, the dressing-room but out on the field. And judging from the reaction of the goys, roysh, it's actually mind-blowing stuff, better than any drug. We all get into a huddle, roysh, and I go, 'This is the biggest day of our lives, goys. We've been through a whole lot of shit together but we'll probably never be all here together like this again. When we leave Castlerock, most of us will go on to five-grand-a-term private colleges, where we'll be given qualifications without having to sit exams. We'll all get jobs through people we share a shower with at the rugby clubs we play for. We'll keep on scoring the birds,' and that gets a roar and I'm like, 'until we reach our mid-thirties. Then we'll marry the youngest and prettiest of them and continue to sleep with all of her friends. We all have big futures to look forward to, because we are the élite. But today is the last time we will ever have to work hord for anything in our entire lives. So let's make it count this time. Let's do it for Fehily. Let's do it for Castlerock. But most of all ... let's do it for us.'

I swear to God, roysh, those goys would have walked through fock-ing walls for me by the time I finish. I have to say as well, roysh, that I have never heard such an atmosphere at Lansdowne Road, not even for internationals, and the Newbridge goys, you can see it *by* them, they're crapping it. I make sure to walk up to them one-by-one as they're doing their warm-up, roysh, and I go, 'History,' and they're all bricking it, I can see it in their eyes.

They've brought a bit of a crew up with them from, I don't know, Kerry or wherever the fock Newbridge is, but the best they can do is, 'DADDY'S GONNA BUY YOU A BRAND NEW MOTORCAR,' and straight away, roysh, our goys are like, 'DADDY'S GONNA BUY YOU A BRAND NEW COW,' which we can actually hear on the field.

We just know, roysh, that we are not going to be denied. I've never actually seen Christian play a better match. He's dancing around them like Michael Flatley, roysh, but he's also putting out fires everywhere in, like, defence. Even Fionn, roysh, who I'd have had difficulties giving any kind of compliment to in the past, I turn around to him halfway through the first half and I go, 'Rugby is actually an easy game to play when you've got goys like you on your side,' and he high-fives me and it's just like, RESPECT!

JP scores our first try, roysh, running pretty much the whole length of the field to score after an intercept ten yords from our line. I pop over the points and within five minutes we basically flatten them with our rolling maul, shoving them from pretty much halfway, right to the other end of the field for Oisinn to put the ball down. Then Christian gets one and suddenly we're storting to relax and, like, enjoy ourselves.

A very funny thing happens in the second half, roysh. I grab a couple of tries myself, flukes I kept telling people afterwards, the whole false modesty bit. But to score the second, roysh, I basically have to run for, like, thirty or forty yords with one of their goys pegging it after me. And I have to say, roysh, he's fast this goy, but I've got a headstort on him and I know I've got just about enough in my legs to carry me over the line before he can, like, get in a tackle on me. Anyway, roysh, as he's chasing after me, I'm talking to him, giving it, 'Come on, catch up. You really need to eat more bacon and cabbage,' and then I'm going, 'Are they rugby boots you're wearing or wellies?'

Anyway, roysh, we end up beating the focking muckers 46-12 and it's, like, big-time celebrations. We really, like, deserved this and we're all bawling our eyes out and hugging each other. They go up to get their medals, roysh, and I end up standing at the bottom of the steps and I say to each one as he comes down, 'Fock off back to Bogland.' Then I go up to get the Cup from Christian's old dear. I ended up telling her that my old dear broke both her legs playing tennis, which was more wishful thinking than anything else. She hands me the Cup, roysh, and she kisses me, not on the cheek, roysh, but actually on the lips and I'm thinking ... No, forget it. I just grab the Cup in, like, both hands, roysh, and I go, 'FOR FEHILY! FOR ROCK! FOR GOD!' which probably sounds a bit wanky, roysh, but it was the first thing that came into my head and the crowd didn't seem to mind, they went totally ballistic.

We peg it back down the steps, roysh, and we do a lap of honour and then Wardy comes up to me and he asks me can he have a few words with the winning captain for tomorrow's paper. I'm there, 'Shoot,' and he's like, 'Okay, first of all, how do you feel?' I'm there, 'Can't really put it into words, Tony. This has been our dream now for two years. And today that dream became a realisation.' He goes, 'I notice you had a word with each of the Newbridge players as they came down the steps with their medals. What did you say to them?' and I'm there, 'I just told them they did themselves, their school and their way of life proud. I told them that the people who said they had no right to be here had been proven wrong and that it was actually our toughest match of the whole campaign.'

He goes, 'And finally, I suppose you and the goys will be having a quiet night in this evening, Ross?' and straight away I'm like, 'Yeah, roysh. AS IF!'

XXX

Picture the scene, roysh. It's two o'clock in the morning and we're in, like, Annabel's and Erika is wearing the face off me, but I'm pretty much numb from the amount of drink I've knocked back and I couldn't tell you whether she's a good or a bad wear. But I suspect it's bad. There doesn't seem to be any, like, passion in it. We both seem to be just, like, going through the motions. After about fifteen minutes, roysh, she finally pulls away and she goes, 'You're nothing to write home about, Ross. I don't know what your little girlfriend's been talking about all these years. I had tickets for the National Concert Hall tonight. The Lyric Opera production of *Nabucco*.'

XXX

Relinquishing testosterone addiction. Stage One, Preparation. For this you will need: one room which you will not leave for the entire month of April; one mattress; roast pumpkin and hickory bacon soup, ten tins of; Marks and Spencer green Thai curry soup, eight tins of, for consumption hot; ice cream, triple chocolate dream, one large tub of; Pringles, sour cream and chive, eight pipes of; mouthwash; vitamins;

mineral water; Lucozade Sport; photographs of Isla Fischer and Bianca Luyckx; one bucket for, like, crap, one for piss and one for Huey; one television; two parents who will basically wait on me hand and foot and get me whatever the fock else I want.

And now I'm ready. All I need is a final hit to soothe the pain while I'm waiting for the old dear to bring me my focking dinner.

XXX

All the goys have been wondering why I decided to bring Fiona, as in one of the O'Prey triplets, to the Leaving Cert Results Ball when (a) she's not exactly catwalk material and (b) she generally says fock-all from one end of the evening to the other, having no basic personality to speak of. Picture, No Sound, the goys call her, but it's when we're all piled into the limo on the way to the Berkeley Court, roysh, that the goys see the method in my madness. Oisinn's with Anna Cotes, a total honey who was head girl in – of all places – the Virgin Megastore in Rathfarnham and at this precise moment in time she's, like, straightening his bow tie and picking bits of fluff off his tux jacket, we're talking maximum attention here. JP brought that Anita Prentice, this bird from, like, Loreto on the Green, who he's already asked to our actual debs, even though it's only the end of August and the debs is still, like, two or three months away, the sap, and there's a major boyfriend-girlfriend vibe going down there. Fionn's brought some focking hound he met at some UCD open day or other and they're busy crapping on about whether or not Clinton should be, what was the word, impeached – your guess is as good as mine – and they haven't a clue what's going on around them. And Christian seems all loved-up with Sophie, a mate of Sorcha's who we've all been loved-up with at one stage or another.

What I'm basically saying here is that the field is pretty much clear for me to walk away with the top prize tonight, as in Miss Roland, this new French teacher who's as loose as, I don't know, Oisinn's trousers would be on me. JP pours me another brandy from the minibor, then slides the little hatch across and asks the driver to go twice more around the block. Fiona tries to, like, link me, roysh, but I shake my orm free and give her a look, to basically remind her she should be grateful just to be here and that I've no interest in going into this race with a weight handicap.

We're on the way in, roysh – red corpet, the works – when Oisinn pulls me back and he goes, 'I know what you're thinking, Ross,' and I'm there, 'You do?' and he goes, 'You think you're going to lick the pot. Just to let you know, I'm not out of the game and neither is JP,' and I end up high-fiving him, as if to say, I don't know, may the best man win. So we morch into the ballroom, roysh, totally ignore the seating plan and all decide to sit at this table smack bang in the middle of the room, which means telling these two Chess Club geeks and their ugly birds to basically hop it. One of them, roysh, a little tosser with glasses – a mate of Fionn's probably – he actually has the cheek to turn around to me and go, 'These places have been pre-assigned,' and without even having to think, roysh, I go, 'Now they're being reassigned. To the stars of the Castlerock senior rugby team,' and I rip off his glasses and drop them into his drink – a Coke for fock's sake, to celebrate his Leaving Cert results? – and the four of them fock off, muttering something about reporting us and we're all like, To who?

The meal arrives, roysh, and all the birds at the table are doing the usual, seeing who can eat the least. Christian, JP and Fionn are too busy knocking back the beers to think about food, but Oisinn wipes every plate on the table clean, roysh, basically breaking the world record for the most Chicken Supremes eaten in an hour. Then he eats everyone's Tiramisu and a few from the next table as well. Fiona's struck up a bit of a conversation with Anita, which is good because I want her to have SOME happy memories of the evening.

Miss Roland's sitting at the next table, roysh, and of course we're all trying to get a good eyeful without actually getting snared. She looks basically incredible. I might have mentioned that she's the spit of Uma Thurman, we're talking twenty-four, maybe twenty-five, and she looks hot tonight in this, like, black dress, which is, as Fionn points out, showing off an unwise amount of cleavage for a teacher taking her first step on the career ladder. I can see Fehily giving her a talking-to about it next week.

There's only one reason, of course, why a teacher would come to a school ball looking that good. She has the hots for, like, someone. Can't be one of the other teachers, roysh, because they've all either got BO, flaky skin, comb-overs, or all three and there isn't one of them under fifty. So she must have it bad for one of us and, not being big-headed or anything, but the smort money's on me, especially given the way she's, like, looking over. That cabbage-breath focker Crabtree's boring the ear off her, probably about Hitler or history or some other horseshite, and I catch her eye and she sort of, like, smiles and waves at me and I give her this, like, disapproving look, as if to remind her that us students are, like, forbidden fruit as far as she's concerned, just, like, focking around of course.

Haven't mentioned it, roysh, but I'm drinking the old non-alcoholic gerbil's piss, determined to keep a clear head. The other goys are already half hammered. We all want the same thing here basically, but I'm the only one with a game plan and the big-match temperament. Hope I'm not coming across as, like, arrogant or anything, roysh, but there's a reason why I always get the girl and it's the reason I'm the best young kicker of a dead ball in Ireland, according to Wardy, and that reason is focus. I suppose you could say that the goalposts in this case are Miss Roland herself and the ball is my ... whatever.

When she catches my eye again I give her a little wink and she sort of, like, blushes, and I know she's basically putty in the hand. Oisinn is asking Christian how much money he'd give him if he lit one of his forts, which means he's pretty much out of the game, roysh, while JP is shouting, 'EAT THE POOR!' which suggests to me that he's in no frame of mind to basically chat anyone up either.

Fiona turns around to me and she goes, 'I still can't believe that out of all the girls you could have invited here tonight you asked me,' obviously thinking she's in the big-time frame for the ACTUAL debs in November here, so I go, 'Don't read anything into it. I'm using you. I basically needed a Plain Jane who wasn't going to distract my focus. Not being a bastard or anything, but there's no attraction whatsoever,' and of course on go the focking waterworks then. Birds do my head in when they stort that shit so I hit the bor for another bottle of piss – Fiona's got half a vodka and Diet 7-Up there, she can make do with that – and who's up there, roysh, only Miss Roland herself and she's pretty locked from the way she's pouring that white wine into her glass.

I'm there, 'Hello there. Looking good,' playing it totally Kool and the Gang, and she looks up and goes, 'Oh! Hello Ross. How are you?' and I'm there, 'All the better for seeing you here tonight. What can I say? You look ... really well,' and she goes, 'I'll take that as a compliment,' and of course I'm wondering what other focking way she could possibly take it but I don't say that, I just go, 'I got into UCD,' and she looks at me as if to say, you know, did you accidentally get someone else's Leaving Cert results or something? To be honest with you, I didn't even bother my orse sitting the Leaving this time around because, well, I got the offer pretty much straight away after the Schools Cup final. I'm there, 'It's, like, a scholarship? We're talking sports management? You don't need, like, brains or anything,' and she nods like she understands. The thing is, roysh, I couldn't stay at Castlerock forever either, and I did the old maths – UCD, we're talking ten thousand students, more than half of them female – and I was like, Lemme at 'em.

Miss Roland goes, 'How was your summer? Did you get a chance to practice any of your French?' and instead of going, 'I don't focking have any to practice with,' which is what I was SO tempted to say, I go, 'As a matter of fact, yes. I spent the whole summer in ... what's the capital again?' and she's like, 'Paris,' and I'm there, 'How could I forget?' and it's all total bullshit, of course. I basically spent the summer in Kiely's, Annabel's, Reynords and the Club of Love, bringing pleasure to the lives of attractive women. That was a major, I don't know, incentive to get clean again. There I was, locked away in my room, and hearing all these stories about Oisinn and JP and Fionn – Fionn, for fock's sake – scoring all around them, roysh, and I just decided basically that I wanted the old Ross back. The birds had been too long without me.

Miss Roland goes, 'So you worked there for the summer?' and we're talking full eye contact here, the big-time hots for me. I'm like, 'No, I was mostly chilling actually, just basically doing French shit.'

Then there's this, like, lull in the conversation, roysh, and I end up going, 'Can I be honest with you, Miss Roland?' and she's there, 'Stephanie,' and I'm there, 'Okay, Stephanie then. I'd like to be with you,' and suddenly, roysh, she drops the whole flirty act and she's, like, looking over her shoulder to see if anyone's, like, listening. She goes, 'I can't believe you ...' and I'm there, 'Don't play the innocent. You want me as much as I want you,' and she goes, 'Ross, I could lose my job,' and I'm going, 'So you're not denying you're attracted to me.'

She storts, like, fidgeting with the wine glass. I go, 'I've got a room booked at the Radisson,' and she looks at me and she goes, 'For you and whoever you happened to pick up tonight?' and I'm like, 'No. I booked it in the hope that it would be me and you basically going back there.'

She doesn't say anything for, like, twenty seconds, roysh, then she just knocks back the rest of her wine and goes, 'I'll leave now. Follow me at a discreet distance. And I mean DISCREET, Ross. No one can know about this,' and I'm like, 'Hey, I'm not the type to kiss and tell,' and she's like, 'I hope not,' and she heads outside. Of course I'm straight over to the goys, roysh, putting my orms up and going, 'HE SHOOTS, HE SCORES!' and of course they're practically focking dizzy it happened so quickly. I'm there, 'At this moment in time, she's in the cor pork waiting for me.' Oisinn goes, 'You mean Roland?' and I'm like, 'Please. It's Stephanie.' JP goes, 'What's the deal? You said you were leaving it till Buck Whaleys?' and I'm there, 'Love doesn't work to a timetable, JP.' Out of the corner of my eye I can see Fiona bawling her eyes out on Anita's shoulder. I go, 'Anyway, I've entertained you losers long enough. I'm off to make mad passionate love to a member of the teaching staff. *Asta la vista,*' and I head out with chants of, 'LEG-END! LEG-END! LEG-END!' coming from our table and three or four others as well.

I go outside, roysh, and she's, like, waiting for me. She goes, 'Are you sure no one saw you leave?' and I'm there, 'Hey, I've got a bit more class than you're giving me credit for,' and she goes, 'I'm sorry. It's just, I really love my job and I don't want ...' and I just go, 'Ssshhh!' and I go to throw the lips on her. She goes, 'Wait till we get to the hotel,' and I'm like, 'Your wish is my command,' the one-liners just falling out of my mouth tonight.

She goes, 'The Radisson? You really believe in pushing the boat out, don't you?' and I think, 'FOCK!' and while I'm driving, roysh, I'm sending a text to Christian, and it's basically:

> **Yo! Ive a techer here who wants my dck bad. Ring d radison in stilrgan n book me a suite. Quick. She wants me NOW!**

And of course twenty seconds later I get a reply, roysh, and I realise I've actually sent it to my old man by mistake, what with Dick Features coming immediately after Christian in my phone. I open his reply and it's like,

No probs, Kicker

the tool that he is. So there we are, roysh, pegging it down the Stillorgan dualler, Stephanie in the passenger seat, Lite FM's Friday Night Love Affair on the radio and me texting the goys, roysh, telling them all the various things I'm going to do to her when I get her back to the hotel, when all of a sudden – OH! FOCK! – I hear this, like, siren behind and sure enough it's the focking Feds. I pull over, like you're supposed to, roysh, and in the old rear-view mirror I can see the copper putting on his hat and, like, walking towards the cor and of course Stephanie's losing the rag, roysh, going, 'If they ask, I was giving you grinds,' and I'm there, 'In that dress? Just leave the talking to me, hon,' thinking I'm basically fireproof tonight.

I wind down the window and I can't believe my focking luck, roysh. It's the same cop who was gonna lift me here before. I remember him from his thick neck and his big cabbage head, the focking bogger. I'm just hoping he doesn't recognise me. I wind down the window and I'm there, 'What seems to be the problem, officer?' but he's in no mood for my shit. He goes, 'Have you your licence?' and of course I know that if I show it to him he's sure to remember me from before, so I just go, 'It's at home. I'll present it at my nearest Gorda station within ten days. Is that everything?' and he's writing away in this little pad, roysh. He goes, 'Is that everything? Let's see. Driving at sixty miles per hour in a forty-mile zone. Texting while in charge of a vehicle. That comes under ... driving without due care and attention. I think that's everything, yes. Oh and there's a smell of alcohol on your breath. I'd like to breathalyse you. Unfortunately, the equipment I've here with me is a bit banjaxed, so I'm going to have to ask you to accompany me to the station.'

I'm like, 'I SO haven't been drinking. The smell is just ... I've been drinking that non-alcoholic shite all night. Look, whatever the fine is for the texting and the speeding and whatever, don't worry, my old man's good for the money,' but I make the mistake then of appealing to him sort of, like, man to man. I'm there, 'Look, I'm kind of on a promise here,' but that just makes him determined to lift me.

He goes, 'There's a reception area in the station. She can wait for you there. Otherwise, one of our officers can drop the lady wherever she wants to go.' Stephanie leans across me and goes, 'Garda, I was just giving him grinds. I'd really appreciate a lift back to Harold's Cross,' and he's like, 'That'll be arranged.'

I still don't know whether the focker recognises me from the time I gave him all that lip. He storts, like, writing in his notebook again, roysh, going, 'Now, name?' and I decide, fock it, I'll give him a false one, roysh, because I'll be out of there the second they find out I haven't been drinking. I end up just going, 'The name's Fionn—' but he just cuts me off and goes, 'Ross ... O'Carroll ... Kelly ... you said I'd remember it. Looks like you were right.'

Fock.

DO YOU WANT MORE OF THE MAN? ...

I know you so do ...

Book 2 in the ROSS O'CARROLL-KELLY series

Ross O'Carroll-Kelly, The Teenage Dirtbag Years
(As told to Paul Howard)

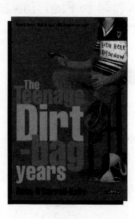

So there I was, roysh, class legend, schools rugby legend, basically an all-round legend, when someone decides you can't, like, sit the Leaving Cert three times. Well that put a focking spanner in the works. But joining the goys at college wasn't the mare I thought it would be, basically for, like, three major reasons: beer, birds and more birds. And for once I agree with Fionn about the, like, education possibilities. I mean, where else can you learn about 'Judge Judy', fake IDs and how to order a Ken and snog a bird at the same time? I may be beautiful, roysh, but I'm not stupid and this much I totally know: college focking ROCKS!

Book 3 in the ROSS O'CARROLL-KELLY Series

Ross O'Carroll-Kelly, The Orange Mocha-Chip Frappuccino Years
(As told to Paul Howard)

So there I was, roysh, enjoying college life, college birds and, like, a major amount of socialising. Then, roysh, the old pair decide to mess everything up for me. And we're talking TO-TALLY here. Don't ask me what they were thinking. I hadn't, like, changed or treated them any differently, but the next thing I know, roysh, I'm out on the streets. Another focking day in paradise for me. If it hadn't been for Fionn's aportment in Killiney, the old man paying for my Golf GTI, JP's old man's job offer and all the goys wanting to buy me drink, it would have been, like, a complete mare. TOTALLY. But naturally roysh, you can never be sure what life plans to do to you next. At least, it came as a complete focking surprise to me.

Ross O'Carroll-Kelly, PS, I Scored the Bridesmaids (As told to Paul Howard)

So there I was, roysh, twenty-three years of age, still, like, gorgeous, living off my legend as a schools rugby player, scoring the birds, being the man, when all of a sudden, roysh, life becomes a total mare. I don't have a Betty Blue what's wrong, but I can't eat, can't sleep. I don't even want to do the old beast with two backs, which means a major problem, and we're talking big time here. Normally my head is so full of, like, thoughts, but now I'm down to just one: Sorcha. I'm playing it Kool and the Gang, but this is basically scary. I mean, I'm Ross O'Carroll-Kelly for fock's sake, I don't *do* love.